GUNFIRE MEN

Center Point
Large Print

**This Large Print Book carries the
Seal of Approval of N.A.V.H.**

GUNFIRE MEN

A Western Trio

L. L. Foreman

CENTER POINT LARGE PRINT
THORNDIKE, MAINE

This Center Point Large Print edition
is published in the year 2013 by arrangement with
Golden West Literary Agency.

Copyright © 1952 by L. L. Foreman.
Copyright © renewed 1980
by the Estate of L. L. Foreman.

The text of this Large Print edition is unabridged.
In other aspects, this book may vary
from the original edition.
Printed in the United States of America
on permanent paper.
Set in 16-point Times New Roman type.

ISBN: 978-1-61173-728-8

Library of Congress Cataloging-in-Publication Data

Foreman, L. L. (Leonard London), 1901–
Gunfire men / L.L. Foremann. — Center Point Large Print edition.
pages cm
ISBN 978-1-61173-728-8 (Library binding : alk. paper)
1. Large type books. I. Title.
PS3511.O427G84 2013
813′.54—dc23
2012050626

Last Stand Mesa

Chapter One: LOST AND GONE

IT WAS AT PENASCO that Mike McLean realized at last that his long flight was ended. He could escape no farther. Penasco was the closed door, the end of his trail.

Where the Rio Bravo made its last loop southward, from old Fort Craig down to Mesilla and thence to Mexico, the great bulge of country that it skirted lay as a high plain slanted gently toward it. Yellow clumps of flowering chamiso patched the bare, sun-glazed earth of the plain, but some thin brown grass furred the higher levels over toward the sharp-cliffed mountains that walled the east. Few men traveled this route south, preferring to follow the loop of the river—unless wishful to avoid notice from the Rio Bravo settlements and such law as might be watching the stage road. Mike McLean rode south across this plain.

He guessed he might have made it over the stage road, with benefit to his horse and himself. It was scarcely likely that they'd be on the lookout for him there as yet. His flight had been aimed straight for Alamogordo and through the mountain passes to Texas. It was his logical course, and the hunters knew it. It was a matter of speed, of staying ahead. What the hunters didn't know was that he had been delayed. They passed him unseen in the dark, on the edge of the bleak Lava Beds.

His delay was the fault of a Mexican goat-herd. That damfool *cabrero*! Broke a leg while clambering around searching for a no-account baby *chivo* caught in a crevice. Nothing else to do but lug the fool to his cabin and fix him up. Later that night, with the certain knowledge that by then posses would be guarding every pass south, Mike McLean decided upon an abrupt shift in his course of flight. It had to be done.

"*Mil gracias*!" The old goatherd lay on his rawhide cot, food and water within reach. He knew the look of a hard-pressed fugitive when he saw one, and he said fervently, "*Vaya con Dios, hijo mio*! God be with you, my son!"

To the thanks Mike replied, "*Por nada.* For nothing." As for the blessing, he thought grimly, *It's the Devil who goes with me!* He rolled a few cigarettes for the injured man. "I go now. To those who may come asking of me, you will tell nothing, eh?"

"*Nada, hijo—nada*! Old Manuel will be deaf and dumb and blind."

"*Adios*!"

He cut west, crossed the San Andres, and dropped down onto the plain in bright morning sunshine. The plain showed a vast emptiness, no distant feather of dust pursuing him. No tiny dots of riders to left or right, trying to race around and cut him off, spreading the word of his flight, his description, his price of capture.

He breathed deeply, and quit bedamning his delay. His luck was strained, but maybe still good for another notch. It had been hell, crossing the San Andres in the dark. Shelving rock, loose shale, an unknown trail. They wouldn't figure he would have tried it, much less made it. He stroked a hard palm on the neck of his dun horse.

"You're okay," he told the dun. "You're about played out, but you're okay. I'll have to turn you loose soon an' get a fresh mount. When I do, then from me to you it's *vaya con Dios, hijo mio*! I don't know this country any too good, but she sure looks nice an' private. Let's take it easy for once."

It was good to drift along in the sun, after the harried days and nights behind him. Mexico was maybe his best bet at that, if he could get there. Tough trek, though. Somewhere ahead, below the Cristobals, there lay the *Jornado del Muerte*, the journey of death. He recalled hearing that nobody tackled the *Jornado* without a stout wagon, spare animals, and a couple of filled water barrels. And prayer.

He shrugged. Prayer would have to do for his equipment.

He made a dry camp that night near Penasco, a town he'd only heard of, and next morning he rode in, forced by the desperate need for water, grub, and grain for the dun.

Almost as soon as he entered the town he sensed

a sharpness around him, an element of tension. Vigilance was his toll for the privilege of living, and he sent his stare ranging for evidence of impending trouble. He was not long in detecting symptoms.

At this hour the old men, the grave old *paisanos*, should have been taking the sun in the little plaza, thinking quietly of the first glass of wine for the day. This was the heart of the Land of *Poco Tiempo*, where time sauntered, where the thunderous invasion of the Spanish warriors-in-armor three centuries ago forever overshadowed the affairs of these slumbering days. Yet it could be awakened occasionally for a lively spell, and many times had been, for it was also cattle country, and cattlemen never slept, as anyone knew.

The plaza was deserted. Sudden events lurked in the unnatural hush. Somebody was coming due for a jackpot. *Me?* Mike wondered, and thought it possible.

He held the dun to its walk through the dusty plaza. There was nothing to be gained by turning back now, and he had skinned through too many tight spots not to have developed some fatalism. He angled over to a crooked side street off the plaza, sighting a building along it that he took to be a hotel and livery. It was so silent that the hoof-beats of the dun raised soft echoes along the street.

A weathered sign on the building proclaimed it to be the Silver Bell Bar and Hotel. The livery adjoined it, and across the street stood a black-smith's shop. Three men, armed, lounged outside the livery, facing one man standing near the blacksmith's closed door opposite. The street was narrow and without boardwalks.

Not me, Mike decided, sizing up the situation. With grain for the dun on his mind, he pushed on to pass between the trio and the lone man. Three pairs of eyes scanned him briefly, and leveled again at the victim across the way.

The victim, too, glanced at Mike. He was a rakish-looking old ruffian in a shabby frock coat. A fake diamond flashed feebly on the chest of his soiled white shirt, and his ancient stovepipe hat had as many creases as a Mexican concertina. He was obviously a tinhorn gambler from way back, and his puffy eyes and shapeless red wad of a nose bespoke a long and thorough devotion to the bottle. Mike hoped charitably that he ran true to type and packed a loaded derringer up his sleeve. It was a tough trio bracing him. They were set to strike. The hush of the town had its focus in their coldly considering eyes.

Perceiving Mike's intention to pass, the trio exchanged rapid glances. The tinhorn heaved a sigh, fished out a cigar stub, and in lighting it he brushed back the threadbare cuff of his left sleeve an inch or two. The lighted match trembled badly in his cupped hands, but the expression on his life-battered face reflected only a moody resignation, the wry readiness of a gambler who was set to play out his last poor hand against aces in a stacked deal.

Mike took notice, and contempt seasoned his opinion of the gun trio. Three efficient toughs against a solitary and probably friendless old booze-busted gambler, and there they waited for a lucky break to favor them. He moved up abreast of them on the dun. The livery stable was just ahead, and damned if he was going to turn back to avoid getting in their way.

They eased forward, closing in, using him and the dun as their shield. In that maneuver they eliminated risk, made a calculated business of their gunplay. The old tinhorn stopped chewing on his cigar stub, as if holding his breath. He stood straight, and for that moment he displayed a hint of tarnished grandeur, a regal defiance to defeat and death. It was that, as much as anything else, that caused Mike to rein in the dun.

Mike said to the three in a biting growl, "Hey, back up, *hombres*! Don't use me for your *'buscado*! I won't like it!"

They paused, eyeing him, giving a closer inspection to what kind of man he was. In their preoccupation with the problem of violence they had accepted him merely as a chance asset. Now his voice and presence were suddenly dominant and intrusive.

They took his measure and saw him as a large,

sandy-haired stranger, rawboned, lean to gauntness. His deepset eyes held the marble stare of a tired man, and between the brows ran a small and crooked scar that gave him a quizzical frown.

He was dusty and unshaved. The gun and its low holster, hung at his right hip, were clean, the only gear about him that still bore evidence of care. A hard case. One of the kind that occasionally dropped into Penasco, rested a spell, and departed unobtrusively, glancing back sharply over their shoulders as they rode south to try their luck against the *Jornado*.

They had to be more than desperate to hit the *Jornado*. Their bones made landmarks for the next hunted wayfarer. Penasco was the last oasis, the end of the false trail beckoning them to Mexico—*independencia y libertad*!—that brave slogan minted on the silver peso. It drew to their deaths men who had nothing more to lose but the hope of dodging the penalty of lawless, wild-spent lives.

But they, too, were hard cases, the three. They were on their home ground. The challenge that he bluntly gave them was not to be ignored. It grated on them.

One, a pale-eyed youth with assurance, drawled, "All right, pilgrim—travel!" He took a kick at the dun.

The tinhorn rasped, "Look out, feller, here we go!"

Resenting such treatment to the horse that had

13

carried him over the San Andres safely in the dark, Mike acted promptly and instinctively. He did three things more or less together. He spun the dun, thrust out a boot, and plucked his gun clear. His gun, a heavy Colt's Walker, long in the barrel, speared its red roar as the dun skittered around, but not at the pale-eyed youth. That young killer was flailing the dust, on his back, knocked there by Mike's boot.

A big-brimmed hat sailed, slapped by a bullet. Its owner grabbed for the forty-dollar headgear. Mike's boot caught him next, hinderly, and sent him in a floundering header against the livery. Mike's gun blared again, and the old tinhorn, coming in a shambling run to pitch in, got off a shot from a sleeve-gun about the size of a watch but with a caliber big enough to clean the barrel with a thick finger.

Another of the trio was abruptly minus his hat, but didn't have time to grab for it. Mike clouted him with a long swipe of his gun barrel, and the tinhorn let off a second load that put him out of business.

The stout marshal of Penasco appeared, cradling a shotgun, and Mike broke up the party. Doorways were slamming, filling with citizens who didn't seem to appreciate a stranger's horning-in on local talent. Mike heeled the dun on down the crooked, narrow old street—farewell to grain, some grub, and a few hours of rest.

It was the *Jornado* for him. On a tired and hungry horse. Not a chance to make it. He bedamned the tinhorn as he had the goatherd. His luck had run out. For a moment he almost wished that he had never stuck up the bank at Estancia. There had been no profit in it, finally. He was broke and on the long dodge.

"A helluva country, this!" he muttered, dusting south out of Penasco, more sorry for the tired dun than for himself.

Clear of the town and glancing back, he spied the dust of a single rider fogging along his trail. In no humor to ruin the dun in a race, he reloaded his gun and waited.

The rider turned out to be the old tinhorn. His horse, the gambler admitted cheerfully, was one borrowed from a Penasco hitchrack without consent of the owner.

"Me wee pistol shot itself off in the doin'," he announced in a rich Irish brogue. "Be pure accident, y'unnerstand! An' I left that poor marshal yelpin' wid a hole in his leg! Ah, the pity of it! Me name, sir, is O'Burrifergus. Tim O'Burrifergus, 'Ould Burro,' they call me, me frinds do."

"Mike McLean, me. Howdy."

Ould Burro doffed his stovepipe hat. "Michael McLean, Esquire, a gintleman an' I don't doubt a scholar! Ye head for south? For Mexico? Well, now, they're foine folks, the Mexicans. But ye'll not git there this route, on a weary horse an' ye plainly weary yerself. Yer good bones would decorate the *Jornado*, an' mine with 'em. An unworthy fate for the likes o' yer grand self, Mister McLean, though fit enough for me. Those three buckos had me, till you spilled in. I'd made the mistake o' takin' up for a young lady they were botherin'. Purely unprofessional. Matter o' common chivalry. Top of it, I'd long wore out me welcome in Penasco, as you did in remarkable short time."

"Looks like we're up a stump, then," Mike observed. "We can't go south, you say, an' we sure can't turn back. Well?"

Ould Burro replaced his hat with a flourish. "Mister McLean, you pose the problem in spare and succinct words. It's a hostile land we're in. 'Tis in me mind to hie to greener pastures an' brighter prospects—to land maybe more suitable to our special an' peculiar talents. We'd do well to slant over to the *Llano Fuentes* range, away from the river. Where cattlemen feud an' fight with cattlemen, without benefit o' law. A good place for us! *No es verdad, señor?*"

"*Es verdad*! Nothing else for it. You know the way?"

"That I do. Mister McLean, I have a bottle. Let's drink to the damnation o' death an' our enemies, an' to life's everlastin' promise. Here's the bottle."

Mike drank. "To life's everlasting promise," he said. To himself he thought, *Life's promises broken. I'm lost an' gone. Me—Mike McLean.*

Chapter Two: LAND OF GUN-PROMISE

OULD BURRO dragged his stolen horse to a halt. "Divil of a country, so far," he remarked. "Dry as hell's bones an' not a drink in the house! What would those fellers comin' from yonder want with us? Is it the majesty o' the law? Ah, no. There's no law here on the *Llano Fuentes*, praise be!"

Two men approaching them reined in and waited for them to come up. They were armed. Their impassive faces and stiff manner hinted sharply at authority. Far behind them a group of other riders trooped along at a walk, angling westward.

"Where are you headed an' what's your business?"

The query was harshly offensive. Mike met the stare of brittle eyes, and thought bleakly, *There's a Jonah on me, sure 'nough. Trouble everywhere I turn.* With the cow-country habit he inspected their horses. Good-looking animals. Both wore the same brand, a triangle enclosing a T. He'd heard of the Triangle T, but knew little about it beyond the hearsay that it was a pretty big outfit, Eastern-owned.

To the question he gave a dry retort. "We're headed sort o' yonderly. Our business is mindin' our own. What's yours?"

They took stock of him, up and down. The one

17

who had spoken gave his verdict. "A raggedy pilgrim on the dodge, an' a busted tinhorn, coyotin' for quick pickin's!"

He was large, but not fat. His partner wasn't skinny, either, though a narrow face made him appear so at first glance.

"Our business is keepin' the range clean. This country is closed. You tail right back the way you came! *Sabe* that? *Sabe* this?" Blued metal flashed in the sun.

Mike sat motionless in the saddle, his gaze on the covering gun and the man holding it. Here was as sudden a jackpot as he had ever got into. It occurred to him, not for the first time, that when a man carried as much sign of trouble as he did, it was hard to avoid further trouble. He bore the stamp. He was like a fang-scarred pariah dog that couldn't hope to stray by its own kind without a snarling fight. It had come to that.

The narrow-faced man spoke for the first time. "Maybe," he murmured, "they should be ear-marked." He began lifting his carbine out of its saddle scabbard, smiling, his eyes contemplating Ould Burro's sizable ears.

"Not a bit needful!" hurriedly protested Ould Burro. "Yer friend's argyment, there in his hand, settles the whole matter! I take off me hat to it." He doffed his hat ceremoniously.

The trick that followed displayed practice and dexterity, and helped to explain the many dents in the old stovepipe headgear. It skimmed from his hand spinning. The narrow brim evidently contained a metal stiffener. Its edge cracked smartly on the bridge of the would-be earmarker's long nose.

The large man started to laugh surprisedly at his partner's expense, and changed it to a grunt. His partner was rocking back and forth in pain, both hands clasped over his nose, tears streaming. And Ould Burro was capping the trick, plucking his murderous little pistol from his sleeve. Mike sent the dun lunging forward.

The dun still had a jump left in him, and Mike fetched it out with a dig of his heels. He crashed broadside into the Triangle T horse, knocking wild the shot of its rider. He had his gun stroked out, and he reached far over and took a long swipe with the heavy barrel.

Fighting to keep from taking a spill with his horse, the large man jerked his head away. He caught the blow on the side of his neck, and over he went, gurgling.

Mike dismounted fast. Holding on to the dun's reins, gun cocked, he was ready to work the job out. But the man he had hit knelt on the ground, gasping and retching, his head at a crooked angle as if he might have caught a stiff neck.

Ould Burro, poking his derringer at the other sufferer, proclaimed somewhat pompously, "Injury I can take, but I draw the line at indignity! Earmark me, would ye? It'll be a long time before ye do more'n snuffle wi' that sniffer! They gen'rally break when I hit 'em. I trust yours is no exception. Mr. McLean, what disposal d' we make of 'em? Days o' drouth!" he exclaimed admiringly. "What did ye do to yon man? Bust his neck?"

"No, just bent it, is all. Let's take their guns."

"The spoils o' war," Ould Burro approved. "An' the good Lord knows we'll need 'em, if yon folks comin' is their pals!"

The group of riders in the distance had changed course and were slowly approaching. Mike said to the Triangle T pair, "You can hereby inform your boss, whoever he is, that we ain't in the right humor to turn back today. Furthermore, where we go an' what we do is nobody's damn business!"

"So you think!" The one with the crick in his neck lurched to his horse and climbed aboard. He and the other one started off. "You'll be hearin' from us!"

Ould Burro, loaded down with two six-shooters and a carbine, plus cartridge belts, retrieved his stovepipe hat and clapped it on his head.

"Here they come. What a country! What manner o' wild an' hostile beasts does it breed? I'd no idea! Well, now, we'll do our best, Mr. McLean, eh? Strategy, as the feller said, is the art o' bluff. Never, f'r instance, let the enemy know ye're out o' ammunition, but just keep on shootin'. Let's face 'em like great Brian Boru scowlin' down at the Pygmies!"

The group of horsemen came steadily on, raising a long stream of dust from the dry plain. At a decent distance they shuffled to a halt and sat eyeing Mike, Ould Burro, and the retreating pair of Triangle T range cleaners. There were seven of them, obviously cowmen. Not one was fat. They didn't appear any too prosperous.

Mike beckoned for them to come on, seeing that they seemed to wait for an invitation. They had some reason for their wariness. Ould Burro, following his own advice, had put on the stance and expression of a fire-eating badman craving blood. Mike, also strung with enough lethal hardware to keep three hands occupied, was plainly a dangerous lobo in their eyes. He felt like one.

They advanced slowly. There were saddle guns among them, strapped down in worn scabbards, but no six-shooters. Their leader, a graying man whose face was deeply engraved by time and toil, gazed woodenly at Mike and Ould Burro. He had the frowning stare of a suspicious, intolerant man, soured by angry frustration.

"You did a fool thing!" he announced bluntly.

"So did they!" Mike scanned the horse brands. A mixed lot. Not a Triangle T among them. "My name's McLean. Yours?"

"Peter Hardy. These are some o' my neighbors—

Llano Fuentes, the Middle Range, is our *querencia*." Peter Hardy sent a somber stare after the two Triangle T men. "The one you clouted is Art Garnett. The other is Homer Allen. Top men in the Regulators—Roone's Regulators—Triangle T payroll. They'll all be after you, give you my word. Don't look to us to hide you out. We got our own troubles. An' frankly, we don't have much place for—hum —gents out o' law."

"Well, now!" Ould Burro shoved in. "Out o' law, sez he! Us? Me dear Mr. Hardy! We do not carry our importance on us like jinglin' medals, to be sure, for we're modest men. Also we've had a little rough wear gettin' here, yer damned country bein' what it is. But after we locate the kind o' range we seek, for the outfit which Mr. McLean owns—"

"Whoa, Burro!" cut in Mike.

The old bluffer was not to be stemmed. "Of which outfit I have the honor to be manager," he continued firmly, "then will ye see followin' behind us the biggest herd that ever tracked the land! The finest horses! Aye, an' the scrappiest crew o' cowhands that ever busted open a closed country!"

"Now, Burro!"

"Mr. McLean, I'm as modest as yerself!" stated Ould Burro. "But I'll not stand by while ye're insulted! Gintlemen! Ye think yon triangular teacups are tough? Hah! For the game of it, our boys will run them an' their kind clear across the dry *Jornado*, an' the sweat o' yer so-called Regulators will start the grass growin' where it never grew before!"

Peter Hardy blinked, awed by the grandiose claims. "You mean you're cattlemen? Scouting for a fresh location? Where you from?"

"Why, Texas, naturally," responded Ould Burro glibly, after running a rapid glance over their gear. "Texas, where the best cattlemen come from! An' the best men, for that matter."

"H'm!" Peter Hardy turned and exchanged glances with the men around him. "That's diff'rent. We're mostly Texicans, too, origin'ly."

Ould Burro inclined his head. "So I—ah—thought. We'll feel right at home. Ye'll love our boys. Texas wildcats, all!"

One of the group pushed forward. "Hey, Hardy! There's room for 'em at the *Llano*. Eh, fellers? Mr. McLean, I'm Ed Horner, Five Bar X. This is Gray Adams. This is Boy Pete—"

"Boy?" Mike shook hands with a blond giant.

"Peter Hardy's son," explained Ed Horner. "We called him Boy when he was a button, an' we never bothered to change. Fellers, let's go back an' hold that meetin'. Hell with the Triangle T! Hell with Roone an' his Regulators! Yeah, an' Brokus, too!"

"Wait a minute," Mike put in. The sudden shift to warm fraternalism aroused a vague and uneasy suspicion in him. Texans were generally friendly to other Texans, all right—but not quite this friendly. These cowmen were just too suddenly full of the milk of human kindness. "What meetin'?" He had become somewhat shy of crowds lately.

Ed Horner drew a breath and announced, "Special meetin' o' the Cattlemen's Council o' the *Llano Fuentes* Middle Range." When he first showed up with the group, Mike had ticked him off as merely a lanky man with a dispirited face. Now Ed Horner had a bright and optimistic air, and had become spokesman. "We were havin' it at the Caven place. Some o' the others will still be there, if we jog smart. Let's go!"

There was nothing much else to do but jog along with them. Mike sent a dour look at Ould Burro. He had a dark premonition that the old liar had talked up some more trouble.

The Caven place turned out to be a fairly large ranch house, in need of some repairs. The corrals held only a half-dozen horses. A good outfit, gone downhill, from the looks of it.

Lindsay and Jana Caven—brother and sister, Mike learned—lived alone. No crew. No cook. Their father had built the outfit, and after his death the life and force had drained out of it.

Mike thought, surveying Lindsay Caven, *Strong father—weak son. Shirt sleeves to shirt sleeves in*

24

a couple o' generations. Oh, well. We're what we are, all of us. I'm no credit to my name.

Lindsay Caven had the look of a young man who was exploring dissipation diligently and finding no release in it. Nor much pleasure. His sister, Jana, was younger. She had a quiet prettiness, and an air of self-control that was tense and likely to break under pressure. Mike felt sorry for her. She was the kind of girl who needed a man for support. All she had was a drunken brother, an educated failure.

The main room held a score of men who listened attentively to what Peter Hardy and Ed Horner had to say. Their eyes, hope awakening in them, shifted constantly to Mike, the stranger, the man who had whipped Art Garnett. The man who owned a big, scrappy Texas outfit that was coming down to run Roone's Regulators out of the country, if he tipped the nod.

"A Texas cattleman, wantin' new range!" Ed Horner argued loudly. "Here 'tis! Him an' his *segundo* knocked the horns off Garnett an' Allen, no trouble a-tall! I say there's room here for that outfit!"

Jana Caven and Boy Pete Hardy were holding hands and standing close together, thinking themselves unnoticed. It came to Mike that nobody could escape the notice of soft consolation, nor the hard condemnation of watching eyes. Love, like hatred, was always naked. It couldn't hide itself under any cloak. It shone too brightly.

Boy Pete called out, "Give 'em range, I say!" And then he flushed redly, a youngster who had dared to raise his voice among the elders.

Peter Hardy's eyes were intolerant and condemning. "Violence begets violence!" He looked around. "I'm against it. We're not gunmen. I've preached in our church against bloodshed, as you all know. Who lives by the sword, dies by the sword! You'd have this man—this stranger and his crew—fight for us? Shameful! I'll never vote for it, though my own son does. Violence is not my way. Nor yours. We put away our guns a good many years ago, by vote and consent of the majority. I stand by that, whatever comes!"

In the babble of voices that broke out, Mike raised a hand and got some attention. "This meetin' was called earlier, wasn't it?" he queried. "What for? Who broke it up? An' what the hell's goin' on here, anyhow?"

It was Lindsay Caven who answered him. Lindsay held a glass in his hand. He said, a little thickly, "Correct, Mr. McLean. There was a meeting. Its purpose was to solve the problem of how to sneak some cattle out to market, and get some needed money. We're all broke. No solution, as usual. And Garnett and Hall broke up the meeting. They ordered us to shut up and go home."

"Two jiggers busted the meetin'?" Mike asked.

"Twenty Texas cowmen or more? I can't see it! Hell, Burro an' me beat their horns down without much strenuosity to speak of!"

Lindsay Caven chuckled and drank. "That perplexes you, Mr. McLean. The answer is simple. We've lived here too long. We've grown used to security. Peace. Some of us took out our warlike, conquering urge on those nearest to us. My father, for one." His face darkened. "My father was a petty tyrant, like most of the rest here. A tyrant to me. To everybody he could batter down and dictate to. Hell have him, and welcome!"

A sigh of prim disapproval swept through the crowd. Jana Caven, tightly holding Boy Pete's hand, shook her head helplessly at her drunkard brother.

His mood had changed to angry scorn. "You know it's true! You all know it. He sacrificed everything to his greed! Property was his god! Damn him, I say! Damn his ranch! Let it go to hell after him!"

Here were sour undercurrents, living son against dead father. Bitter memories, resentment channeled into a blind desire to destroy what the father had built and worshiped. Mike, not overly interested, and a trifle embarrassed for the girl, thought it time to change the subject.

"If your earlier meetin' settled nothin', what's the reason for this one?" he asked. "An' just what is your big problem, anyhow?"

Again it was Lindsay Caven who spoke before anybody else. "I'll tell you that, too! The problem? How to drive cattle out to market, against the opposition of the Regulators—Amery Roone's Triangle T men, that is—and the Brokus bunch up on Alta Mesa. The solution? You!"

"Me?"

Lindsay grinned mirthlessly. "Yes, you, Mr. McLean. And your big crew of Texas scrappers. You're elected to pull our chestnuts out of the fire, in return for range which we don't own and you'd have to fight to take and hold! There's your answer, and my good neighbors are all glaring at me for putting it in plain words. Look at them! Ah, hell—"

He slumped into a chair, sank his head onto his crossed arms on the table, and quietly passed out. Mike eyed him for a moment, before ranging a regard over the crowd. These men were in a bad way, so much so that they were ready to compromise with their pride and trick a stranger into taking on their troubles.

"When the drink is in, sometimes the truth comes out," Mike remarked. "Doesn't he own any cattle himself?"

"Sure he does," Ed Horner answered awkwardly. "Maybe a thousand steers. Don't know how much mixed stuff, some branded, some not, scattered around. He never bothers about the stock. Hates everything about the outfit, an' he's lettin' it go to

28

pieces. Sold most o' the horses after his pa died, an' paid the hands off."

"What's the setup about these Regulators an' so forth?"

"Roone proposed organizin' a law force to keep stock thieves an' such out o' the country. We agreed. But he only used his own men, an' now they boss the country. His Triangle T claims range on three sides o' the Middle Range to the river, or anyhow as far as Alta Mesa, roughly. When we try to trail a beef herd out, the Regulators claim we're in trespass an' they turn us back. It ain't legal, but what can we do? They tell us to take the west route around Alta Mesa. They know damn well we can't."

"Why not?" Mike queried.

Ed Horner shrugged. "If you knew this country you wouldn't ask that. Ever hear o' Bloody-Wire Brokus? He'd like real well to see a herd comin' into his territory. Save him goin' out to get it! That's his business. So we're blocked all round."

"What's Roone's game? The markets are good, an' enough for everybody."

"Sure they're good. That's why Roone wants to increase his stock. To do it he needs our Middle Range. An' to do that he's got to squeeze us out first. Brokus has got his eye on our range, too, lately, as well as our cattle."

"An' that," said Mike, "is the jackpot you'd steer a poor unsuspectin' stranger like me into!"

Chapter Three: CATTLE GAMBLE

"GINTLEMEN, ye're the victims o' graspin' rascals!" Ould Burro observed indignantly. "How long can ye hold out?"

His rum-red face was innocent of guile, or as innocent as it could ever look. Mike suspected, though, that the shabby old adventurer was feeling out the situation, on the alert for any prospect of turning it to his advantage. He was getting to know Mr. O'Burrifergus.

Ed Horner stroked his nose. "We-ell, I dunno, maybe—"

"Ah, let's tell the truth of it!" broke in Boy Pete. "We're all about finished! We're all broke! If we don't get a herd out soon, we've got to quit and take anything Roone offers us!"

Peter Hardy frowned at his too-frank son, muttering that it wasn't as bad as that.

Mike said reminiscently, "I've bossed a trail herd or two through some tough country. There's been a big new strike, I hear, over in Torreon. Crowds o' miners an' newcomers there, all hungry for good beef. That's a market that would pay high, an' it ain't too far. I'd consider it, if I was you."

They shook their heads. "Torreon," Ed Horner pointed out, "is west. There's the river, for one thing. Deep, too fast to swim, an' no ford for seventy miles. How about that?"

"Build a log raft an' line it across the river with our ropes. Ferry the critters over, a few at a time."

"It can't be done!" Peter Hardy said positively. "It would mean driving around Alta Mesa. Brokus would jump us, take the herd, and chase us back!"

"Not if I had a crew o' men, he wouldn't!" Mike responded. "I've got an idea about how to get by your Brokus booger. But I said men—not nursemaids!"

Ed Horner slapped his hat on his knee. "That's talkin'! That's old Texas talk, an' high time we heard some! McLean, count me in!" He stopped, and asked cautiously, "What would you want?"

"Five thousand dollars! You got it?"

"Hell, not five thousand pennies!"

Mike nodded. "All right. Seein' I've got nothin' much to take up my time just now, I'll take a gamble. We'll hold a roundup an' shape a herd of around three thousand head. That ain't too many for a short drive, an' about right for the Torreon market. A thousand o' these steers are to go in my name an' under my brand." He held up a hand. "Now, wait a minute before you bubble off!

"They can be Lindsay Caven's steers," he went on. "If, as you tell me, he's lettin' his stock go wild, then I guess he'd take my note for 'em at five dollars a head. If I don't get the herd out, then I lose. If we reach Torreon, I win what profit I can make on his steers, over an' above the five dollars

31

a head which I'll pay him from the proceeds. You got nothin' to lose."

They talked it over. One. of them asked, "Wouldn't it be better to wait till your outfit comes down?"

Ould Burro handled that question. "We'd have to trek way back to guide 'em here. Take time. An outfit the size of our NS travels slow. Account o' grass an' water, ye know. By then, some other enterprisin' cowmen will have got to Torreon with a herd, an' that market will be glutted, for even miners can eat only just so much beef. It has been suggested here that ye want others to pull yer chestnuts out o' the fire. 'Tis a fallacious wish, gintlemen, I've always found. Whilst ye wait, yer chestnuts burn!"

They held further consultation, and voted agreement.

The vote went against the stubborn antagonism of Peter Hardy, who declared, "It's a mad and dangerous scheme! It means fighting, I tell you! Violence begets violence, McLean—as I'm sure you know! You and your man, there, are gunfighters, but we're not. We older men gave up wearing guns years back. Our young men hardly know how to strap on a holster!"

"Time they learned," Mike countered. "I'll give 'em a few lessons. Quit bawlin'! You've got nothin' to lose."

"Only our lives!" retorted Hardy. He addressed

32

the meeting. "Do you follow this man? You'll regret it! I know his kind! He'll lead you to disaster! He'll make gunmen of our sons! He's just said he would! A roundup now will bring on war!"

Ould Burro inquired, "Since when did cowmen lose their right to gather up their cows on their own range? The shame of it!"

Peter Hardy flushed. "I stand for peace! Let the wolves fight and devour each other!"

"A wishful stand, sir. Meantime, where's self-respect? The wolves, I grant ye, may fight to death over a rabbit. Aye, an' between 'em the misfortuned rabbit lies torn to flitters. The rabbit gains a moral triumph—an' much good it does him!"

Ed Horner shouted, "Damn right! Me, I'm sick o' bein' the rabbit!"

This was revolt. The peace-inspired leadership of Peter Hardy was in sudden discredit. Others joined Ed Horner in his rebellion, particularly the younger men, yelling assent and nodding approvingly at Mike.

Boy Pete was one, and he called out, "Let's start roundup tomorrow! I got a little bunch o' my own that I'll throw in!"

Peter Hardy, defeated, worked his lips. Bitter hurt in his eyes, he looked at Mike. "If anything happens to my son—if you drag him and the others into a losing fight—I think I'll try to kill you, McLean! I haven't always been a peaceful man. There was a time when I could take on the likes of you and lay you in the dust! Bear that in mind!"

He stalked out of the Caven house, shaking off the restraining hands of friends who wanted to talk matters over with him. At the door he snapped, "He may be a cowman, but to me he's a gunman on the make! I warn you all!"

They had a tiny settlement, too small to be called a town, that for some forgotten reason was named Fifty. Only one room was to be had in it, and that behind a log saloon titled not too surprisingly the Log Cabin. Ould Burro said it was mighty convenient, and after a constructive trip to the bar he joined Mike in their room.

"A poor brand o' whisky," he remarked, "befittin' the brand o' men inhabitin' this barren excuse for a country. Michael, ye're foolish. Ye could have made a better deal. They'd have signed notes for Caven's cows, themselves. Ye were soft. Why?"

Mike, boots off, rubbed his feet. "I hate the Roone breed. I had a ranch once. Lost it to a Roone kind o' man."

Ould Burro sighed. "Sentiment. An unprofitable emotion. I like yer gamble not one damn bit. There is no fondness in me for Mr. Peter Hardy. An upright man, yes. Out o' credit now as their leader. But, Michael, they've listened to him a long, long time. They'll listen again to him, should ye fail just once. These peaceful folks are wildcats when they start. I know! An ye'll teach 'em how to fight? Lord save us!"

Mike scowled. "Quit dealin' me misery. What you got against these folks?"

Ould Burro wagged his head. "Their whisky speaks against 'em! An' Mr. Peter Hardy strikes me as a man o' total abstinence. A benighted Pythagorean! A nephalist! An Encratite!"

"Chew it up finer so I know what you're sayin'," Mike told him. "I think you're prejudiced, pard."

"Prejudice," declared Ould Burro, absently drawing forth a newly acquired pint, "is the offspring of ignorance. I'm not an ignorant man, Michael, believe me!"

Grass was sprouting on the Middle Range, and cowmen were up and about. Organization for the roundup was completed. Mike was elected *caporal*, and Ed Horner and Boy Pete were his *segundos*. Here in the deep Southwest everybody used the old Spanish terms, though often stumped when it came to exchanging weather observations with a Mexican.

Chuck wagons had been repaired and put in order, saddle horses gathered and a few shod, cowhands given their orders, and wranglers delegated to handle the *remuda*. The roundup crews went to work on the beef-herd hunt. The range was large, brushy in parts. The cattle, after too long a time of running wild and feeding on good grama, were snuffily inclined to dispute any influence toward discipline.

There were five wagons and their crews. Forty-odd cowpokes. The cattle had congregated mostly on the outwaters, on the water holes and spring lakes. The drive had to ride out twenty miles to round some of them in. In clouds of dust, the work went on, cutting, trail-branding, gathering, and shaping up the herd for Torreon.

It had to be good, the herd, to sell straight to the Torreon miners' market without benefit of feeder middlemen. These steers had to be right for the butchers.

A scorching sun beat down on the cowhands by day. At night, sitting cross-legged by the battered chuck wagons, smoke from the cookfires blew into their unshaven, work-worn faces. The hands and owners, all of a kind, were working against time, together. Except in humor, the title of "Mr." was out of use, and "boss" was a forgotten word. This was a cow camp. It was doing okay.

The growing beef herd contained all sizes, all colors, from black to white and in between. The sweating, swearing, ragged roundup hands sawed their horns off, earmarked and laid on the hot irons, did their messier work, and ran them into the gather. This was work. Sixteen-hours-a-day *work*. Sit the spooky nag and spin the rope nimble. Cussing won't help, but it seems to.

Although no move had yet been made by Roone's Regulators, Mike kept Peter Hardy's solemn warning in mind. He took what time he could to train the crew into a potential fighting force. It wasn't easy.

Some of the older men thought they knew a thing or two about handling a gun, and they clung stubbornly to their ways. The younger ones were willing to learn, but they were apt to think that they'd mastered the whole idea when they could hit a mark four times out of five. The matter of a mere two or three seconds' lag in their speed didn't mean much to them.

On the other hand, some of them had heard of how to fan a gun—slapping the hammer with the free hand while holding the trigger pulled back. Proudly they sprayed the landscape in rapid bursts, after which they sucked hammer-torn palms and privately decided to wear a stout leather glove next time.

Patiently, Mike taught them that marksmanship was one thing, speed another, and neither talent was worth a damn without the third ingredient, when it came to a fight. He said, "You've got to balance speed with marksmanship, an' not get fussed."

He meant, but didn't want to put it too bluntly, that the third ingredient was nerve. Any gun-fighter knew that a wasted shot or a split-second of fumbling could spell his finish. He couldn't allow that knowledge to stampede him. He had to get his gun out fast, but unflurriedly, and fire with care, all his concentration fixed upon the single purpose of accurately shooting a man in the shortest possible time. That was the difference between a gunfighter and a shooter.

Boy Pete proved to be a promising pupil. He could shoot fast and well, and was too phlegmatic by nature to be bothered by nerves. But he had a fatal fault. Too often he dug his big hand at his holstered gun instead of stroking it out, and he'd mess up the draw and have to claw it clumsily free.

Surprisingly, Lindsay Caven showed up at the roundup camp occasionally and put in some work. Sober, he was a quiet young man, a capable rider and roper. More surprisingly, he promptly out-classed the others with a gun. He cocked as he drew, and as the barrel came level he fired at once and rarely missed. Respect for him, which had fallen low, rose somewhat among the crowd.

Drunk, he was sardonically merry, a jeering, sarcastic bystander. He and Ould Burro got together frequently over a bottle, usually winding up as a hilarious and irresponsible pair of nuisances keeping everybody awake half the night. Mike couldn't quite decide which was the worse influence on the other. He was sorry for Jana Caven. All she had was a worthless brother and a ruined ranch, and big, simple Boy Pete.

• • •

"Any coffee, Burro?" Mike called, riding over into camp from the *parada* ground.

The beef herd was shaping up. In the cutting and branding, dust billowed in the hot sun, cows bawled constantly, dirt-caked men cursed, and the gentlest horse was apt to uncork a bonehead notion. It was a tough time for all.

Ould Burro answered sourly, "There's the pot." He heartily despised the cook job that Mike had talked him into taking on. It entailed entirely too much labor for his taste. He was sore at Mike, and hitting the bottle hard.

Lindsay Caven sat against a wheel of the chuck wagon, drinking. Mike scowled.

The scowl registered in Ould Burro's fuddled consciousness. "What's the trouble wi' ye?"

Mike heaved his sweaty body out of the saddle, and got some coffee. "This damn outfit! Oh, they know the work, sure. They know it all! Every order I give, they want to argue it over. I wish this was a reg'lar crew o' hired hands. I'd fire some right now. You, for one! An' as for that other booze walloper there—"

"Say no more!" interrupted Ould Burro. He hurled an iron ladle at the cook fire. "I resign, Mr. McLean! I concur fully wi' Lindsay Caven's opinion o' cows an' all fools connected! Lindsay, me boy, is there a shot left in that canister? I desire to celebrate me sunder from the bedamned bovine business!"

Lindsay waved the bottle. "*Por si, viejo*! Come and get it! 'For let us laugh and never think, and live in the wild anarchy of drink!' I've misquoted that, I believe, but let it go. It was what the revered Ben Jonson or somebody meant, when he wrote with ponderous pen—"

Whatever it was that somebody meant, it went with the drifting dust, for just then Ed Horner and some others came loping over, calling urgently, "Hey, McLean, look! There's a bunch comin'!" Half a minute later Ed Horner exclaimed, "Lord, we're in for it!"

Chapter Four: KING OF ALTA MESA

MIKE FINISHED his coffee. The alarms and anxieties of these Middle Range cowmen no longer pricked him. They had cried wolf too many times. Only when he grew aware of a heavy silence did he glance around. Ould Burro was sidling behind the chuck wagon. Ed Horner and those with him had the look of taut-nerved cats backing off from a pack of dogs.

Nine newly arrived horsemen sat gazing around over the camp. The racket in the *parada* ground had deadened the sound of their coming. They were well mounted and heavily armed, but none of their horses bore the Triangle T brand. Mike took in that much, before giving regard to a bearded man who met his eyes with a straight and mockingly humorous stare.

He was huge, as big as Boy Pete. He had a royal tilt to his long-haired head, massive strength in his frame, and supreme arrogance in the thrust of his bearded jaw. His wide green eyes held assurance of power. His voice roared at Mike.

"What the hell are you up to here?"

Instant irritation sparked Mike's reply. "What does it look like? Who the hell are you?"

The big horseman shoved back his hat. "Boys, he don't know me. He honestly don't. He's a stranger in a strange land, so overlook his

41

ignorance an' don't hurt him! Young cockerel, what's your name?"

"Mike McLean. Yours?"

"A damn Scotch-Irisher! I knew it! Are you the wampus who put the crick in Garnett's neck? Man, you're all right! I'm Brokus. Ol' Bloody-Wire Charley. I've wrecked more fence than a man could ride in a year o' paydays! Mike McLean, you're wastin' time on this roundup, I'm tellin' you!"

"Want to bet?"

"Don't be foolish. From your looks I judge you've bet the limit already. You can't win. I'm sorry to say it, for I kinda like your style. You can't win, because your backers, here, they won't back you all the way. They'll pull out in the pinch. Hell, I know them an' their kind!"

Ed Horner and the others stayed mute. Mike said, "We'll make this roundup. We'll get a herd out."

Brokus wagged his great head indulgently. "Ah, to be young again! You do me good, McLean! A pity you're on the wrong side. But when you've lost out an' they turn against you—as I know they will—come to me, hear? I'll have a place for you."

"Where?"

Brokus boomed a laugh. His men, double-gunned, chill-eyed, listened and looked on, unsmiling. "Alta Mesa. Give a good yell as you come. We only welcome those who're invited."

Irony was heavy in his tone. "It's a rare honor!"

Mike guessed he was being mocked. He didn't appreciate it. "I'll get along without that honor, thanks. No reason for it, that I can think of."

"No reason?" inquired a rider alongside Brokus, a slim one with a smooth and youthful face shaded under a wide-brimmed sombrero.

Mike let the query go, wanting no gun-itchy stripling to build an excuse to cut down on him. There was no profit in that. The other riders of Alta Mesa would be certain to pitch in.

The slim one lifted a hand to the big sombrero, a slow deliberateness in the movement. Mike remembered Ould Burro's hat trick. But the sombrero came off, was slapped to knock the dust off, and then was used idly as a fan. The sun shone on the uncovered head of a girl.

She had dark hair, thick and soft. Released from under the sombrero, it tumbled to her shoulders. She brushed it back with a deft flick of a gesture that was wholly feminine. Her skin had a warm, rich hue, almost dusky.

Mike automatically shed his own stained and fire-spotted hat. He stood bareheaded, his hair all tangled and sweat-plastered. Nobody else paid the girl that courtesy, and Brokus's stare at Mike grew curiously blank for an instant. Ed Horner and the Middle Range men had dismounted. They stood behind their horses.

She asked again, "No reason?"

Mike held her level gaze. Scanning her eyes, he discovered that they were a deep jade-green, not black as they had seemed in shade. He guessed she was beautiful. His mind wasn't in a state to reach any calm conclusion about it. What he did know for sure was that her presence was a sudden, vivid impact on his senses.

Imps of tumult jumped brightly alive in him. "I take that back," he said, still holding her gaze, while his eyes frankly signaled the masculine dare. "Right this minute I've thought of a real good reason!"

Brokus exploded a laugh at the girl's flush, and whirled his horse around. Abruptly, the nine rode off. Brokus's voice came bellowing back. "Watch your step, Mike McLean!"

It could have been either a warning or a threat. A man the type of Bloody-Wire Charley Brokus, though, Mike reflected, wasn't likely to indulge in threats. That great lion of a man was the kind who pounced at the right moment—no preliminaries.

Mike peered through the hoof-stamped dust and beyond it, toward the high, flat-topped edge of Alta Mesa in the distance.

"So that's Brokus! Friends, I suspect you've still been holdin' out on me! What kind of outfit does he run, an' what's his stake in this range?"

Ed Horner answered uncomfortably, "We— uh—told you."

The rest of the crew from the *parada* had come

riding in as soon as Brokus left. Among them Boy Pete called, "Tell it all, Horner! No, I'll tell it! Brokus is a cattle raider, McLean. It's an outlaw spread he runs up there. Got a crew of twenty, thirty—hard to say how many. Always comin' an' goin'. Gunmen, rustlers, road agents, all kinds. It's a hangout for wanted men. They stay a spell, then they're gone. Some stay. Those you saw are just a sample."

Peter Hardy, who had finally and grudgingly consented to work with the roundup, put in, "Brokus has been operating from the mesa for years. Never bothered us till lately. Too much law an' barbwire have blocked him in the west an' south. So he wants to take over the *Llano* now an' settle down as a rancher. He does everything in a big way. Not a chance of a herd getting out past him! If any cows of ours reach Torreon, Brokus's men will be drivin' 'em!"

"Then why this roundup?" Mike demanded.

Peter Hardy struck a thumb at Ed Horner. "Ask him, not me! I've been against it from the first, and everybody knows it."

Ed Horner muttered, "McLean, we been hopin' maybe your outfit would get here in time to give a hand. Your crew must know you're somewhere down here."

Mike gazed speechlessly at Ould Burro, who, taking a swig from Lindsay Caven's bottle, husked, "Chestnuts!"

It was no use flying off the handle. Mike swallowed his feelings and said, "Brokus was right! Who was the girl?"

"His daughter."

"Daughter? H'm. Name?"

"Flame. Outlandish name for a girl, but it suits her. She's gen'rally called the Cheyenne Flame." Ed Horner curled his lip. "Her mother was part Cheyenne, they say, an' part French. Some Mexican, too, likely."

Mike frowned at the tone. It was becoming harder to hold his temper. "I've had some fine Cheyenne friends," he mentioned. "A French Canadian set a broken leg for me once. I've rode with Mexicans an' shared grub an' smokes with 'em. Miss Flame Brokus strikes me as quite some young lady!"

"She's no lady. How could she be, livin' with nobody but outlaws around her? Maybe that's why she kind of attracts the men! Some kinds o' men, that is!"

"Like me, you mean?" Mike gazed at Ed Horner thoughtfully.

"I didn't say that."

"All right. I'll still say she's a young lady. Want to argue it?"

Ed Horner shook his head. "No. Say, what's the chance o' your outfit gettin' here soon?"

"Don't bet on it!" Mike advised.

Lindsay Caven, who hadn't moved from the

wagon wheel, uttered a strange laugh. Mike glanced at him, and caught a knowing glint in his eyes. From some corner of his whisky-inspired brain a flash of the truth had come to Lindsay. Or else Ould Burro had let out a few careless words. Lindsay knew. And if he spilled it, the lid would be off.

Jana Caven drove out early that evening in a buckboard, to take Lindsay home. She had done it before, able from past observation to predict when he would be ending a bout and too drunk to ride. Mike and Boy Pete loaded him in.

Lindsay opened one eye, cocked it up at Mike's face, and chuckled. "Ugly big son'f a gun! You've got 'em kidded—but not me! Own a big outfit, eh? The mighty NS. Sure. The mighty None Such! You won't get that herd to Torreon! You know it!" He closed his eye and curled up in the buckboard to sleep.

Mike chilled. He avoided the eyes of Jana and Boy Pete, until Jana whispered dismayedly, "What did he mean? Won't we be able to sell the cattle? We've got to! He's got to have some money to get away! There are too many bad memories for him here! That's why he drinks."

Mike couldn't stand it. He said rashly, "That herd's goin' to Torreon!"

He turned away while she and Boy Pete kissed good night. Jana drove off with Lindsay. Boy Pete came up beside Mike, and they stood for a moment, not speaking.

Then Boy Pete said very gravely, "I won't ask you any questions. But if you let her down, you better look out! I sure hope you're straight, 'cause I like you. It sure would hurt me to kill you."

All Mike could find to say was, "Keep your shirt on, Pete. I'll do everything I can to get the herd through. My oath on it."

Boy Pete nodded. He was terribly in earnest. "Okay. I'll keep my mouth shut, too. I mean, about what Lindsay said. He was awful drunk, after all, wasn't he?"

"Yeah. Awful drunk—"

The shaping up of the beef herd was about completed near the end of that week, and Mike called a meeting.

"I've been talkin' hard to myself," he told the crowd, "an' I still think there's a way we might get the herd out. Both the Roone an' Brokus mobs will be watching for us to start the drive. First sight of our trail dust, they'll be onto us. Only question then is which jumps us, an' where. Right?"

They nodded moodily. Lindsay Caven, sober the whole day, for once, was watching him and listening closely.

Mike continued. "But who can spot dust a couple miles off at night? Yeah, I know—a load o' grief, startin' off a new herd in the dark, I grant you! With luck, though, we can be way out o' sight next morning, if we push. An' we push from there on, fast an' regardless. We'll lose beef, but that can't be helped."

Peter Hardy spoke up. "You're crazy! It can't be done!"

"Why not?"

"Why? Do you think Brokus doesn't know the herd's ready? Do you think he and his bunch go to bed with the birds? They're watching us day and night!"

"I'd be surprised if they weren't," Mike agreed. "So here's what we do. We announce roundup's over an' we're ready to start the drive come Monday."

"What? Give Brokus notice?"

"Sure. An' we put on a *baile* somewhere, a big Saturday-night dance, to celebrate. That's natural. When it gets goin' good, we slip out, two-three at a time. We come back here an' start the drive right away. That's one night when neither Brokus nor Roone will expect us to work. Who ever quit a *baile* to go fool with cows in the dark? We'll be the first who ever did it!"

The younger men grinned. Some of the older ones nodded agreement, their eyes pensive and faraway in memories of laughing girls, swishing skirts, music. It was long since the folks of Fifty had held a *baile*. Too long. Clean joy had become a stranger in this land. It had no value in the struggle for survival, and its face was blurred.

Lindsay Caven raised his hand. "Friends, neighbors, gentlemen, and others! I hereby announce a dance at my place Saturday night. Come one, come all! Bring the ladies. Spread the glad tidings hither and yon. Burro, prince of guzzlers, what became of my last bottle?"

"Lindsay, baron o' boozers, we finished it this mornin'!"

"You did, eh? Oh, well—"

Chapter Five: BULLET BAILE

MIKE DIDN'T INTEND GOING to the dance, himself. He had too much to do, he told them, to be cutting capers. The fact was, the only clothes he owned were in rags and he hadn't the money to buy others. He didn't mention that.

"I think you should show up, at least," Lindsay urged, "if only for the looks of it."

"I don't," Peter Hardy disagreed flatly. "You've made him *caporal* and it's his job to stick close to camp."

Because of Hardy's tone, Mike said, "Maybe I'll drop in, Lindsay, if things here look okay."

He didn't mean a word of it. Saturday night, though, his thoughts kept turning to the party in spite of stern resolution. The men had spruced up and departed long ago, all but the couple of discontented night guards circling the herd, and Ould Burro at the wagon comfortably settled down to a bottle that Lindsay had charitably slipped to him. The herd was a dark and peaceful mass, the humming of the night guards a monotonous, lulling sound.

Mike smoked by the small fire. He got up, stretched, squatted down again, and drank some more black coffee that he didn't particularly want.

Music and lights. Dancing. Long skirts swirling. Girls' flushed faces— "Damn!" he muttered, and got up and stretched again. It had been a long time.

Ould Burro growled amiably, "Michael, ye're that twitchy an' restless, ye get on me nerves! All work an' no fun is yer trouble. It'll ruin any man."

"What would you know about it?"

"I was a young buck once meself, full o' ginger an' energy, as I recall, gifted wi' the good sense never to miss a dance if I could help it. Go to it, man! This camp needs ye no more'n a graveyard needs a brass band."

That was about all the persuasion necessary. Mike caught up his saddle. "Guess I ought to see how it's goin', at that. Okay, I won't be long. Try to bring you back another pint."

"A generous thought! This'n will last me an hour or two yet, so have yer fun. Ye deserve it."

The *baile* at the Caven place was swinging right along when Mike arrived. All he would do, he'd promised himself, was take a brief look. Nothing more. A window would do. Just a look at the crowd, the lights, the faces. A minute to listen to the music and the laughter and the rhythm of dancing feet.

It was so durn lonely out at the camp. A man could get to delving too deeply into his thoughts at times, letting memories ghost up around him, doing him no good.

Horses and rigs filled the yard. Some of the older

men had a fire going and were grouped around it, passing a jug back and forth, talking cattle and occasionally cracking a joke. Peter Hardy was one of them, staid and severe, unsmiling when the point of a joke was earthy or on the ribald side. He didn't notice Mike. Married women sat in the rigs, their gossip a highly confidential murmuring.

A good time was being had by all.

Inside, hanging lamps shed a mellow light. Men in their Sunday clothes stood packed along the walls, roving-eyed. The girls, far outnumbered as usual, had their pick of partners and were queens this night. At the opposite end from the musicians and the leather-lunged caller sat the inevitable elderly ladies, the Death Watch, the self-elected chaperons who guarded the proprieties, nodding approval of plain and prim girls, and passing whispered judgment on those pretty and popular ones who lacked the benefit of being their kin. It was a fine *baile*. Nothing was missing.

How he ever happened to get inside, Mike wasn't sure. Somehow, after a glance through a window, he found he was being pushed along by a mixed group entering the front door. So he went on in, feeling that it was only polite to co-operate with the inevitable, his powers of resistance having become temporarily puny.

The dresses of the girls and the men's colored shirts presented a constantly changing pattern on the dance floor. Mike stayed close to the wall and behind some of the men, keenly conscious of his stained and ragged attire. The musicians were a fiddler and a guitar player, both of Mexican blood, dressed in their party finery of tight pants and short black jackets, silver-scrolled.

Mike soon figured to leave. It was a little too much for him, all this. It made him tingle. He'd had his look-in. Now he was on his way. He wished he were scrubbed and shaved, spruced up, able to prance over to some pretty girl and ask her for the honor and pleasure. Durn the cows.

The press at the front door was too tight. He edged on along the wall toward a door at the rear that would let him go through the house and out the back way. He overheard a man he passed mutter anxiously to another, "Look who's come! Them! They ain't welcome here, an' they know it!"

Occupied in easing unobtrusively along the wall, Mike suddenly realized that he was pushing past the unwelcome newcomers—eight men in a group, stiffly alert, coldly inspecting the crowd. Eight Regulators. They had entered by the back door.

Garnett was one, his neck still knotted, head tilted, eyes brilliantly malevolent.

"Hiya, stranger!" he called to Mike, and silence spread.

The Regulators didn't move, yet they gave Mike an impression of jumping to attention. Their eyes fastened on him and searched him. Lack of visible weapons meant nothing. They displayed bulges under their coats. Mike, bowing to social custom, had left his gun behind.

"Ah, there," Mike casually returned Garnett's greeting, and moved on. He hoped to stall off trouble by getting out. To hurry, though, might prompt them to act.

Near the rear door somebody nudged him and said softly, "Not that way. More of them out there. I just looked." It was Lindsay Caven. Mike felt the butt of a gun pressed against him. "I'm afraid they've come for you!"

Mike took the gun and hid it under his brush jacket. He asked without moving his lips, "How many out back?"

"I saw four. The women don't yet know anything's wrong. If anything happens, it'll be sheer hell in here!" Lindsay paused as Ed Horner joined them.

Ed Horner whispered bitterly, "You said you weren't comin'! If you weren't here, they'd leave soon, after lookin' us all over. But you're here an' Garnett's their *caporal*. All these women! God help us!"

"I'll try to bait those *hombres* out o' here," Mike promised.

The rear door was no way out, if four Regulators had it covered, so he circled on around the room, back toward the front entrance. A quick glance told him that the eight were following him. One of them slipped out through the rear. The rest came on, thrusting, creating a stir along the crowded walls.

A whisper reached Mike, from Boy Pete.

"Watch yourself! One's gone out to tell the others!"

Abreast of the two musicians and the caller, Mike halted. Some kind of disturbance was cropping up at the front door. The men crowded there were turning to stare, and making way for somebody coming in. There were strange expressions on their faces.

Somebody exclaimed, "Almighty Lord—it's the Cheyenne Flame!"

The name rustled all through the room in repeated whispers. The dancers stopped like an intricate machine brought to a shuffling halt. The caller shut up and the musicians got their chords tangled and quit embarrassedly.

What the Regulators had failed to do, the Cheyenne Flame had accomplished merely by stepping into the house. She caught and held instant attention.

In the frozen silence only she retained poise. The staring eyes must have conveyed to her like a slap in the face the naked truth of how she stood with these people. Yet she stood erect, apparently unshamed, looking as fully bulwarked in her pride as a princess. She wore no range garb this night.

She was a girl clad in feminine glory, a girl who knew how to adorn her young body in color and grace, for men to admire and women to hate.

Her dress was turquoise, the clean and vivid blue beloved by the Navajo and Taoseño. That was all Mike knew of it. He knew that she was beautiful, as polished ivory was beautiful, and crystal emerald-and-rose tourmaline, and the dusky, lustrous opal.

There was something more that he knew. Beneath her cool composure she was fighting to hold her nerve and grip, as hard as any gunfighter in a jam. She had known how she would be received here, and still she had come, perhaps hoping that in the gay, unguarded hour the frigid intolerance might lessen a little.

It was something else than brazen defiance, Mike thought. She lived in a hangout of lawless men, the daughter of a veteran lobo chief. But she couldn't help having a girl's natural dreams. He guessed it was terribly lonely for her sometimes, up there on the isolated and shunned Alta Mesa. He knew about loneliness.

Damn 'em! he thought in a rush of anger. *Damn 'em all, she's payin' 'em an honor! Why can't they offer her a decent greetin', at least? Can't they see?*

He met her gaze across the heads of the silent crowd. For a second it seemed to him that her eyes dropped their cool mask, as if glad to see a friend in a hostile house. Mike noticed then the four Mesa men following her in.

One of the four stepped up close behind her and placed a hand on her arm. He was a tall, lean man, strikingly handsome, the touch of rakish elegance in his garb enhanced by a tiny gold concho holding together the chin strings of his Mexican-style sombrero. He had been one of the riders with Brokus at the roundup camp, and Mike later heard him spoken of as Colorado Jack, one-time leader of a notorious road-agent gang, now *caporal* for Brokus.

Smiling faintly, Colorado Jack steered the Cheyenne Flame onto the dance floor. He had a superb sureness of himself, no question of that. But the fiddler and the guitar player were hastily packing up to go, and the caller had discreetly withdrawn. So the couple paced forward without music, while others vacated the floor.

Colorado Jack raised his eyes from the girl's face, a swift scowl replacing the smile. It was then that he spied the Regulators. They had already spied him.

Unruffled on the surface, betraying no hint of startled worry, Colorado Jack released his hand from the girl's arm and motioned behind him to the three Alta Mesa men, who had taken up positions just inside the doorway. The trio at once sent darting stares over the crowd, saw the reason for his signal, and stepped apart. They had come openly armed, like Colorado Jack. He turned with the girl and started back toward them, unhurriedly.

The Regulators were strung out along one wall, some of them sheltered unwillingly by Middle Range cowmen. They had shifted their regard from Mike, concentrating it on the Brokus men. The feud between Roone's Triangle T and the Alta Mesa mob wasn't an affair of grudges and patched-up truces. The Middle Range and the control of all the *Llano Fuentes* was the prize. Any accidental meeting could culminate in only one result. There was a rumor that both Roone and Brokus had privately posted cash bounties on the members of each other's crew. The Middle Range cowmen didn't count. The winner would shoo them off at leisure.

The women grew aware of the impending explosion. The sharp-eyed chaperons of the Death Watch caught on first. One of them let out a smothered scream. It sounded loud and foolish, but it stamped a stark reality onto the tragic thing in the making, and cowmen's faces grayed. In a minute the women would panic and rush the exits. Someone among the gunmen was sure to take advantage of the diversion and slam a shot at an enemy. These men were wild like wolves. In this crowded house a blazing gunfight would result in as much haphazard disaster as a charge of dynamite.

Reaching the front door and his three ready

men, Colorado Jack swung around, a dashing figure of a man, his glance twinkling darkly at the Regulators. Mike inwardly cursed the man's reckless pride. The Alta Mesa *caporal* wasn't big enough to back out of a fight, with a crowd looking on and a beautiful girl by him, though it might cost the lives of frightened women.

In the tensely quiet moment Mike spoke to the guitar player. "Strike up, *amigo*! Play somethin'! Play"—for some macabre reason he could think of nothing better than—"*Festivo del diablo*."

It was a hell of a choice: "The Devil's Holiday."

The guitar player, eyeing Mike astonishedly, picked up his huge guitar and hit the strings. The sonorous, plaintive ring of the opening chord brought all eyes to him. The fiddler hesitated, shrugged resignedly, fitted the heel of his fiddle under his chin, and joined in.

A hell of a tune. Probably nobody here knew how to dance to it—the slow, gliding steps and sudden whirls of a Spanish waltz composed long ago by a *gitano* who sang his gypsy songs before Emperor Maximilian ever attempted to introduce a refining French taste into the rich music of an ancient people. Poor Max died before a firing squad. They said it was because he ran into the Monroe Doctrine. But Mexicans, a musical people, always did manifest their artistic criticism in a definite kind of fashion.

Mike struck off across the floor. The beat of his

worn-over boot heels on the boards was an unconscious metronome spacing the music's tempo, double time. He was between the two gunmen groups. They had their eyes on him queryingly, not knowing what he was up to. Fight was their trade, not music or dancing. Not now.

The eyes of the Cheyenne Flame met Mike's before he came up to her. Unlike those of every other woman in the place, hers were not senseless with fear. Her look was understanding. Even in this moment Mike felt the strong attraction of her.

He took her arm, hearing Colorado Jack expel a breath of outrage. He stepped out with her onto the emptied floor. She had lived in Old Mexico. So had he.

There was music, light, a girl's swirling skirts and a girl's flushed face. They swung easily into the strong, graceful rhythm. Her bare arm was smooth to his roughened hand. Her slim waist yielded to his guiding pressure. A warm and vibrant life ran deep in her. He sensed it. Fire ambushed behind the cool mask of her jade-green eyes.

He was a man, having all his share of faults and vices, Adam instincts, impulses good and bad. He forgot his torn, unclean garb. He could easily have forgotten the presence of the gunmen, too, if some fool hadn't upset a chair with a crash, hurrying out.

The music, their dancing, had broken the frozen

tension, given some excuse for movement. Fear was still rampant, but the peril of panic was lessened. People were pouring out through the front door, women first.

Colorado Jack and his trio stood apart, letting the crowd scurry past, themselves too proud to join the exodus. Across the room the Regulators, as proud as they were, waited along the wall. They had their coats and shirts open, readied.

The two Mexican musicians—Mike blessed them—played on, though edging for the door. They knew the pattern of the game. There was going to be shooting. They weren't too shy of that, but this was none of their affair and they were unarmed, and their *charro* party clothes were expensive. Also—*por Dios!*—the fiddle and the guitar were very fragile.

Chapter Six: THREE IS A CROWD

WHIRLING THE GIRL slowly around, still dancing, Mike guided her over toward the wall that the Death Watch had vacated. "I guess we better take the window for it," he murmured down to her, and wished they could go on dancing The Devil's Holiday to its stirring gypsy climax. The front door was jammed with the departing crowd.

Her full skirt billowed in a wide ripple as she tilted back her head to look up into his face. "Yes, the window." Her voice was low-toned, warm, and in her eyes he plumbed a mood that was cheerfully making light of peril. She had a gay courage. "I've never broken out through a window before," she confided. "You don't know what a quiet and guarded life I spend."

"Your life is still guarded—but as for quiet, I sure can't guarantee that!" said Mike.

He had no sooner got the words out than a gun exploded a report and changed the place into a rioting madhouse.

The four Alta Mesa men crouched together, not too close and not rattled, firing unflinchingly. Through the rising screen of smoke Colorado Jack flashed a white-toothed grin over his thudding guns. The last of the crowd burst through the door, and the two-man orchestra shut down and streaked out after them.

The Regulators had split up and spread out, showing the cool efficiency of a trained posse, shooting while keeping on the move. One of them stumbled, raised a hand halfway to his head, and went down. None of the others paid any heed to him.

Garnett came trotting along the wall. Mike glimpsed the look on his face, and tugged out the gun that Lindsay Caven had slipped to him. Garnett's bullet cut the collar of his brush jacket. Mike got off a quick one and saw from the result that Garnett was cured of his stiff neck and all else that ailed him.

A smash of glass brought Mike twisting around with the lively recollection of the other Regulators outside. But it was Flame doing the window-smashing, with a chair. The ladies of the Death Watch had closed that window tightly against the night draft on their backs, and the quickest remedy was to break it.

Mike helped her through and dived out after her. The front yard was a pandemonium of screaming women, shouting men, and horses scared out of their senses. The gunfire in the house thundered on.

Mike pulled Flame away from the light of the shattered window. "Did you come in a rig?"

She shook her head. "No rig on the Alta Mesa. I rode. My horse is tied at the fence in front. I'm wearing Levi pants under this skirt," she added simply. Her voice quickened. "*Cuidado*! Some-body coming!"

Mike aimed a look along the shadow of the house and made out two figures, one ahead of the other, coming around from the rear. The foremost one, intent on finding the handiest-placed window through which to shoot, almost passed by Mike and Flame in the shadow before noticing them. The upswing of his gun wasn't finished when Mike hit him.

A shot sent the second man limping hurriedly back. "Let's get out o' here!" Mike hurried Flame on to the front yard. She had promptly bent over the clouted Regulator and got his gun.

The front yard was emptying fast, and outside the fence was wild and noisy confusion. Men, mounted and afoot, were dodging the wheels of women-laden rigs pulling out fast. Tethered horses were doing their best to snap their tied reins. They were all caught by the panic, horses and humans alike.

Peter Hardy planted himself in Mike's path, a mob of angry cowmen backing him. "What d'you mean by this, McLean?" he blared. "You're a trouble maker! You an' this Brokus wench—"

Mike sliced his gun up, changed his mind, and struck with his fist. Peter Hardy rolled back and somebody caught him. He sagged, shaking his head.

Mike said soberly, "I don't like hittin' any man that's older'n me, but he asked for it."

Ed Horner shook his fist. "So you take up for her against us, huh? Why, she's—"

"Don't finish that!" Mike warned him, and Horner didn't.

Flame turned quickly away. She gathered up her skirt and without aid swung aboard a fine sorrel that instantly hung its head and corked off its aroused temper as if it had all the wide world to buck in.

Mike's horse, discomposed by the excitement, also had to get a few kinks out of its system before allowing Mike much saddle comfort. The place was in a worse turmoil than ever by the time Mike and Flame got their mounts lined out in a lope away from there.

A weak sliver of moonlight lay over the west section of the *Llano Fuentes*, etching in pale silver and black the hollows and folds of the range. Ahead loomed Alta Mesa, towering higher and higher against the night sky as the distance decreased, its plunging cliffs darkly gashed by jagged arroyos and crisscrossed with long outcrops of ledge rock.

Mike scanned the forbidding great bulk while he and the girl jogged along together across the plain. Those cliffs looked impossible for any horse to climb, but he knew how the eye could be deceived in this country of level plains and abrupt mountains. And the girl was sure of the route. She rode with her head high, her face turned to the sky as if in deep meditation.

Breaking a long silence, she said, "I know I shouldn't have gone to that dance. They all think I only went to spoil it for them, of course. But I didn't. I went because, well—" She gave her head a slight shake and didn't go on.

Mike said, "I know."

She flashed him a startled glance, and looked away. "I do hope the Caven house hasn't burned. Some lamps got smashed."

"I hope the same. But if it has, that Colorado Jack *hombre* an' his three playmates are bound on a hot route for a celebrated place that's some hotter, from all accounts. Somehow I doubt if that would hurt my future sleep much."

She smiled. "You don't know him. I wouldn't vouch for the others, but Colorado never fails to turn up without a scratch." A moment afterward she remarked, "That's probably Colorado coming up behind us now. We'll know soon. He'll give his yell when he catches sight of us—long before we catch sight of him. He can see in the dark like a cat. I mean a wildcat!"

They pulled in, listening to the furious pounding of a wildly ridden horse. A screeching yell rang out, but it was a moment more before Mike could glimpse the oncoming rider hurtling through the darkness.

Colorado Jack maintained his mad gait to the

last, swerved around them, and hauled to a jolting halt. He laughed at Mike through the plowed-up dust, misreading his wince. It was the abused horse that Mike winced for. That kind of riding was senseless and showy, ruinous to good horses.

Colorado Jack's eyes shone like the gold concho dangling under his chin. His large gestures and brittle laugh were signs that he was drunk with the night's bloodshed.

"Hi, Flame, little *querida*!" he drawled, leaning forward on his saddle horn. "We sure busted up that *baile*, eh? Have a nice time?"

"How are the others?" she asked.

"They don't say." His tone was amused. "Nor a passel of those Triangle T jiggers. They're done regulated! Your good ol' Colorado was last to leave the party—as per habit an' inclination, an' strictly accordin' to his justly famed reputation. McLean, you can go now. I got delayed some in performin' my social duties, but here I am to take up the welcome load again. G'night!"

Mike said, "Social duty is serious to me, too. Givin' this case my full consideration from all sides to the middle, I just can't see how I can get out of escortin' the lady home."

The top gunman of Alta Mesa eased upright in his saddle. "It's a point," he allowed softly. "But don't push it. Frankly, I don't like you too much. It would take awful little for me to—"

"You've forgotten something," Flame interrupted

him. "You forget that I have something to say about it." The gun that she had picked off the Regulator was in her right hand. It was pointed in the direction of the gold concho. Her tone contained a cool authority.

Colorado Jack switched his gaze to her and dropped it to the gun. "Would you shoot me, *querida*? Aw, no!"

"I certainly would!" she responded. "And ease off that *querida* talk. I don't like it. Nor Dad. And you know it."

"Now, look! Who took you to the *baile*?"

"You and three others. On Dad's orders because he wouldn't allow me to go alone—least of all alone with you! I'm not riding back alone with you, either, don't fool yourself!"

Colorado Jack stared fixedly at her. The dim moonlight showed his handsome face quivering uncontrollably. Mike tensed, ready to draw and shoot, sure that the man's fury would burst. A monstrous vanity had been pricked. Flame must have caught the same foreboding. The hammer of her gun clicked to full cock.

But Colorado Jack released a gusty breath, dug in his spurs, reined his horse around, and went riding off. As he rocketed past Mike he didn't even glance at him. His eyes were wide and glaring straight ahead, blindly, like those of a rabid dog. With that puncture in his vanity, and the aftermath of the gunfight gripping him, there was no knowing where he would go and what he might do tonight in some insane effort to work off his rage and rebuild his pride.

Mike had seen other such men go berserk like that. And animals. Killer broncs. Outlaw bulls. He took his hand off his gun butt.

"That *hombre*," he commented, "isn't just as easygoin' as he might be."

Flame shrugged. "He's all right until he can't have his own way. Then he's loco."

"Had his own way too often?"

"I suppose that's it. Until he came here, that is, as he had to. He's wanted everywhere. But Dad can handle him. Dad's had his own way a good deal longer."

Her words indicated a casual acceptance of a way of life in which raw might and lawlessness ruled, and danger was a common element. Yet it was apparent that she found such a life less than satisfactory. She had the wish to follow another, more normal, way. She was an astonishing mixture.

They rode on side by side, saying little, and their silence itself became a strengthening bond. There was no need to talk. They glanced aside at each other, and exchanged smiles without any spoken reason.

It passed from Mike's mind that he was a hunted man trying desperately to raise a stake. For this little time he was once more a cowman, owing

70

nobody more than he could pay, owning a free man's right to see a girl home from a dance. And, furthermore, with the right to pay open and honest court to her, if she didn't object too convincingly.

The high cliffs of Alta Mesa rose near. Mike absently took note that there appeared to be no trail here on the hard, gravelly slope, although he and she were riding straight up to the foot of the mesa.

As if reading his thoughts she said, "I'll take my private path tonight. The regular one is about a mile farther on. You couldn't miss it, but there are always a couple of guards out. This one is my own. I discovered it two years ago, after heavy rains and a flash flood cut it. I said nothing about it, not even to Dad."

"Why?" Mike asked.

She answered after a silence, haltingly, "Nobody knows the future. I may have to leave, some day. Fast and alone. Dad can't live forever. When he dies—" She lifted her slim shoulders in a shrug that was weirdly like that of a fatalistic gunman.

Mike nodded. "Yeah. Men like Colorado Jack."

"Yes. They're badmen. Well, we're all what life has made of us, good and bad." She pointed upward. "Here's the first arroyo. One cuts into another, right to the top. Not easy on the horse. Have to get off and lead him in places. We part here, Mike."

He looked up at the cliff. "S'pose I came tootlin'

71

up sometime, callin' on a young lady by the name o'—"

"No." She looked into his face. "Not unless something happens and I can't get down. If that comes, remember this private path of mine, won't you? I haven't showed it to anybody else. And now—thank you. For the dance. It was grand. For everything."

"Hold it!" He kneed his horse after her. "In about fifteen days I'll be back from Torreon. Could I call?"

She shook her head. "I may be married by then!"

"What?"

"Yes. To Amery Roone."

He laughed shortly. "You scared me for a minute! Good night, Flame."

"Good night, Mike," she called back, softly and somberly, and he watched until she vanished on up the first arroyo.

Chapter Seven: FIGHTERS OF FIFTY

SHE WAS GONE. Mike turned his horse, feeling lonelier than he had ever been in all his life. He was still a young man, as years went, but his years had been crammed with experience, not all of it good and most of it tumultuously unpeaceful.

As a kid he had seen his father die of diphtheria—*el garotillo*, as the Spanish-speaking neighbors called it—on a San Saba homestead. He had roped down and milked wild cows, a half pint per indignant cow, when his mother lay ill of the ancient malady that brought the thin cheeks and hacking cough. He had buried both of them, and, not yet old enough to know about the Burial Service, he'd said, "God bless you, Pa." And, the short time later: "God bless you, Ma." And wiped the sweat off his face, onto his arms resting on the spade.

Perhaps as a recompense, nature had made of him a strong and healthy male, able to do a man's work at fifteen and ride into camp with his head not lolling. Nature could not, though, erase from his young memory the bad and tragic days, nor ease the hard times ahead. Nor, without a helpful shove from what Mike had heard was Divine Providence, save him from taking on a tough frame of mind, a tough philosophy so close to cynicism that the difference couldn't be measured.

Mike McLean was tough and cynical. He knew it and believed in it. Not heartless. That was another thing. Only the weak and spiteful were heartless. But he had never in his life heard soft words addressed to him, as he could recall. Never seen the shine of a woman's eyes turned lovingly, trustingly, softly to him. He had missed out on much. Once in a while he sensed it. He figured he was too tough to get along with any nice woman.

He drew away from Alta Mesa, disturbed, attempting to analyze his feelings toward that girl—that girl whose father was an outlaw, whose only acquaintances were outlaws.

Dammit, I'm way out o' the law, myself! he remembered.

The remembrance brought his mind to realities, to harsh, cash-value realities. Cattle! A thousand steers were his, if he could get them to the Torreon market. His, at ten-fifteen dollars a head. Maybe twenty, twenty-five, if the Torreon miners were hungry enough for beef. He stood to win anywhere from five to twenty-five thousand dollars. Enough to clear him and supply a fresh start.

He heard a thunder, a rumbling that resounded and echoed over the plain. It was made by cattle on the jump, he knew. After listening to it he gigged his horse and set out on a dead run for the roundup camp. Something had gone wrong there. It was from there that the rumble came.

He rode into a deserted cow camp that guarded

nothing but a dust-hung and empty *parada.* The herd was gone.

He cursed. But even in his cursing he admitted the fact to himself that he was at fault. The life he had lived had the virtue of pointing the finger inexorably at the stark law of cause and effect: *As ye sow, so shall ye—* He never should have left the herd. It was his responsibility. He drew up, staring around.

From under the chuck wagon Ould Burro called hoarsely, "Gone to hell an' yonder, Michael! That madman—Colorado Jack, I think he's called—came like a thunder-gust! Yellin' an' shootin'! Those cows jumped to their feet an' stompeded in all directions! Lord knows when Jim Henry an' Half-Star Ralph will turn up. It took 'em by surprise, an' I s'pose their horses bolted with 'em. For me, I stayed right here, seein' every horse in the *remuda* had took off with the herd. It was the *remuda* he spooked first, that feller."

Mike gazed speechlessly at the empty expanse of the *parada* ground. In one stroke a rage-crazed killer had wrecked everything. There would be no drive tonight, or any night. It would take weeks of patient work to catch the horses and gather in the cattle again. The Middle Range cowmen were out of patience and dead-weary.

He became aware after a while of other riders dusting into camp. He gave them a dismal hail, and met them. They greeted him with hostile eyes.

"Damn your triflin' soul to everlastin' hell!" rasped Peter Hardy. "While you went off playin' round with that girl, Colorado Jack stompeded our herd! He rode into Fifty an' bragged about it, shouted it out an' dared us all to start something! We'd only just got back from the Cavens'. Boy Pete had a gun. He took him up on it. He never would've done it, till you taught him your cussed gunman ideas!"

Mike shivered, thinking of big, simple Boy Pete pitting his clumsy courage against the trained technique of Colorado Jack. He asked, "Did Pete make out—or did he dig?" But he knew the answer.

"He dug!" said Ed Horner bitingly. "You didn't teach him good enough! Colorado Jack shot him in the wrist. An' while Boy Pete stood there, he shot both his legs. An' laughed at him fallin'! It's the only time I ever wished I was a damned gunman!"

"You've ruined my son!" Peter Hardy spoke in a low and trembling monotone. "Made a cripple of him! Yes, you, McLean! It never would've happened, but for you. I can't kill you—you're too gun-smart for me—or I would! But I'll curse you to my last day! My boy—crippled! An' no money to get him a doctor down from Albuquerque or get him to a hospital there. Oh, God!"

He turned and rode off. The others followed, muttering, casting angry glares at Mike.

Crawling unsteadily out from under the wagon, Ould Burro observed, "'Twould appear we're finished here, Michael! A hasty *vamoose* is in order, *no es verdad*? When yon departing gents get to augurin' amongst themselves they'll work up a hot stew. But where do we go? We've run right out o' geography, dammit!"

Mike sat slumped on the wagon tongue. "Can't blame 'em. I'd feel the same. Hardy is right. A trouble maker—that's me. I'm a Jonah." He rose wearily. "Got to raise some cash somehow."

"A noble decision!" approved Ould Burro, shaking an empty bottle and sighing. "I don't know how ye'll go about it, but count me in."

"Not this time, Burro. It's for Boy Pete. For hospital an' doctors. Hardy's right about that, too. The blame's mine that Pete got himself shot. I see only one way to raise the money."

"Ye sound mighty solemn about it, Mr. McLean!"

"That's how I feel, Mr. O'Burrifergus!"

In the morning, after a sleepless night of long thoughts, Mike rode into Fifty. Ould Burro insisted on going with him, mentioning his urgent need of a drink to nail himself together, and adding pensively the information that he lacked the price. Mike had a dollar and gave it to him, causing the old gambler to eye him searchingly, troubledly, before heading for the Log Cabin Bar.

Mike called at the plain little Hardy house. Like most of the small cowmen, Hardy lived in Fifty and ran his cattle on the open range.

Answering Mike's knock, Peter Hardy grunted at sight of him and started to slam the door. Mike jammed a foot against it.

"Hold it, Hardy! I've got something to say."

"I've got nothing to say to you, McLean, that can be said on a Sunday! Get out!"

"Wait a minute. How's Pete?"

Peter Hardy breathed hard. "I'm tending him best I can. But I'm not a doctor. It's surgeons an' hospital care he needs."

"I'm here to tell you how to get the money," Mike said, and paused. The hot sun felt good. The surrounding plains and far mountains looked good. It was a good land.

He said, "I'm worth a thousand dollars up in Estancia. I stuck up the bank there. I'm bound to be caught, soon or later. Somebody will earn it. Let it be you. I give up. Let's start north in a wagon with Pete. You turn me in at Estancia, collect the thousand, an' take Pete on to Albuquerque."

Peter Hardy's eyes flickered. "You don't own any cow outfit, eh? I suspected it. You're on the dodge. Why would any bank robber do this?"

Mike looked away, scowling. "It's not my trade, robbin' banks. Stickin' up that one wasn't smart, but I figured I had good reason. Drennan, man who owns that bank, caught me short on a note for two thousand. Took my outfit, worth five thousand at bottom. So I collected the difference—three thousand."

"Where did that go?"

"I got caught near Manzano by the local marshal an' some citizens, while I was asleep. The marshal was a poor man an' I made a deal with him. He let me break out for three thousand dollars. Well, never mind that." Mike swung on his heel. "You get a wagon ready. I'll be at the Log Cabin. Don't take too long. I could change my mind, if the weather stays nice!"

Striding to the Log Cabin, Mike came face to face with Amery Roone.

He had never met Roone, and had only a scanty description of him, but he guessed immediately that this was the man, the Eastern owner of the Triangle T, boss of the Regulators. He based his conclusion on the stiff-brimmed hat, whipcord breeches, and tailored coat. Besides, five gun-slung Regulators rode at heel behind him, the brand of the Triangle T on their horses.

"Are you McLean?"

It was more of a snapped command than a query. There was sharpness in Roone's eyes, a suave and chilly assurance in his manner, and hardness beneath. His keen face showed no humor. It looked incapable of emotion. Here was a man utterly unswayed by the wayward influence of human passion.

Mike said, "Yeah. You Roone?"

Perhaps nobody before had ever addressed Mr. Amery Roone in so unceremonious a fashion. The eyes of the five Regulators stabbed at Mike.

Amery Roone, however, chose to let the disrespect pass. He said in his clipped voice, "Heard of you, McLean. Understand you roughed up my best man. Leaving this country? You'd be well advised!"

Mike said, "Fact is, I am. Not on your say-so, though."

Men of the Middle Range were looking on from some distance along the street, and trying to listen.

Amery Roone smiled frostily. He put his horse up closer to Mike and held out his hand. "Yes, I'm Roone. Let's shake hands. I like a man with independence."

Mike shook hands with him. It would have been small to refuse. And he knew that the cowmen of Fifty, suspicious now of anything that he did, were watching and whispering.

"Good luck, McLean." Amery Roone withdrew his clean white hand. "This isn't your country. You joined the wrong side. Where do you plan to go from here?"

That, the positive opinion and the rank out-of-line question, sparked Mike's temper. Mike said distinctly, "Where I go is no man's damn business. I reckon you ain't been long here."

Into Amery Roone's cold face crept an added

pallor. That was all. "Excuse me. For a moment I forgot"—his thin lips perked—"the sensitive reactions of men who are on the wanted list. I'm afraid I'm ignorant of the—hem—etiquette of outlaws."

He and his five armed warriors rode on. Mike proceeded toward the Log Cabin, not in a gentle temper.

Into Mike's path stepped Ed Horner and several others. "McLean! What's between you an' Roone? We saw you shake hands with him. Looks mighty funny to us!"

Mike's temper began cracking. "Don't pull that snuffy tone on me, Horner! I won't take it!"

Behind him some horsemen walked their mounts briskly up the short street. He supposed they were Roone's Regulators coming back to witness a promising row that had him on the short end, and he knew now that Roone's handshake had been done with malice aforethought.

He didn't look around. Ed Horner and his friends were plainly on the prod, ready to pile into him if he offered them an opening. The gun he wore was all that was restraining them. Ould Burro's prediction was square on the nail. They looked as if they had been up all night, holding a stormy session, and worked themselves into an unreasoning rage. Disappointment and disaster had become intolerable.

The horsemen halted behind Mike. Their silence

gave him the creeps, and he snapped at the cowmen before him, "Out o' my way! I'm in a hurry!"

One of the horsemen at his back drawled, "You *been* in right smart of a hurry—but not from now on! Lift your hands, straight up an' clean, an' quick!"

That drawling voice registered. Even as he jerked around, the knowledge flashed into Mike's mind that Peter Hardy would never earn that thousand dollars' reward. It was already earned. The hunters had caught up with him at last.

George Pringle, sheriff of Estancia, spoke over a leveled gun. "Your hands, Mike, pul-*ease!* Kindly excuse my insistence, but I know you too well to take ary a chance."

He was a leathery old lawdog who liked to affect an elaborate politeness, especially during critical moments. His long, sardonic face and disillusioned eyes gave him something of a sinister aspect, but it was on his record that he was as honest as a bloodhound and just as uninterested in any phase of law outside of the tracking down of fugitive lawbreakers.

Flanking the sheriff were his two best deputies, guns drawn, regarding Mike with grave detachment. They knew him. He had been on good terms with them. As casual friends, they might have been glad for him to have made good his get-away, he knew. As lawmen they would strain the last notch to take him in. He knew that, too.

Still, it was some better than being taken by strangers. He raised his hands. " 'Lo, Bert. 'Lo, Webb. All right, George, no hard feelin's. You can take my gun. Sure wish you'd got here a little later, though. You've put me in a plumb embarrassin' position. I promised a man my reward."

Pringle leaned over carefully and got the gun. "Are you tellin' me you aimed to give up? You? Why?"

"I owe him the money."

"Well! Y' know, Mike, I could have a foolish inclination to believe you, only it's my recollection you departed Estancia with three thousand dollars!"

"I didn't keep it."

"No?" George Pringle narrowed his eyes thoughtfully. "I think I can guess where it went. That Manzano jailbreak smelled! There'll be no gettin' the money back. Pity. It would've helped you at your trial. Mr. Hebard Drennan has a sentimental attachment for that money." He motioned behind him. "Mr. Hebard Drennan is about to become awful sore an' vengeful!"

Mike looked past the sheriff. Down the street he saw Roone and his men coming slowly along. And among them rode Hebard Drennan, banker of Estancia, merchant and dealer in anything of value, and expert manipulator of mortgages.

George Pringle smiled at Mike's expression.

"Yeah, you've guessed it. Mr. Drennan an' Mr. Roone have some business connections. Mr. Roone it was who sent word you were here. He's a man who gets all the news, like about who's wanted an' what for, him bein' sort of volunteer high constable hereabouts. So he notified Drennan. Drennan notified me an' decided to come down with us, to personally thank friend Roone for his help, an' to vouch for us so we could come in by way o' Roone's Triangle T without somebody tippin' you the word. Also, to personally collect his three thousand dollars before anything further misfortunate might happen to it. No, Mr. Drennan ain't goin' to be pleased!"

Chapter Eight: **KNIVES IN THE DARK**

THE COWMEN HAD STOOD listening puzzledly. Ed Horner asked, "What's this all about? Are you lawmen? You arrestin' him?"

George Pringle gazed at them solemnly. "We're lawmen an' we're arrestin' him, as you have so shrewdly guessed. Mr. McLean in an absent-minded moment happened to rob the bank at Estancia, for which misguided whim he will be wearin' gray whiskers when next he appears in our midst."

"What?" Horner exclaimed. "Why, he's a big Texas cattleman!"

Pringle shook his head sadly. "Mike McLean, you've sure gone bad! First it's bank-robbin', then lyin'. You're on the downward road to perdition. To be a cattleman means to own cattle. Which at this present time makes you totally not a cattleman!"

Mike rubbed his nose. "Well, I came close to bein' one here. I had it all figured, George. I was goin' to make enough profit on a cattle deal to pay Drennan if he'd drop the charge. An' some over for a fresh start."

"At our expense!" Horner burst out. "Why, you—you—"

His rage spilled. His fist caught Mike high on the cheek and knocked him stumbling sidewise away from the lawmen.

The shout and the blow uncapped the fury of the cowmen. Ordinarily as fair in their ways as most, for them to attack a disarmed prisoner was against all their principles. But principles had fled along with reason. The final exposure of Mike as a penniless outlaw, robber, and liar, on top of their bitter anger and disappointment, was too much.

They went bronco. They charged at him. Disregarding the lawmen's guns and plunging horses, they swamped him, all trying to get in a lick at him. It came to Mike that he, who had worked to arouse a fighting spirit in them, was the first victim of his own teachings.

More men came running to the riot, caught by mob fury, craving to tear the scapegoat apart. Angry voices reached a swelling roar.

"Get him!"

Using fists, elbows, boots, Mike fought to his feet. Some inspired rioter hurled a hammer at him from the open door of the blacksmith shed. He saw it coming, ducked, tried to catch it, and failed. A heavy clout sent him floundering. He bounded up again, handed Horner a belt in the jaw, and knocked two men down in a headlong lunge to the Log Cabin. He got his back against the saloon front, slamming at all corners.

For once George Pringle didn't seem to know quite how to handle an urgent situation. Nor did his two deputies. The three of them were shouting, vainly attempting to force their horses forward, but their horses had different ideas. Knowing little of the previous circumstances, to the lawmen the riot exploded as a completely unexpected development. To shoot into the berserk mob was too extreme a step. These men clearly were respectable citizens, or had been, up to this minute. Now the respectable citizens were trying hard to share up Mike among them.

Roone and his men came up and sat looking on, making no effort to interfere. Drennan, his baggy eyes bulging, kept saying something to Roone, who smiled frostily and shook his head.

Ould Burro barged out of the Log Cabin, derringer in hand. "Hold the fort, Michael, I'm comin'!" he clarioned. Somebody fetched him a terrific smack and he took a backward header into the barroom and stayed there.

Mike landed his fist on a burly cowman, and teetered against the saloon wall for balance. He was as mad now as any of them.

He crouched, his unruly hair tumbling over his broad forehead, butted an onrushing man in the middle, and kicked the feet out from under another.

"Fight, is it?" he snarled. "You forty-to-one warriors, I'll give you a fight!" He dived into the thick of them.

Back on the San Saba, and in Dodge City, various points between, and widely separated other spots where life galloped to a fast tempo—

including Estancia—there were men who could agree reminiscently that Mike McLean was well able to give a fight that satisfied most applicants. Struggle and battle came naturally to him, he not having known much of anything else.

The dust-hung air was full of fists and feet. He toppled three men to the ground with him, reared up with another hanging to his back, jackknifed, sent that nuisance overhead, and dived in again.

They didn't give way. They came at him like hunting hounds at a mountain lion. The thud of blows given and taken beat a dull tattoo to their shouting. His face and knuckles bloody, Mike smashed on. He took a punch that rang bells and got spraddle-legged from it. Recovering dizzily, he handed one back to the giver and sent him colliding into those behind him. But they pressed on, cramping him in close.

Someone on the ground clutched his legs. He tried to kick loose, and a fist got through and rocked him badly. He struck out, making awkward efforts to keep his footing. If he went down under this pack, it was farewell. There were faces as bloody as his around him, eyes glaring as savagely as his own.

Down he fell, those clutching arms vised around his legs. The cowmen piled onto him. Striking, kicking, he gave back what he could. The hold on his legs loosened. He used up all he had left, getting to his feet. He was about done up.

George Pringle quit tussling with his fractious horse. "Mike McLean!" he yelled wrathily. "Here's your gun back! Catch!"

It was a good throw. Mike caught the gun by the barrel. He rammed the butt at a lunging head, flipped the gun over in his hand, and triggered two shots, not caring much where they went.

Another shot cracked from a different gun, then another and another. Mike became aware of men plowing their horses right into the crowd. Cold-eyed, reckless-looking men, who rode as if they didn't give a damn how many respectable citizens got hurt.

Those hitting at Mike split up and fell back, suddenly self-conscious. Bruised and bloody, dazed, one eye swollen shut, Mike couldn't see much. He got a poke at the nearest man, and set himself to start all over.

Then he saw, with his good eye, the foremost rider pushing toward him.

The Cheyenne Flame kept an easy seat in the saddle of her rearing horse. Reins wrapped around her wrist, she reloaded a smoking gun. She wore range garb—Levi's and flannel shirt—and her big sombrero. Back of her rode Bloody-Wire Charley Brokus, laughing his huge laugh, and the gunmen of Alta Mesa.

Brokus bellowed, "As pretty a scrap as I've seen since ol' Montana Monte took on the crowd at Trinidad! They make men yet, hell scorch me if they don't! McLean, you revive my faith in human nature!" He pointed his beard, in the old-timer manner, at Flame. "She was for hornin' in sooner. Likes your style. So do I, but I wouldn't let her stop good fun. Man, your face is a mess! Ah, to be young again!"

He waved scornfully at the glowering cowmen. "*Vamoose*, you uninitiated amateurs! Begod, you met a man! Hey, McLean, who're those three? They wear the offensive look o' lawmen, to me. They after you?"

Mike nodded groggily and steered an unsteady course to George Pringle. "George, you gave me my gun. I 'preciate that. I'm givin' it back."

Pringle took the gun. "Thanks. You don't take advantage, do you, Mike? Dammit to hell! I wish you had that three thousand. You could make a deal if you did, son. It won't make me happy, takin' you back to Estancia for trial."

"Trial for what?" demanded Brokus.

"Bank robbery," said Pringle quietly. He nodded at Drennan. "There's the banker. He's out three thousand. McLean ain't got it. Spent it on his getaway. I'm George Pringle, sheriff of Estancia, where the robbery was done."

The great head tilted regally. "I'm Charley Brokus, boss o' the Alta Mesa. You don't take McLean! I like him. An' I got twenty-odd men here, you'll notice! *Sabe, senor*?"

"I *sabe*, Mr. Brokus." Pringle eyed Mike.

"Seems you've already made good friends an' bad enemies here. Well, that's you! But I'm here to take you in. I aim to try!"

Mike said. "Okay, George. Brokus, let's not have any trouble, eh? George an' Bert an' Webb, they kinda been friends o' mine."

Brokus quirked an eyebrow. "I know how that is. Makes it tough. But look." He grinned affably at Amery Roone. "Mr. Roone, have you got anything against McLean that you can't forget? No? *Bueno* to hell! You an' me, we've come in to make our peace. Ain't it so?"

"It is so, Mr. Brokus."

"You bet! Is it okay with you if I pull this boy out o' his jackpot?"

"Perfectly, Mr. Brokus," replied Roone. "However, my friend, Mr. Drennan, here—"

"He's out three thousand, the sheriff says," Brokus interrupted. "A dirty little three thousand dollars. Chicken feed. I got the answer to that. But I can see where my *caporal*—" he snapped a hand on Colorado Jack's wrist—"is wishful to shoot Mr. McLean! It make me curious. D' you mind, Mr. Roone, if I take time out to get at the root o' the matter?"

Mike said, "That root ain't deep. Your damned *caporal* stampeded our herd last night. He gunned a friend o' mine, too. You turn him loose, an' I'll take him on!"

"Ah!" breathed Brokus. "So you did it, Col! Not

91

on my order, blast you! You rebel son, I got a mind to let that boy have you!"

Colorado Jack glanced at Flame, who was looking at Mike. His eyes flared. "That would suit me fine!"

"I'd put you in hell where you belong!" Mike promised.

Brokus nodded amiably. "Two fine men spoilin' for a fight! I'm all for it. But, McLean, you're that banged up I doubt you could hit a barn an' you inside it! Boys, put 'em in the blacksmith shed, the door shut an' no light. Take the guns off Col. Let 'em keep their knives an' no more. McLean, it'll give you a more even chance, you blind in an eye as you be. In the dark you won't need good sight. An equable arrangement, Mr. Roone, don't you think?"

"Quite as equable as could be arranged," Roone agreed. "Some of my men would welcome, I'm sure, the opportunity to step into your man's place. My foreman was shot last night at a dance. They tell me it was this McLean fellow who did it."

"Yeah? Well, well, boys will be boys, Mr. Roone!"

Mike felt for his knife. It was a cowman's clasp knife, keen, but not designed for fighting. Colorado Jack had a ten-inch bowie on his belt, a sticker of the size to whack off a bull's head.

They stepped into the blacksmith shed.

Colorado Jack walked to the far side and stood with his back to the plank wall, his eyes glittering. Mike heard Brokus commenting that he had once settled a quarrel in this manner, in Quebec.

"They took up that Frenchman's mortal remains in a sack," Brokus related, "an' I left Canada on a fast horse. He had many friends. Ah, but I was young then an' full o' the devil. Anybody want to bet on who comes out o' the shed? Name your fancy, boys!"

The door closed. As the light was blocked out, Mike sensed rather than heard Colorado Jack's rapid shift. He dropped to a squat. A pair of heavy tongs whammed the wall and clanged on the floor. Colorado Jack obviously wasn't limiting himself to his big bowie knife. The shed, black dark, was rich on potential weapons. Mike stayed motionless.

He had no liking for this type of prowling murder. But he was in it now. He remembered what Flame had said, that Colorado Jack had cat's eyes. It didn't make him feel any better. For his part, he couldn't see in the dark any more than a blind mule. Nor in broad daylight right now, the way his eyes were puffing. He bedamned Brokus for fixing up this silent, crawling duel in the dark. It wasn't his style of fight. He didn't like it.

He heard George Pringle say, "Mr. Brokus, you sure do take liberties with my prisoner!"

"Prisoner?" Brokus echoed. "He's a free man!"

Soon Mike felt that he was staying too long in one spot. Reason warned him that his safest play was to stick, that Colorado Jack couldn't locate him as long as he remained motionless. But impatience prodded him. Waiting and safe playing had never held much appeal for him. He slid noiselessly from his position and started edging around the shed in a blind stalk after Colorado Jack.

He wished that he could have impressed upon his memory the layout of the shed and its contents, as Colorado Jack must have done as soon as he entered. There wasn't a sound from him.

Mike's head brushed against something dangling from a rafter, and he ducked instinctively. It swung, and let out the soft clang of an iron tire lightly striking wood. A single thud, just above and behind his head, puzzled him momentarily, until he heard Colorado Jack whisper a curse.

"Lost your long blade, *hombre*?" Mike inquired. He reached up and felt it; stuck hard in the plank wall, and he left it there. It had been a lightning throw, terrific force behind it, the distance judged accurately.

"You know it," came the reply. "An' if you're any part of a fightin' man you'll chuck yours away an' we'll slug it out."

"That's more in my line," Mike agreed. He discarded his knife and stepped forward, abandoning stealth. "Come on, where are you?"

"Right here!" Colorado Jack's voice crooned a fierce mirth. "Comin' right up!"

Mike spun half around. A forearm swept past his face. He sucked a breath in sudden pain, his chest ripped by a stab meant for his neck. It hadn't occurred to him that Colorado Jack would carry a clasp knife as well as the long bowie.

"You dirty damned—"

He jumped back to avoid the next slash of the knife. The backs of his legs fetched up against the anvil in the darkness and he toppled across it, rolled off, and got snarled up with the black-smith's open-head water barrel. The blacksmith had the usual habit of hanging all his variously shaped and sized tongs around over the edge of the barrel. It was like falling onto the spiked ends of a bundle of iron picket stakes.

The jangling clatter brought a laugh from Colorado Jack. "Howya doin'? I'm goin' to cut your ugly head off an' boot it out the door!"

Falling off the barrel, Mike dragged loose a pair of tongs and let fly. They hit a rafter, but evidently bounced off onto Colorado Jack, judging by his change of language. Mike sent another pair going. He kept flinging tongs until the supply ran out, sailed a couple of sledge hammers after them, and switched to horseshoes.

Outside, among a rumble of talk, Brokus boomed, "How can two men raise that much racket? If I didn't know, I'd swear it was forty wild broncs an' a bear in there!"

Keeping up the bombardment, it wasn't possible for Mike to know if he had scored any hits where they mattered, but once or twice he thought he heard a yelp. He figured he had hit just about everything in the shed. Colorado Jack was staying clear. Getting down to the last horseshoe he could find in the dark, Mike gripped it in his fist and went looking for him. Not finding him, he thumbed a match alight. A slight sound took him on another couple of paces.

Colorado Jack stood leaning against the wall, one shoulder lower than the other and the arm dangling, his face, like Mike's, glistening with sweat and blood. They glared silently at each other over the match. Letting his pent-up breath out gaspingly, Colorado Jack lurched forward, the knife in his left hand jabbing for Mike's neck.

Mike hit him one blow with the horseshoe.

He couldn't locate the door. He was all turned around. "Open up!" he called hoarsely.

They let in light and he stumbled out. He was shaking, racked by pain, blood-soaked all down his chest. He peered through one puffed eye at misty shapes of men.

"Go drag your man out! I don't know if I've killed him, but he sure ain't walkin' around!"

Chapter Nine: BOUGHT AND PAID FOR

BROKUS ROARED, "Pay me, boys! McLean, I bet on you. What was all the racket?"

"We pitched some horseshoes, among other things," Mike said, "an' I hung a ringer on him." The crowd was blurring worse. He was having trouble keeping upright.

Brokus slapped his thigh, laughing. "Look at him! Ain't he a sight? Ain't he a beaut? Hung a ringer on Col, he says! Haw! Sheriff, what's he worth, anyhow?"

George Pringle fingered his long chin, scanning Mike reflectively. "He stole three thousand dollars. If he had it, which he hasn't, I think Mr. Drennan could be persuaded to—"

"Cheap at the price!" said Brokus. "Sheriff, you look like a reasonable man, one o' the old grain. You know you can't take him if I say no, don't you? An' I do say no!"

Pringle coughed gently. "The weight of the majority is on your side, sir, that I admit. Furthermore, I grant I'm a fair stretch outside my bailiwick. Hum. In the haste to get back to my regular duties at Estancia, it's possible a warrant could get lost, under certain conditions. Like after a tiresome day's ride, y' know. Hungry. Dark evenin'. Not thinkin', and sort of absent-mindedly starting the fire with it. There's another certain condition, too, though, without which I doubt the mishap could occur."

"Sheriff, you're a man o' broad understandin' an' rare good judgment," Brokus complimented him grandly. "Wish they were all like you. Sure, I'll foot his bill. Three thousand. You hear, McLean, or are you as fogged as you look?"

Mike was fogged. But there was a thought that stuck in his head. "Make it four thousand," he said, "an' I'm your man. A thousand for me. I need it."

Brokus laughed again. "Can still crack a joke an' drive a bargain, huh? Yeah, you're my man. Four thousand it is. But, as the sheriff put it, under certain conditions. Namely, that while you work it out you'll have to take my orders without any question, an'—" he blinked thoughtfully up at the sky—"guard the interests o' me an' mine at any cost."

He apparently relished the phrase. "You'll guard the interests o' me an' mine at any cost!" he repeated, and added for good measure, "So help you God!"

"You an' yours," Mike mumbled. "S' help me."

He missed a clutch at the blacksmith's door and keeled over. It was George Pringle who caught him. The last Mike heard was Pringle muttering, "Boy, I hope I've done you good! But I sure got misgivin's—"

• • •

The Brokus house on Alta Mesa was an adobe mansion, a mud palace of many rooms, three floors high at one end. The outside walls, four feet thick, kept the interior cool on the hottest day. Here and there in angles of the building were little odd-shaped *placitas* that, in the Southwestern Spanish fashion, should have contained flower gardens, but didn't. This was a place of men, and there were limits to what one girl could accomplish with such an immense household.

The structure had grown more or less haphazardly through the years, Mike learned, as Brokus's prosperity and number of followers increased. No bunkhouse existed. The men's quarters were in the long wing of the house, and everybody ate in one great room, at hand-hewn log tables that would have needed a team of oxen to drag.

It was pleasant and restful to sit lazily in the shade of a red-flagstoned *portico*, smoking and gazing out over the plain at the purple-hazed mountains, cool water in an Indian clay *olla* hanging within easy reach.

Mike said to Brokus, "So you an' Roone are buryin' the hatchet, eh? That was what your meetin' with him was about in Fifty?"

"Right." Brokus sent him a bland glance. "I told Roone I thought it was mostly my fault, the bad feelin' between us. Like an old fool, I'd set out to be boss o' the whole *Llano*. In that smooth way o' his, he said, 'Mr. Brokus—' to which I said, 'Call me Charley.' He said, 'Thank you, Charley, I will. Charley,' he said, 'we're only human. Much fault has been on my side.' That was real generous of him, wasn't it?"

"Yeah. You, too."

"Sure." Brokus sucked a tooth. "So in that happy light o' mutual confession an' trust, we made a deal. Roone gives me free hand to run off those cow-squatters an' take over the Middle Range. After which, we share the whole *Llano* like good neighbors, an' stand together against anybody tryin' to move in. United we stand! How's that? *Bueno*, huh?"

"Oh, sure." Mike yawned, and stretched cautiously. The knife-slash across his chest had about healed, but too-energetic movements twinged reminders of it. And his face had reshaped to about normal, a bit bulged and dented here and there, but good enough to do ordinary service.

"Yeah. *Bueno* to hell," he said. "Like dreams o' payday!"

Brokus grinned. "Speakin' o' pay, what did you do with the thousand I gave you? You sure didn't spend any on clothes. Did it go with your Burro man on a certain mysterious trip to Fifty that you sent him on?"

"It went to pay a man what I owed him."

"Begod, you don't welsh on your debts!"

Mike changed the subject. "I don't quite see you an' Roone pullin' together. You don't match, an' you're both too durn ornery. I foresee a split soon. Do I miss the right time to keep quiet, maybe, though? Let me know."

Brokus banged him on his shoulder. "I'll let you know when. Don't worry, Roone won't be any trouble. I spread him a nice deal an' he liked it. Who's tryin' to sing? Your Burro man?"

Mike nodded. "Mr. O'Burrifergus is drunk again. You should keep your whisky locked up. I'm not sure you did right by yourself, bringin' him here along with me."

"He ain't no big help," Brokus agreed carelessly. "But he's an amusin' cuss. I might make him my court jester, like they say the old kings had. King here, ain't I?"

Mike bowed without rising. "Truly spoken, Emperor Charles, Majesty o' the Mesa, Lord High Mogul o' the *Llano*, an' Prince o' Powdersmoke. May I ask your mighty highness how in hell you led Roone into makin' a deal with you?"

Brokus chuckled. "Trappin' was my trade, way back. I still know how to bait a coyote!"

"What bait did you use on Roone?" Mike asked.

The king laid a quizzical look at him. "Flame," he said. "My daughter."

Mike shot out of his chair.

"Huh?"

"What's bit you? Sit down. You'll have jumpin' a-plenty to do next Sunday. That's the day. Roone's had an eye for Flame these two years past. I'm not blind to him. Not blind to you, either! It was for somethin' more than your fightin' ability that I paid your bill."

"She's your own daughter! You'd sell her for—"

"Shut your mouth! I said I'd let you know when to be quiet. I'm lettin' you know!" The iron was in Brokus's harsh command. "You'll take my orders without question—remember? Sit down!"

He leaned back, nodding, as Mike slowly sank into his chair. "Now you listen. Sunday is the day. A quiet weddin', nothin' big an' fancy. I wanted it here, but seein' Roone was still a leetle cagey, I proposed his place. It'll be a fortunate union, he said, of two great houses. A weldin' o' the warrin' clans. The talk o' the man! A—"

"An' how does Flame feel about it?" Mike broke in. "How about her, you daughter-sellin' old—"

"Hobble your tongue, son," Brokus advised, "else I won't like you any more. That would be bad for you! However, I'll answer your question. My daughter is an obedient girl an' she'll do as I say. She's a good girl. I'm more'n fond of her."

"Looks like it!"

"Be quiet, damn you! Keep your mind—an' I use that word loosely—on what I'm sayin'. Listen! In this enlightened land the wife inherits the property of her dead husband, full an' clear.

The common-property law. The widows' law. All right. Sunday afternoon, Flame becomes the bride of Amery Roone. Right off thereafter, due to a sudden an' fatal circumstance, she becomes his widow! Legal owner o' the Triangle T, before her marriage is—hem—consummated. Is that the word? A widow, I mean, the poor child, before she's actually a wife. Ah, the pity of it!"

"You finished?" Mike hunched forward, clenching his fingers. "That common-property law works both ways. If *she* dies, he gets *her* property. Includin' what she inherits from her pa—who could become a late lamented awful quick if he don't watch out!"

Brokus waved a hand. "You're way behind me, son. That's the bait I used on Roone. But the race is to the swift! First come, first served! My daughter will be the cattle queen o' the Southwest!"

"You're gamblin' her life. Roone's no fool. Have you figured that he might be first—yeah, as smart as you think you are, an' maybe smarter!"

"What?" Brokus flung up his head. "I can lick any man at any game. Flame is safe. We'll all be there for the weddin'. An' I'll have the right man there to take care o' Roone soon's I give the nod."

"Is he reliable?" Mike queried.

"I think he is," returned Brokus, "or I certainly wouldn't have paid four thousand dollars for him!"

● ● ●

The voice of the preacher from Alamogordo droned solemnly out through the open windows.

"Repeat after me. *I take this man . . .*"

It was the only definite sound in the hot, quiet Sunday afternoon. In the wide yard the two groups of men idly watched white-coated Mexican servants skurrying with last preparations for the wedding feast spread out on the famed Triangle T grass lawn. China dishes, real silver, and linen tablecloths.

Roone's house, nothing like the adobe palace on Alta Mesa, had been planned by an architect brought from the East, who scorned the age-old style of the country. It was as civilized as a hearse.

Perhaps it was the bride who set the somber cloud over this wedding. Unsmiling, her eyes haunted, she had entered the house, still alone among men, pale with foreboding like a virgin led to sacrifice in some barbaric rite. The men in the yard listened to the service.

"Whom God hath joined . . ."

There was no mixing between Roone's Regulators and the men of Alta Mesa. It was natural that the Regulators should congregate close to their bunkhouse, clannish and stiffly reserved in the presence of old enemies. It was just as natural for the Alta Mesa guests to clot together in the shade of the wagon shed.

Brokus had foreseen and fitted the arrangement

into his plans. Guns hidden under clean shirts, their horses within easy distance behind the wagon shed, the Alta Mesa men waited. They knew what they were here for. The plan had a simple recklessness that appealed to their lawless inclinations. A shot at Roone. That was to be the opener. Mike's job. In the flare-up, Brokus would make a getaway with Flame, helped and covered by the crew.

The rest would be up to Mike to handle. Push the fight and take over the Triangle T right then and there in the name of its new young mistress, if things looked promising. If not, jump to the horses and get out, covering always the escape of the bride.

Either way, it would work out all right. Roone's men were a fighting outfit, but they wouldn't stay with it long, their boss dead and no more pay in sight for them. Old Bloody-Wire Charley would be king of the whole *Llano*, his daughter the princess. He was smart. He had Mike almost convinced of it.

Treachery against expected treachery. Mike had no taste for it. A murderous business. But he had his orders. Get Roone with the first shot, and free the bride. As long as he thought of Flame it was easier to hold the purpose steady. It had to be done, if only for her sake. He knew that Brokus was banking on his feeling that way about it. That scheming old robber had him weighed, figured, and tied. As the bride's father, Brokus was a wedding guest in the house, all dressed up, exuding dignity and benevolence.

Colorado Jack had insisted on coming with the rest, although the effort of riding broke sweat out on him and he wasn't good for much. He was a changed man, his face misshapen, eyes sunken, his right shoulder and arm bulkily bound and strapped. Nobody in the crew paid him much attention. He had been *caporal*, but in the jungle code of the Alta Mesa gunmen the loser went into the discard. Mike was *caporal* now, by right of conquest.

The voice of the preacher ceased, was replaced by a medley of others, topped by Brokus's booming hearty congratulations and good wishes. The ceremony was over. The ill-matched two were man and wife.

"They'll be comin' out now," Colorado Jack whispered unsteadily. "Eyes on that front door! Eh, McLean?"

"Right. But, man, how you shake! Why don't you slip out before it starts? It'll be okay."

The broken gun boss muttered something and limped into the wagon shed. There was another door in the rear. He could reach the horses handily by that route.

Mike said to those around him, "Remember, nobody shoots till I do. An' I don't shoot till Brokus sends me the nod. Let's not have any

106

bobble. Act natural. Those jiggers are eyein' us pretty close over there."

Brokus emerged from the house, a magnificent figure in gray trousers, Prince Albert coat, and fine white shirt. Smiling, the picture of a proud father well satisfied with his daughter's choice of a husband, he betrayed no sign of being at all conscious of the eyes fastened on him. He had always lived a dangerous life.

Perfectly at ease, casually lighting a cigar, he beamed at the laden tables on the lawn and called over his shoulder, "Amery, you surely do things up right! My, my, do I see champagne? Come on, let's have a toast or two to start with!"

"Of course, Charley, of course!" responded the cool, clipped voice of Amery Roone from inside the house. "Nothing will please me better."

But still nobody came out after Brokus. He stood there alone. He puffed his cigar, waiting. He turned, looking back inquiringly. He frowned slightly and glanced at the Triangle T men at the front of the bunkhouse. The cigar in his teeth went motionless. He had sensed something wrong. His eyes flicked swiftly, shifting their regard to the wagon shed.

His genial expression froze. He whipped a hand under his Prince Albert coat to his armpit. On the instant he was bad old Bloody-Wire Charley Brokus again, the hard-bitten outlaw chief.

A shot whanged loudly inside the wagon shed.

Brokus frowned deeper, finished his armpit draw, and fired. A sobbing sigh joined the ringing echoes in the shed. Mike spun around and saw Colorado Jack, his gun trailing smoke, falling out of a buggy. While Mike looked at him, gunfire in the yard shattered the remaining hush of the Sunday afternoon.

Inside the house, Roone was calling, his tone unchanged, "A toast, Charley, by all means. Here's to your demise!"

Chapter Ten: THE KING IS DEAD

AN ALTA MESA MAN fell heavily against Mike.
Mike shoved him off, slung two shots at the
bunkhouse, and backed into the wagon shed.
Others hurriedly dived in after Mike.

The open yard was an execution ground.
Roone's men, too, knew what they were there
for and they had their orders. They had dropped
instantly at the first shot and opened fire. And
from the upstairs windows of the big house a half-
dozen hidden riflemen got busy.

Brokus, his fine white shirt pitted and dis-
colored, shouted, "Get to the horses, boys!
'Buscado!" He lumbered across the yard, fell, and
pushed himself up again. "McLean!"

Mike ran out to him. Those who had made it
into the wagon shed were piling out through the
rear door. They didn't panic, being what they
were, but they recognized a jackpot when they
saw one. They just stampeded for their horses,
every man for himself and the Lord take care of
any noble fool who elected to stand and get
killed. The men at the bunkhouse promptly cut
around to liven up the rush. The Regulators were
clearly drilled to handle any eventuality, and this
was their home ground. They knew every inch of
it.

Brokus, falling again, bumped into Mike and

hung on. He even gave Mike a hard grin. "We still got a chance, boy, if the horses don't spook off. We'll come back! We'll show these sons!"

The horses danced, some breaking away, Alta Mesa men chasing them. Rifle fire continued relentlessly from the upper windows of the house. Mike straight-armed a man and took his horse, rode down and caught another, and circled back to Brokus.

"Climb on, quick!"

The Alta Mesa men streamed head-long down the ranch road. The brush along both sides burst noisily alive, gun smoke spurting. Roone had overlooked no bets. Men and horses spilled as if on trip-wires.

Brokus reined his horse around. "Satan's sins, what next! Look at 'em go down!" He swayed and jolted clumsily in the saddle. "Hey, I got trouble sticking on this nag!"

"Too bad, damn you!" Mike spurred by him. "I'm goin' to try for those hills. Hang on an' follow if you're able, Mister King, you so-smart son—"

Darkening the earth and changing the mountain to blue-black silhouettes crinkled with red streaks, sundown at last masked hunted from hunters and ushered in the quiet hour of evening. A coyote howled its hypocritical mourning, ending in sharp yaps, summoning friends to the business of the night. Somewhere far off a bull bellowed mighty challenge to any other bulls that might be hanging around.

Brokus was dying.

He said, "Boy, they were ready, weren't they? All set to go. That tricky Roone. Col sold us out. He had his gun lined on your back. Glad I got him. Should've known he'd turn Judas, after you beat him an' I made you *caporal*. He couldn't take a lickin', ever. Guess he aimed to bolt with the horses an' leave us all in the lurch." He rasped a breath. "My oath, we took a lickin' this day, though, didn't we? It all went wrong."

Mike said, "Yeah, they were ready. They beat us to it." He didn't mention that he had feared it might happen. He only thought it. After all, Brokus was dying.

They lay hiding in an arroyo, their horses drooping near by, Brokus's saddle blood-caked. Bloody-Wire Charley drew another shuddering breath. He stretched out, his boots scraping the sandy bed of the dry arroyo.

"I think I'm through. That Roone! I've whipped a score the likes o' him. I must be gettin' old. Ah, to be young again! It's up to you now, son."

"What is?"

"To get my daughter out o' that jam, damn you! What else? Listen!" The old outlaw's eyes narrowed. His scheming brain still worked. "She won't be at Roone's place. My crew's busted, an' Roone will want to take over the Alta Mesa right

111

away. He'll want to take Flame there an' show her he's boss. We only left three men on guard. Yeah, that's what he'll do. You get her out, hear?"

"How?"

"How the hell do I know? You do it, that's all!" Brokus stared up at Mike. "It's an order!"

"I don't need any order," Mike said. "Not for that. I don't know how it's to be done, but I'll try."

"*Bueno*!" Brokus slapped him weakly. "*Bueno* to hell, boy!"

He was dead half an hour later. Mike took his gun and the better of the two horses, and rode down out of the hills, wishing he had some help. A lone hand didn't stand much whack, going against Roone and his victorious Regulators on the conquered Alta Mesa.

Not much whack at all. But there was nobody else left to try.

In the hope of borrowing some ammunition, he took an extra chance and dropped in at the Caven place. Being supposedly unarmed at the wedding, he and the Alta Mesa crew had gone without cartridge belts, and all he had left of his pocket supply was a scant handful.

Lindsay and Jana Caven stared as if seeing a ghost when he walked in on them at supper. He had come up warily without their hearing him, a gun ready, not knowing what to expect.

"Anybody here besides you two?"

"No."

"Good." He began a brief account of what had happened, but they already knew.

"We had a visitor," Lindsay told him. "An Alta Mesa man, hurt and in a hurry. Begged a fresh horse. Gave us the story. What a shoot-out that must have been! He said you and Brokus got cut off and left behind, and a minute later he and some pals rode into an ambush. Not many broke through without damage, I gather, and they're skinning out of the country. They rightly figure that Roone's Regulators will organize a hunt, come daylight. How about Brokus?"

"Dead. The Alta Mesa is busted."

Lindsay nodded. "We heard a bunch riding by toward there, late afternoon. The Triangle T, no doubt. They didn't come back. How about Brokus's daughter?"

"I guess she was with that bunch. Roone would take her along, if only to show the way up."

"M-mm, yes, if only that." Lindsay and Jana looked carefully away from Mike's face. "Guards?"

"Three. An' Ould Burro, dead-drunk. No opposition, that, to the Roone crowd." Mike stuck his gun away. "It was quite a weddin'."

"Glad you survived it. What do you need?"

"Shells. An' I could sure use a drink."

Lindsay looked embarrassed. "Shells, yes. Not a drink in the house, though. I—er—I'm experimenting with sobriety. Sorry. Coffee? Jana, please—"

"I'll heat it up. Sit down, Mr. McLean."

"Thanks."

"The mail came in this morning at Fifty," Lindsay remarked. "Letter for us from Peter Hardy in Albuquerque. You know, he took Boy Pete there to hospital. Pulled out so quick, he didn't tell anybody where he got the money. He tells us in his letter. Mike, may I bow to you?"

"Save it." Mike glanced at the coffeepot. "I bet that's hot now, Miss Caven. How's Pete, did Hardy say?"

"The doctors," said Jana, raising radiant eyes, "promise that Pete will be all right. He won't be crippled. You take it black, Mr. McLean—Mike? I'm Jana. To you."

He watched her pour the coffee. And, forgetting, he ground out an oath. "Goddammit! If those folks o' Fifty only had some sense! An' guts! Here's their chance! Roone's jiggers will be celebratin'-drunk tonight, I bet. Roone, he'll take over the Middle Range, cows an' all. A dozen good men could bust him tonight, but not later. An' if I went into Fifty they'd try to tear me apart. Oh, the damn fools!"

Lindsay regarded him strangely. "Granted. Why bother about them? Think of yourself, man! You've got some fast travel coming up. Where do you go from here?"

"Me?" Mike sipped the hot black coffee. "The Alta Mesa, o' course! Where else d'you think?

Get me those shells, will you? I'll 'preciate it."

Lindsay exchanged a glance with his sister. He slapped his hands on the table, sighed, and got up. "I was afraid of that. All right. The shells. I'll get 'em."

He returned carrying two double-holstered gun belts, filled to the last loops. Mike said, "One is enough, I guess, for me."

"Yes," responded Lindsay gently. "I think so. The other one is for me. Yes, Mike. I can shoot, remember? I'm going with you. Aw, shut up! I wouldn't do it if I weren't so stinking sober! And that's your fault, if you only knew!"

They climbed the arroyo path that Flame had showed Mike, their horses abandoned a mile back on the plain. The rain-gashed arroyos were gravelly, rough, studded with rocks and steep in places. It took a good rider. Even on foot the going was tough. Lindsay, too much whisky behind him, puffed like a spent runner.

At the top Mike paused, getting his bearings, and climbed onto level ground. A light in the distance marked the Brokus house. He set out toward it, whispering back, "You okay, Lindsay?"

"Hell, no!" gasped Lindsay. "I'm fagged out and far from home. But keep going, friend. I'm toddling along right behind you, fool that I be. Do I perceive a welcome light?"

"It's a light. I don't speak for any welcome."

Mike stalked the house with care, examining all shadows. Lights shone from most of the downstairs windows, and the noise of loud voices in the big dining-room was a comfort. Roone was not a careless kind of man, but tonight he was letting his men relax. He was on top, and had nothing more to worry him.

A clatter of dishes resounded through the open door of the kitchen. To approach the house without risk of being spotted, all the lights on, was impossible. Mike sprinted to the kitchen door. He halted there, listening, and peered in.

"Mr. O'Burrifergus," he said, "you're a helluva servant, to be spittin' that way in the wine glasses!"

Ould Burro, so engaged, whirled around. "Michael, I thought ye were dead!" he exclaimed. "What d'ye do here? Have a drink!"

"In a clean glass, please, and another for my friend. No spit!" Mike eased into the kitchen. "When did you aspire to serve the high aristocracy, anyhow?"

"I'm havin' to learn fast," Ould Burro confessed. "I woke up an' there they were, grinnin' at me. They made me their lackey, point o' gun. From their talk I fear there's been disaster."

"Yeah. We got licked. Where's Flame?"

"She flung a dish at Roone an' tried to scoot. The celebration is goin' on without her. Roone's tryin' to be one o' the boys, this once. He thinks

116

the occasion calls for it, I s'pose." Ould Burro snorted. "Takes more'n a weak drink an' a stingy smile to be a man amongst men! By that measure, as well as others, he's more mackerel than man!"

Lindsay, slipping into the kitchen after Mike, commented. "How true. Did he spank the naughty bride for her—hum—display of domestic dissatisfaction?"

Ould Burro bushed his brows at him. "You, is it? An' sober? Now I know everything's turned upside down! No, he did not. It was all he could do, with some help, to rush her up to her room and lock her in. There's been some jokes behind his back about what further help he'll need. They're a rotten, rock-hearted mob. No more decent chivalry than wolves. I'm in horror for the girl."

"Her room," said Mike, "is on the second floor, isn't it?"

Ould Burro lifted the laden tray. "It is, an' to get to it you'd have to go through the dinin'-room. Not a chance, Michael! Oh, I know how 'tis with ye. I was a bright young bucko once, meself. An' there was a girl. I didn't get her." He shrugged. "Better off, perhaps. Git out o' here while ye're still alive. G'wan, beat it, the two o' ye! I got me damn job to do."

"Don't spill those drinks," murmured Lindsay, backing out, while Ould Burro bore the tray into the noisy dining-room, leaving Mike alone in the kitchen.

Half a minute later, four shots and Lindsay's yell outside broke up the brideless wedding party.

Chapter Eleven: POWDERSMOKE PROPHET

A BROKEN WINDOW tinkled a brief overture to the roar of startled growls, tumbled benches and chairs, and men charging out to get at the shooter.

"There he goes—there around the quarters!" A gun spat rapid reports. "Hell, he made it!"

"Only one? Must be he's lost his nut!"

"If he ain't he's sure gonna!"

The hurried talk faded to a muddle of running footsteps and half-drunken profanity, the only sober voice that of Roone, irritably snapping orders.

Mike poked his head into the dining-room. Its only remaining occupant was Ould Burro, rising from the wreckage of the tray of drinks and grumbling disgustedly, "Fooled me that time! He *is* drunk!"

"No, he's not," Mike disagreed, whisking by him. "You stray-brain, he did that to draw 'em out so I could get through!"

"Then he's as crazy as you! Her room's the third door on the left, top o' the stairs there. Hurry! I don't reckon Roone's gone far."

The stairs led onto a gallery that had become a closed-in corridor after the addition of the upper rooms. Lacking any outside windows, it was half dark, the only light coming up from the big room below. Mike tried the third door on the left. Due to the gloom, he couldn't tell at first how it was fastened. There was no knob, and the inside doors of Spanish-Southwestern houses rarely had locks. Nor the outside doors, for that matter. This was a country of hand-wrought iron latches and drop-bars.

He finally found the iron latch was bound down with a piece of wire. By that time his fumblings had caught Flame's attention. Her whisper came muffledly through the door.

"Who is it?"

"Me—Mike McLean."

"You? Oh, Mike! Oh—"

"Quiet, now!"

A gun thundered a single discharge in the downstairs room. There was the sound of a body falling, and Ould Burro asking painedly, "Why did ye do that, Mr. Roone? Why have ye shot me?"

"You frauding old tramp, you know why!" came the reply. "Somebody ran through here from the kitchen. I saw him cross that broken window. Somebody you were hiding! Who? Where is he? Men," he yelled, "come back here! Somebody's in the house, and I think it's McLean!"

Mike tore the wire off the latch and threw the door open. Before him Flame's face was dim in the darkness, her figure a shadow framed by a pale oblong of window. The darkness couldn't hide the shine in her eyes, and he thought she must be smiling and it didn't surprise him. Her nature and environment had combined to give her a ready optimism and a sense of values stripped down to immediate essentials. Outlaws couldn't afford to worry much about their future.

"You okay?"

"Yes, Mike. Can you spare me a gun?"

"Here. What's outside that window?"

"The gallery that overlooks the only *placita* where I've been able to have a garden. Roone had a man nail the window shut, though. And it's a long drop to the ground. I would have broken the window and tried it, but the noise—"

"Can't be helped. They'll look here first, anyhow. Break it an' climb out. I'll lower you down off the gallery. Here they come!"

A group of Roone's men came trotting up the stairs, as sternly purposeful as a military squad. Mike tripped a cocked hammer, and the close-range flash and report shook their businesslike efficiency. The first two to top the stairs jumped back and collided into those coming up behind them. The noise then resembled that of a military squad falling briskly downstairs. It almost drowned out Flame's breaking of the window. Flame was getting the knack of smashing windows neatly at one bash.

Mike felt good until a man leaped up into the corridor, two guns blazing wildly. He pulled his head in, rocked back on his knees, and waited for the man to come barging abreast of the open door. But another door banged and the two guns quit.

Flame spoke behind Mike. "There's a man in the next room. He's Osbee, Roone's new *caporal*."

"The heck with him!"

"I agree. The window of that room opens onto the outer gallery, like this one. He's standing there with two guns."

Mike slung another shot along the corridor. "Out to make good on his new job, huh? An' drunk, the way he busted up here. You hold this door a minute while I— Is that him yellin'?"

"Yes. He's calling to some of the others to run around to the garden." Flame took Mike's post. She swept her hair back and smiled up at him. "If they tramp their big feet on my begonias I'll never forgive them."

"You should put a sign up, 'Beware the begonias.' You do that, next time."

Mike went to the broken window, looked out, ducked in again, and carefully drew a sliver from his cheek. Osbee's bullet had splintered the windowframe.

"H'm! Fast an' ready, him. Wonder did he close his door?"

He left the window. He bent over Flame and said, "Here's some more shells. How they behavin' on the stairs? Shy? Bust a couple more at the top stair an' make 'em real bashful. I got a call to make. See you on the gallery!"

He stepped swiftly past her into the corridor. A gun flash fleetingly illuminated the head of the stairs. They weren't so shy there. They were only waiting. And he, though crouched, made too tall a target not to be seen.

The bullet got him between his left shoulder and his neck, high, through the muscles. It caused him to flinch and dodge so that he lost balance. The door of the next room stood open. He blundered through on his toes, falling.

The man at the window snapped around, firing at once. His reactions were fast, and he must have marked the doorway in his mind as a possible danger spot. What he hadn't taken into his consideration was the implausible circumstance of an intruder pitching onto his face before he shot him. His bullets pocked the opposite wall of the corridor at the height of a man's chest.

Mike fired from the floor and got Osbee somewhere in the middle. Osbee hung in the window, and Mike fired again. Osbee slumped out, gasping, loosing a last shot that speared upward.

Mike stepped out over him onto the gallery. He looked down and saw the pattern of a flower garden, adobe walls, and a little wooden gate through which men were swarming. He darted along the gallery, clambered through the smashed window into Flame's room, and said to Flame, "Lord help the begonias!"

She turned her face up to him. "They've got there?"

"Yeah."

"You're hurt!"

"Some." He sank down beside her. "I'll take this. You watch the window. Or is there any way out o' here?"

"The walls are 'dobe. Could be dug through."

"Not into Osbee's room. Get us nowhere. Other side?"

"There's a hall there, and the stairs up to the third floor. Give me your knife."

"Lost it in a blacksmith's shed. Sorry. Guess we stay."

"Guess we do, Mike," she said. "Thanks for coming."

He lined a shot at a rising head above the stairs. "Your dad gave me orders right to the last. Was he a man! I know now that I liked him. We got along."

"Dead?"

"Yeah. I did what I could."

"Sure, I know you did." She stood near the broken window, watching her garden below being ruined by the careless feet of drunken, violent men. " 'To guard the interests of me and mine.' You stayed with it all the way, Mike. You kept your oath."

"My oath!" he grunted, and thumbed two shots savagely at two more heads rising slyly above the

124

stairs. "My oath! Dammit, don't talk that way, Flame! I'd have come, oath or not. Your dad knew it. I told him. It kind of pleased him. Lindsay Caven didn't give any oath, but he came along. There are good men in the world. Lindsay's one, whatever they say. An', by God, I'm another! Yeah, me!"

Born of hopelessness, a flaring temper charred the curtain of his masculine reserve and control. "Good enough to come after you, girl! To take you if I could! Damn the oath! I came here for you, understand? Don't you—"

Incredibly, clearly, in the big downstairs room Ould Burro chanted, "Gintlemen, come an' have yer fortunes told! I'm a dyin' man, an' I have the ancient Celtic gift an' a pack o' cards! Nor do I require ye to cross me palm wi' silver. 'Twould buy me nothin' on me journey or at me destination. Mr. Roone, you first, sir? Surely a man o' your power an' prestige has no fear to peek through the veil o' future fortune?"

"My fortune is in my own hands, you old faker!"

"Indeed it is, sir, an' a grand fortune, too. It may be grander yet, who knows? 'There is a tide in human affairs, which, caught at the flood—' Ye know the rest o' that wise old quotation, ye bein' a scholar an' gintleman. Let me then foretell the tide for ye, that ye may know when to catch it. What's to be lost? Ye're too big an' broad-minded a man not to admit the possibility o' the verity o' mystic divination."

Silence then, except for the soft purr of riffled cards. The men hugging the stairs were evidently looking on, intrigued and curious.

"Three times shuffle, three times cut," intoned Ould Burro. "This first card covers yer fortune. Ah, a splendid card! This one crowns it. Better an' better! This is what's behind, an' this is what's before. Most fortunate sir! Yer troubles are done. For luck, now, come touch the deck before I turn the last card, for on that one everything depends —Thank ye, sir, for yer kind, co-operation—"

A shot thudded dully, muffled by point-blank range, unmistakably from the stubby barrel of a little sleeve-gun that needed a near target to be wholly effective in the hand of a dying man.

"An' here's yer future, ye black-souled mackerel —wi' the compliments o' Timothy O'Burrifergus!"

After the shocked hush, rage broke. The cursing of the men on the stairs ran a choppy under-current to the tardy and senseless blaring of their guns.

"Here's a chance!" Mike muttered.

He meant a chance to do mischief, preferring it to waiting to be rushed. There was no hope left of escaping from the Brokus adobe palace. Roone's men were shooting furiously down into the big room at the corpse of a man who had played a last card trick. In a moment they would swing their attention to the living. Leaderless now, they would charge amuck through the house.

Slipping out into the corridor, Mike crept close to the stairs, held his gun high, and fired. He used the old kick-and-fall method, letting the gun rebound upward from each shot, and thumb on hammer, letting its falling weight take care of the next cocking.

He fired again and again, counting his shots, his weakening left hand groping his belt for fresh loads. Once more the stairs took boot scars from hurriedly vacating men.

He could see down into part of the big room. There were the huge tables, the overturned benches and chairs, broken glasses—and Ould Burro—Mr. Timothy O'Burrifergus—lying on the floor in a scatter of cards, skimpy pistol still in his hand, and Roone slumped dead across his legs. Roone's stiffening forefinger was on a card, the ace of spades. Mr. O'Burrifergus had stacked the deck expertly. A matter of habit, finesse, and grim humor.

A man scuttled past the tables. Some gunfire sounded outside. Flame's little garden, Mike thought. Her begonias. He took a shot at the scuttling man, missed, and the man slithered around and returned the compliment.

Mike lurched sidewise and fell over. It was a fluke shot, endowed with the instinctive accuracy of a man in a hurry who aimed from feel and nothing more. A small boy with his first gun, and a rabbit hopping by, could have done as well. Later the boy would miss, too preoccupied by lessons of sighting, trigger squeeze, and the fine rules of leading.

The bullet had parted Mike's hair and rung bells in his head. The man ran on out. The gunfire outside increased.

Mike heard Flame, crouching beside him, saying, "Hold up, Mike! Please don't die! I'll take care of you!"

He said, "You take care o' that gallery! I'm not dead, not yet. Don't get scared, now!"

"I w-won't be, if you'll get up!"

He got up clumsily. "What they shootin' at out there? Us? Why, the crazy—"

He was talking against a deafening roar. More men ran across the big room and vanished through the front doorway. There was a lot of yelling going on, and what sounded like a running battle.

"They're utter-to-bedamn crazy! Flame, you an' me, we still got some sense left. Especially me. I can remember an' regret most distinctly that I never did kiss you. It takes good sense to—"

"McLean! Where are you?" A shouting man plunged into the big room, others on his heels. "You all right?"

"I'm right as rain," Mike responded clearly. The shouter had some resemblance to Ed Horner, which wasn't sensible. It was his eyes that were wrong. His head was perfectly all right. "Come an' get us," he said, clicking his empty gun, and fell downstairs.

Lindsay Caven said, "I don't mind saying I hit for the way out. Thought I'd try to rouse up the folks at Fifty. But I met 'em on the way. They were roused, no help from me. So I turned around and led 'em up here. I don't know what got 'em started. I didn't think to inquire at the time."

"Your sister," stated Ed Horner, "is quite a gal when she turns loose. Yeah, Miss Jana. She came bustin' into Fifty. She told us off. How she told us! This, she also said, was our last chance. Showed us a letter from Peter Hardy. Told us a lot. It was the letter that did it, I guess, but what she named us— What was it, Books Thomas? I disremember the precise words. Hell, I don't wanna remember!"

Books Thomas, a little man with earnest eyes and a twenty-gauge shotgun, related specifically. "'Poor trash. No more backbone than dough-splatter. Worthless as tick-fevered dogies. Not men at all.' The rest was—er—repetitious, though very strongly enunciated. We resented it. My wife informed me—advised me—that some action in the matter was—er—in her opinion—er—most definitely required. Yes, indeed."

"You'll like Jana," Mike told Flame. "She's okay."

He sat on the bottom stair while she cut away

the remains of his shirt and tried to decide where to begin patching him up.

"I want to know her better," she replied. "I think we could get along. Hold still."

"Those so-called Regulators!" Horner sneered. "We brought shotguns, mostly, an' sent 'em ki-yiyin' off in no time! Gunmen! O' course," he admitted, "you'd already took care o' Roone."

"Not me," said Mike. He got up and weaved a course to the tables, Flame at his side. He gazed down at a grimly smiling, rascally old face. "Take off your hats! Take 'em off to Mr. Timothy O'Burrifergus, a good man!"

The hats came off. He leaned on Flame. "You all looked down on him, a boozer an' a busted old tinhorn. Well, that's what he was. You condemned Flame, the daughter of a man way out o' law. She's that. An' you cussed me for a long rider on the make. That's me. If it wasn't for us, though, damn your smug—"

Flame interrupted him. She said, "Mr. McLean isn't quite himself. He's hurt, as you can see. What he means to say is that we don't want any more bad feeling. There's plenty of range for all of us, if we share like good neighbors. And the trail out to the markets is wide open. Right, Mr. McLean?"

From then on there was considerable talk and crowding around. Some said respectfully, "Miss Brokus." A few said, "Miss Flame." It didn't seem to occur to anybody to call her Mrs. Roone.

"Mr. McLean," Flame said, "you were speaking to me of something that sounded important, and you were interrupted. It was about why you came after me, wasn't it?"

"Yeah." Mike took a hold on the table. He picked up Ould Burro's stovepipe hat and brushed it. "I want to keep this. Why, yeah, I was sayin' somethin' or other. An' didn't you say you'd take care o' me?"

"I did, Mike."

"*Bueno.* Start right now. Help me get out o' this crowd o' fool cowmen. Then I'll finish what I was sayin'. An' the good Lord hide your blushes, girl! I never did court a young widow before, but I'm rarin' to go!"

Powdersmoke Empire

Chapter One: TOO TOUGH TO LIVE

THE FRONT DOOR of the Starbuck Hall swung open a bare thirty inches, and in the backbar mirror Bain Foyle watched Big Mac's messenger, Deputy Pete, ease quickly into the barroom. It was a single door on one-way hinges, not a swing door, so Deputy Pete had to push it shut behind him. Then Deputy Pete had to blink and squint to get his eyes fixed, after the outside glare of sunlight, before looking around.

Everybody in the Starbuck knew Deputy Pete was looking for Bain Foyle. They all, including Bain Foyle, knew what kind of message he had brought from Big Mac. The barroom, already quiet, grew quieter. Sidelong glances touched Foyle fleetingly and whipped off to become blank stares at nothing.

Bain Foyle went on gazing into the backbar mirror, allowing himself a moment of wry wonder and recollection. As a boy on his father's small ranch down on the Nueces in Texas, he had never guessed that some day he would forget how to laugh. Life then had seemed simple and secure. Years after the collapse of that sunny illusion, when he wasn't a boy any more, a diamond-studded gambler's queen said of him thoughtfully, "That Foyle guy makes me think of a bad Indian I saw brought through Tucson once, in chains. Big,

135

bad devil, cool as they come. But kind of sad, too, somehow. His eyes, they looked right through everybody like they didn't count for much. A man, all right. Know what I mean?"

"I know," murmured the gambler, and at the first opportunity he staged a neat gun play, on personal principle. Foyle shaded him, though, and lit out—alone.

Bain Foyle now was tall, big-shouldered, a hard and muscular man. He had a scrapper's ridged brows, a wide, faintly sardonic mouth, and a collection of small scars marked his sun-darkened skin. Men saw only hardness in his eyes. Some women—like the gambler's queen—thought they saw also a kind of sadness there, but they were inclined to be uneasy of him, just the same.

Turning, Foyle asked, "Looking for me, Pete?"

Big Mac's messenger, Deputy Pete, all but ducked at the curt question. He hadn't yet got his eyes to focus right, and it had become more difficult lately to guess at Foyle's mood.

"Yep, for you, Mr. Foyle," he reported. "Big Mac wants to see you right away." While older men answered to nicknames, and Mac M'Cavan was Big Mac to everybody, it was rare for Bain Foyle to be called by anything but his surname.

To stall off a peremptory summons from Big Mac was like flying against providence. Big Mac was the provider. But Foyle said, "Tell him I'll be along later. I don't doubt he's already heard about the jigger tangling with me in here a while ago. Harvey Rose, the new man. That's his gun on the bar. He says he's getting another one an' coming back. I said I'd wait."

He had been drinking. He wasn't drunk, but the mood was in him to pull one more joke on Big Mac. "You tell him," he said, "I'll be with him soon's I tend to Mr. Rose, his brand-new shootin' star!"

Shaking his head worriedly, Deputy Pete sidled up closer. "Now, you know Big Mac's order. No more private fights in town! He specially warned you!" The little man was honestly concerned. Foyle was one of the few, among the Banner toughs, who didn't make him the butt of contemptuous jokes.

He lowered his voice. "Watch y'self, Mr. Foyle! Go the back way. That feller's out front with his horse, an' he's got holt of a double-bar'l shotgun. He'll blast you, you open that door!"

Foyle finished his drink. "*Gracias, amigo*. This shouldn't take long, then!" He slid his empty glass across to the bartender. "Same again, Sam, and ask Mr. Pete what he'll have. Be back in a minute."

The silent crowd at the bar split up, watching him. In this mad town of cutthroat politics and organized violence, Foyle stood high in reputation—Big Mac's top man, the Number One. Little Deputy Pete occasionally wondered if even

Big Mac wasn't a bit afraid of Foyle, when Foyle's eyes got a certain look in them.

Foyle walked to the front door. He stood regarding it, while building with chill logic the picture in his mind of the man who waited for him outside. The hitchrack stood somewhat to the right of the door, at the edge of the boardwalk, facing the painted window. Harvey Rose wouldn't be waiting there. It was too far out of line to catch a man starting out, first shot. And the first shot would spook the horses dozing at the rack, making a second shot chancy.

No—Harvey Rose knew better. One shot, without warning and with the least possible risk of a slip. That was the favored way of his kind. Mr. Rose would have his horse standing broadside to the door. He'd be crouched behind it, using the saddle as a rest for the shotgun. He would want to make certain, too, that it was Foyle coming out, before he cut loose.

This, the figuring ahead, so habitual that it cost no more than a few seconds, was the tariff Foyle paid for staying alive. Some flaming day he would forget, he supposed, and down he'd go like so many he'd seen. Unthinking rage—hot pride—the overconfidence of drink; for such luxuries the price ran high.

He pulled open the door, saying loudly for Rose to hear, "If Big Mac wants me—" and leaped aside.

The shotgun blast spattered the edge of the door and ripped on into the front of the bar. Harvey Rose's horse reared in abrupt alarm, knocking the shotgun upward. It tried to plunge off. Rose, expecting that, had taken the precautions to wrap the reins around his left forearm. He was a lean, quick-moving man, and he instantly planted his feet and hauled the horse around. Thoroughly upset now, the horse backed away in a series of hops.

Sliding in the dry dust of the street, his left arm busy, Rose tucked the smoking shotgun under his right arm, finger on the trigger, and leveled it desperately at the open saloon door. His first shot had gone bad, but he still had another load left to cover his getaway.

Foyle smashed the painted window with one stroke of a drawn gun, and fired. "Sam," he asked, watching Harvey Rose get up and stumble after his horse, "how much do I owe you?"

He swallowed a drink, paid his bill, and left.

When he was gone Sam broke a long silence. "That Foyle," he sighed, "is sure hell round here!"

The men along the bar nodded. "Too tough to live!" muttered one who had felt the rough edge of Foyle's cold temper.

"Maybe that's what Big Mac figgers!" blurted Deputy Pete.

They turned and looked at him in stony inquiry. They all owed allegiance to Big Mac, and not one of them ever went unarmed. He coughed and hurried out, scared by the fleeting insight that had inspired his remark.

In the heat-baked, dusty street, Foyle ranged a blank stare over the town. The prosperity and importance of Banner showed in its big false-front stores, wagon yards, and the brick mansion that strangers always bewilderedly mistook for the capitol building of the Territory. He spat, impatiently hitched up his gun belts to an easier hang, and gave his black sombrero a yank. He was sick of this whole damned place and all that it stood for. Three years was a long time in Banner.

No reaction, either uplift or letdown, touched him from the Rose scrape. The thing was too common. Rose, another fool puffed up with visions of becoming Big Mac's top man by shooting the incumbent, had come at him. He hadn't killed Rose because the man just didn't matter that much. It expressed his opinion, not only of Rose, but of most of the specimens Big Mac had been bringing into Banner these last few months. The old bunch would never have tolerated Rose and his shotgun. Long known as a gun fighters' hangout, the town had become a refuge for thieves, thugs, and back-shooting badmen—under the protection of Big Mac.

He recalled that Big Mac wanted to see him. "Hell with him!" he muttered. But he turned toward the brick mansion, snorting a short laugh of derision at his own words of defiance. Like the rest, he belonged to Big Mac. Had belonged for three years, which was longer by far than any other man had been owned and trusted by the man in the red brick mansion.

They were all gone, the others, the quiet-spoken gun fighters whose peculiar pride demanded that they give a man an even break. He would go, too, in time. Big Mac would drink a toast to his memory and look around for somebody else to ramrod the mob. He had turned in plenty of good work for Big Mac. Not so good lately, perhaps. Too restless.

Pacing up the path to the brick mansion, he wished suddenly to be riding away forever from Banner. As suddenly, the knowledge struck him that Banner had made him incapable of being anything but the gun boss for a political mastermind. An empire builder, was what Big Mac called himself; and believed it.

For satirical amusement, Foyle considered what would be the result if he were to tell Big Mac his plain opinion of him. Big Mac would simply be surprised and annoyed. He most likely would mention that all methods were justified when the goal was a good one. Then, no doubt, he'd pull a blinding-fast trick out of his bag, smiling affably—next day shaking his head sadly at the funeral.

"Too bad. Yes, indeed, he was a good man, the best ever." A fat sigh. A sentimental *ha-hoomf!* into a white silk handkerchief. The merciless Mick-on-the-Make, with the moist eye. "Still, y'know, boys— When the finest dog goes mad. Turns its slavering teeth on you. Best to kill it quick, eh? Yes, indeed. But too bad."

Foyle moved his lips, giving a meager smile to his thoughts as he entered the mansion. He had seen that little act played, and had caught a grain of humor in it. Big Mac could never admit that a hireling of his might grow rebellious and dare to flare up against him. To his nerveless intelligence such behavior was irrational. It signified madness. Therefore, any man who attempted to cross him was mad and had to be killed. The policy of regrettable necessity included decent burial and a few kindly words, containing the gentle hint of warning to anybody else who might feel an urge to blow his conk. Big Mac loved ceremony best when it served a purpose.

The armed man inside the door nodded to Foyle. "He's waitin' for you," he said, keeping his face wooden.

"Hunnh," Foyle acknowledged, but didn't hurry. He remembered again the strict recent edict against private shoot-outs. No excuses. No exceptions. *Meaning me!* he thought.

He broke another edict by going into the office wearing his guns and without knocking. The armed guard at the main door took note of that, evidently, for Foyle heard him whistle.

A shade of coolness flattened Big Mac's usually cordial greeting. "Ah, there, Foyle. You're late."

Foyle hooked a chair forward with his toe and sat down, not waiting for the invitation. "Late for what?"

The huge desk, littered untidily as always with stacks of papers and spilled cigar ash, had a tier of sliding drawers built on it, topped by a row of open pigeonholes. From behind it Big Mac looked at Foyle and deliberately met his eyes. He must have immediately noticed Foyle's guns, for nothing ever escaped his deceptively lazy glance, but he passed no comment. Without breaking his gaze at Foyle, he reached forward, took a cigar from the drawer where he kept them, and leaned back, lighting it carefully. The oversize swivel chair creaked under his weight, and that was the only sound for a moment.

This time— Foye thought. *This time—*

But he felt himself growing smaller. He had taken orders so often in this room. It was he who, inwardly furious, outwardly unmoved, broke the locked glance.

Yet he knew, better than anybody else, the kind of man Big Mac was. He had seen fully the cynical hypocrisy behind the benevolent mask. The utterly unscrupulous machinations of the clever brain. The ruthless ambition that readily employed cheap and shameful tricks. The brutal vices, secret debauchery, weaknesses enough to rot the character of any normal man.

To look once at Big Mac M'Cavan was to believe that here was a man destined for greatness. He had the appearance of a great man, so rare in the truly great—the noble, craggy face, strong-jowled, leonine. The sweeping forehead crowned with a magnificent gray mane reaching to the shoulders. Immense size. Ponderous dignity. The gift of genial courtesy. His voice could throb in deep bass organ or rise to Olympian violin crescendo—depending on whether he was holding forth on hallowed American Womanhood or the Fourth of July.

"You picked a fight with Harvey Rose, I hear," he told Foyle.

Foyle replied, "He picked a fight with me, the fool."

"Kill him?"

"No, he'll live—somewhere."

"H'm! I'm pleased that you followed my warning that far." Big Mac turned on a smile. "That's—ah—an extenuating circumstance!"

Foyle rose abruptly to his feet. Big Mac looked at him, met his stare, and this time dropped the glance to his cigar.

Foyle said, "I'll kill the next one like him!"

Big Mac smiled on. "Now, now! You need action—I've kept you in town too long. Are you broke?"

Foyle shrugged. "Paying for a busted window took my last."

"Sit down," Big Mac commanded. "Listen! When I first came here, this Territory was practically still a no man's land. There was no political organization whatever. I was a newcomer. I didn't even have a dollar to get my boots mended! And now—"

"Now you've got new boots. An' half the Territory has got a political boss. You're halfway there, Mac!"

"Shut up and listen!" Big Mac's eyes shone. "Remember, I told you once I'd be the governor here one day? You believed me. You threw in with me. Believe me now, Foyle, I'll be more than that! Territorial governor? Chicken feed! I'm going higher—a hell of a sight higher! Want to go up with me, Foyle?"

"How much higher can you go?" Foyle asked.

Big Mac blew a cloud of blue smoke. "I'll tell you. This is in strict confidence, mind! The good old whisper, just between us, eh? All right. Listen!"

He creaked the swivel chair forward. "There's a pile of political discontent going to waste all through the Southwest. Not just in New Mexico, mind! All through this country! Look! The Mexicans don't love the rule of the grand and glorious Army of the United States of America! Furthermore, this Southwest is full of foreigners—

adventurers and outlaws—and unreconstructed rebels from the Southern States! You know that. You know the country."

"Full o' bandits an' scalawags, if that's what you mean."

"Foyle, they're men! Fighting men! A force, wasted! Some of us, in—ah—positions of authority, believe that the time is ripe to organize and use that force. Yes, indeed! For the freedom and glory of our beloved Southwest!"

Foyle scowled at the cigarette he was building. "I don't get it. Those long words choke me. Chew it finer, Mac."

Big Mac nodded indulgently. "Our great Southwest," he proclaimed in deep bass, "was surely not intended by the Almighty Lord—" he raised his eyes reverently—"to be ruled by ignorant men back East? No! Our standards are higher! Cleaner than those of the sordid money-changers temple! We have so decided—we of the Secret Committee, the men of honesty! New Mexico! Arizona! Texas! Yes, and the discontented border states of Mexico. Sonora and Chihuahua and Coahuila—they'll join us! Rebellion!"

Foyle made a wreck of his cigarette and flipped it over the floor. "Secession, begod! That's a word I do know, me from Texas! But this is bandit rebellion you're talking!"

"Rebels," observed Big Mac, "are called bandits—till they win. Then they're heroes.

146

George Washington, Oliver Cromwell, the bloody Robespierre—history's full of 'em. All outlaws—till they won. And we'll win, too! Do as I say, Foyle, and I'll take you up to the top with me. Me! Future president of the Rio Grande Republic!"

"Lord God Almighty!" Foyle murmured.

"I've got a very important job for you, Foyle."

"I'm not so sure I want it, Mac."

Big Mac's laugh filled the room. It drowned to silence the listening guards outside the door. "You'll take it, Foyle! You damned-well will, and you know it!"

Chapter Two: YOUR OBEDIENT SERVANT

RIDING NORTH up the wide and interminable valley of the Pecos, Foyle scanned the country constantly. He gave close attention to its possible pitfalls, none at all for its bleak beauty.

The river ran like a gold-flecked blue ribbon, scintillating in the sun, flanked by its narrow margin of green grass and spreading cottonwoods, through the barren, burned-out hills sinisterly resembling a giant's dried mud pies studded with warped cloves. Far off to the west the Capitans ridged purple peaks against the monotonous blue sky. Eastward lay the long plains, furred over by the brownish-yellow of sun-shriveled grama.

Engaging most of his mind was the thought of twenty thousand dollars. That was the sum definitely set by Big Mac. A pile of money. As much as any man could reasonably need for anything—a long getaway, a wild fling, or a fresh start. A stake for anything.

"For Ebb Grimm—delivered alive here to me, in fair health and whole mind!" Big Mac had said. And Big Mac's word was good. It had to be good. Or men wouldn't give him their faith any more. Men's faith was his stock in trade. That was the one thing he dared not cheat on.

"Trouble from Grimm again, huh?" Foyle had remarked. "Mac, that old Pronghorn country has

148

got you licked, I swear! A standout crowd, that—then, now, an' from here yonderly! I'd admire to meet that Ebb Grimm. He must be a Texan! Unreconstructed! I'm a working cowman, says he, an' a free man—an' damn your carpetbag politics!"

"Damn you and him and your rebel sentiments! I tell you, Foyle, that Pronghorn country is holding us up! Ebb Grimm is the trigger up there. Bring him here to me! Alive, mind! Able to sign his name to what we tell him, see? Twenty thousand dollars, Foyle, hard cash! That man's dangerous!"

"Twenty thousand? Hey, look, Mac! Who else you got?"

"Ah, hell!" Big Mac, throwing away two inches of good cigar, picked a fresh one. "Foyle, you're too damn smart. Okay, we've had Red Murrell's bunch on his tail for months. Yeah—Red Murrell. You know him. He's got a hide-out somewhere up there somewhere along Pintada Canyon. Lifting horses is his main game now. He's fallen down on this Grimm job. If you can locate him, tell him I said he's to give you any help you need."

"Anybody else?" Foyle asked.

Big Mac shrugged. "Oh, I've sent three or four up there, odd times. They never came back, not one of 'em. But then, not one of 'em was a Bain Foyle caliber of man. They didn't have your knack of getting things done. And this has got to be done, give you my word! We're pretty sure Grimm has talked the Pronghorn cowmen into making up a cash pool, a war chest, to hire a posse of scrappers from outside—ex-Texas Rangers and the like. He must have heard something of our plans. We've got to get hold of him and break that up. He's the big kingpin up there. We can make good use of him, once we put him in the right frame of mind. I want him here alive! Think you can do it?"

"For twenty thousand dollars, Mac, I'd make a stab to kidnap *you!*"

Big Mac blinked at that, then laughed. "That's the talk, boy! Here's a hundred to go on. Cigar?"

It was a lot of money to think about on the lonely ride up the Pecos. Foyle was used to being lonely, but he liked having something to occupy his mind and keep the ghosts out. The size of the reward for Ebb Grimm was a guarantee that the job was considered difficult and suicidally dangerous. Although Big Mac usually paid well and threw in a bonus for good work, he had never before made a straight offer of anything near such a large sum.

Probably the money was being put up by the undercover group that Big Mac spoke of as "we" —the men who planned to set up an independent Rio Grande Republic.

Foyle pondered on that. If such was the case their plans were past the talking stage. Well, many a smart man had come a cropper reaching for the moon. Unbroken success must have gone to Big Mac's head. He and his powerful backers were crazy.

President Mac M'Cavan! King Mac the First! Foyle shook his head. Maybe everybody was kind of crazy in one way or another.

"Just so their money's okay," he muttered, "they can put on tin crowns to play royal cassino for all I give a damn!"

Beneath the important pondering, he paid part of his attention to a man on a yellow horse coming along behind. The man must have left Banner some time after he did, although he didn't recognize the horse. Since morning, when Foyle first sighted him, the rider had shortened the distance between them, but appeared to be in no hurry to catch up, if that was his intention.

Foyle hipped around in his saddle, scanned the distant figure carefully, and frowned. It was possible that the stranger was hanging back to escape the dust of Foyle's shuffling big sorrel. Or maybe he just didn't care for company. On the other hand, it was somewhat queer that he should be taking this route, if he was from Banner. Nobody from Banner rode casually up toward the Pronghorn country. Banner men were highly unpopular up in Ebb Grimm's bailiwick.

Foyle didn't like having anybody behind him, even beyond rifle range in open country. He watched the man vanish in a dip of the trail. In a spirit of irritated speculation he decided to make a test. He reined his sorrel off the trail, heeled it to a canter around the nearest low hill, and there drew in. That jigger would notice his line of tracks, sure. If he had the right kind of savvy he would take the hint and ride on by.

Cuffing back his black sombrero, Foyle thumbed sweat from his forehead. He slid his carbine up and down in its saddle scabbard, built a cigarette, and patiently waited. That jigger had better pass on and not stare around too inquisitively, if he understood the correct rules of health.

The jigger didn't do that. Foyle was smoking a second cigarette when the muted clop of hoofs in the sand reached him. He pinched out the cigarette, rose in his stirrups, and scanned the trail.

The man on the yellow horse came to where Foyle's tracks bent off. He reined over, following them deliberately, and walked his horse around the hill.

"Mr. Foyle, I believe?" he inquired blandly. His voice was soft and light, like that of a child.

Scowling darkly, Foyle looked him over. He saw a squat little man with short legs and long arms. A broad nose, low forehead, and huge mouth made the face so strikingly ugly it had the fascination of a clown's grotesque mask. Eyes slightly slanted and a tawny skin gave it an Oriental cast. But the eyes shone a pale gray, not the black of a typical Chinese. And there was that smoothly assured voice without a trace of the singsong that Foyle associated with pigtailed cooks and laundrymen.

Foyle returned curtly, "Yeah. Who're you?"

The gargoyle face smiled shallowly. "I, sir, am Fellowstone Gano, your obedient servant." A tinge of mockery crept into the statement.

Fellowstone Gano removed his hat. It had a flat crown, wide brim, and chin strings. His hair was coarse and yellow, as startlingly incongruous as the pale eyes, against that Oriental visage. He smoothed it down with his palm, watching Foyle's expression, and uttered a liquid giggle.

"Weird-looking specimen, aren't I, Mr. Foyle? You see, in technical parlance I happen to be a very rare instance of biological Mongolism."

A deal of elegance, close to dandyism, hung about him. His shirt was of heavy yellow silk, and well made. His boots had the rich look of fine leather, and the Mexican spurs were silver. He wore a gun in a low-cut, businesslike holster. As he made the extraordinary remark about himself, he gazed at Foyle steadily.

Not having the faintest notion of what biological Mongolism meant, and doubting if it was worth knowing, Foyle demanded, "What's your business?"

A brightly expectant glimmer faded in Fellowstone Gano's eyes. He replaced his hat on his head and fingered the long chin strings thoughtfully. It was as if Foyle had in some way disappointed him. His wide and mobile mouth quirked downward at the corners.

"You are my business," he replied calmly. "I am your obedient servant. By order of Mr. Big Mac M'Cavan."

Foyle scowled. "What's Mac's idea? Hell, I don't need any servant! Wouldn't know what to do with one!"

"The idea, I believe," murmured Gano, "is to help you stay alive while you carry out a certain task that is—er—considerably fraught with peril! To that desirable end I am to give you such small aid as may be possible within my poor capacities. If not as a servant in the narrow sense of the word, you may find me useful as a back-watcher. It was with some such thought that Mr. M'Cavan sent me after you."

He coughed gently. "Mr. M'Cavan chose me for my rather special qualifications—or so I flatter myself. Also, he thought it high time that I should repay him for sheltering me in his house. Frankly, I'm wanted."

Foyle nodded. That counted up pretty straight. Leave it to Big Mac to make use of anybody he did a favor for. This odd little jigger with the outlandish name was probably a killer on the dodge.

A strain of something utterly soulless and sinister lurked in his eyes. He was a man lacking in all the usual indications of age, too, Foyle noticed. Fellowstone Gano could have been twenty or forty. Or a hundred, for that matter.

Foyle lifted his reins, shrugging. "Okay, let's push on. No, don't ride behind me! Nothing personal, friend. I don't like it, is all. We'll ride together, if you don't mind."

Fellowstone Gano inclined his head. He glanced questioningly several times at Foyle as they rode along. It was some time before he asked politely, "Why so sad, Mr. Foyle?"

The question, unexpected as it was, barely penetrated into Foyle's silent meditations. "Me sad? Huh! What's there to laugh about?"

"Not much," conceded Gano. "Still, I'm able to laugh—and look at what I am!" His laugh came thin and tinny. "I'm a freak of nature, like a two-headed calf! A biological throwback to some atavistic ancestor, perhaps one of the howling Mongol marauders of Genghis Khan. Or an interesting example of congenital malformation due to glandular disturbance, depending on your anthropological viewpoint. Yet—"

"Why so sorry for yourself, Mr. Gano?" Foyle interrupted.

Anger glittered for an instant in the gray, slanted eyes. Then Gano laughed again, this time without the thin, choking restraint. "I don't

155

believe you even know what I'm talking about! Or care. Do you?"

Foyle shook his head briefly. "To tell the truth, Gano, I don't. Look, if we're to do this job let's try an' get along together. So shut up, will you?"

"Sorry," Gano breathed. "They told me you were—er—a bit strange. And tough. I didn't understand. Yes, I believe we'll get along, Mr. Foyle."

"Okay, Gano. But drop the 'Mister'—huh?"

"Okay, Foyle."

They didn't exchange another word until they made camp that evening. Camp was a dry one, for the old trail that they followed was the forsaken Espejo and it angled away from the river. Few traveled it these days. They camped without a fire, although the air grew chilly after dark.

There had to be no knowledge of their coming. Their first object was to get up into the Pronghorn country—the great cattle land lying between the old Espejo Trail and the Estancia plains—without arousing notice. After that it would be best to proceed openly, acting the part of drifting cowpunchers from east of the Pecos. The Pronghorn Pool had to be smashed—for the glory of Big Mac and twenty thousand dollars.

Returning from staking out his yellow horse, Gano remarked, "Fine bright moon, isn't it? 'How oft hath yonder moon—' " He shivered, broke off that quotation, and murmured another. " 'Till this outworn earth be dead, as yon dead world the moon.' H'm. Deep and somber is our mood!"

"Here, have a cigar," said Foyle. "One o' Big Mac's. I hate to waste it."

"Thank you. Do you actually prefer the chopped straw and horsehair that you call tobacco? Oh, well, every man to his own taste, however depraved."

"You go to hell!"

"I'll arrange to have the red carpet spread out for you there!"

"Okay." Foyle yawned. "G'night, friend."

There was a long silence. Gano shook out his saddle blanket, and, lighting the cigar, lay smoking, arms under his head. Foyle was close to sleep when he heard him say hushedly, "Good night—friend."

On the last word Gano injected a note of strange, lingering query: ". . . friend?" As if the word were new to him and he doubted its meaning. As if he had never used that word before.

The cigar was mashed viciously into the sand. Gano sat up, took a last look around, and got under his blanket. He hissed something that sounded like a curse, and then he breathed quietly, not stirring in the silence, his slanted eyes wide open, glaring palely up at the remote round glob of moon.

Chapter Three: BANNER MEN BEWARE

IN THE TOWN of Van Gaughn the keeper of the general store had no information for the two dusty strangers. He admitted to being a Pronghorn man from way back, and judging by his leathery face he had been a cowman until too many rough horses wore him down.

"Ebb Grimm?" he echoed. He raised a cogitative squint at the ceiling, his elbows on the counter. His drawling voice boomed louder than was necessary. "Of the V Bar, you said?"

Some men idling in the store quit fingering new saddles and Indian blankets. The women filed out, their shopping unfinished, silent for once under the compelling glances of their bowlegged lords and masters.

"Never heard of him!" declared the storekeeper. "Anything you need, gents?"

It was Foyle's doing, this inquiring openly for Grimm and the directions to the V Bar. There was nothing unusual about a couple of men drifting around seeking jobs. And if Grimm was recruiting gunhands, that made it the more plausible. Gano wasn't much sold on the idea, but he was willing to trail along—the obedient servant, with insolent eyes and sardonic hints.

"All right." Foyle slapped a dollar on the counter. There was no sense in calling the man a liar. "Give me—" he glanced along the counter and called for the first thing he saw—"a packet o' pins."

"What size?" asked the storekeeper, taking the dollar, and from Gano came a malicious chuckle.

That was too much. "The hell with it!" said Foyle, and walked out, Gano following him.

It was Saturday and just past the end of the month, payday. The town was fairly full of cow folks. Soon, as the sun went down, the women and most of the married men would be pulling out, buggies and buckboards loaded with supplies, homeward bound to the ranches. Foyle chose the biggest of the town's three saloons. The painted sign said it was the Union Bar. Not a common name, this near to the Texas Panhandle. A Northern kind of name.

The place held a crowd, but it wasn't noisy. Unlike the hard drinkers of Banner, these were working cowmen who conversed in easy tones and counted their drinks. They addressed one another familiarly, in the manner of neighbors who had been friendly for years. This Pronghorn country had been settled a long time. It wouldn't have been possible for two strangers to scout around in it without attracting sharp attention.

Still, Foyle wished that he had taken the trouble to get exact directions to the V Bar, before leaving Banner. His neglect of that simple forethought bothered him. It caused him to wonder if he was growing dull and careless. About all he knew of Grimm's V Bar outfit was that it lay somewhere north a few miles of this Van Gaughn cow town. He had no description of Ebb Grimm. Nobody in Banner had ever got a good look at the man. He could be right here in the Union Bar, among his friends.

"What name?" asked the bartender, filling two glasses. "Grimm?" He thumped the cork back in the bottle. He planted his hands flat on the bar and started to say something. He paused.

The big stranger was looking straight at him. He had mighty hard and chilling eyes. His Chinese-faced partner folded his arms, solemnly inspected the quietly listening crowd, and yawned like a horse, exposing fanglike molars and a huge red tongue. The cowmen stared, hypnotized by that monstrous gape.

More men came in. Some of them were those who had been in the general store. They exchanged nods with the men present, and halted inside the swinging doors, gazing like all the rest at Foyle and Gano.

The bartender shook his head as if to clear it. He passed the buck to his customers. "Anybody know a feller named Grimm?"

He drew no response. The Pronghorn men stood silent, their eyes probing the pair and disliking what they saw. Finally a voice rasped, "Who wants to know?"

The owner of the voice was a heavy, red-faced man of middle age, standing with a group at the dice table. His glazed round eyes, like those of a bull, and the belligerent tilt of his head, were signs of a flaring temper. He was plainly a man of some standing here whose attitude could set an example, for his loud demand started a slow surge of movement. His group quit the dice table and ranged up along with him. The men at the bar eased away from Foyle and Gano, leaving them standing alone in space enough for a square dance.

Those at the door closed rank and stood pat. One of them called across to the red-faced man, "Who wants to know, is right! An' who sent 'em from where! Go ahead, Atchley!"

"Ask me!" hooted the bartender from a reasonably safe position at the far end of the bar. "I can spot Banner buzzards a mile off!"

A lanky rancher observed reflectively, "Well, after all, y'know, it was comin' time Big Mac sent us up another candidate! Maybe some dark an' dreary day he'll get real annoyed at us an' send the big Foyle joker! Wonder what the Chinaman's for? Hell, this ain't washday!"

Foyle and Gano picked up their drinks and swallowed them. It wasn't comfortable to stand there and be talked over by the surrounding mob. It was a lonely spot. These Pronghorn proddies weren't scrappers by trade, but they stuck together and were quick to jump. They had succeeded in

161

defying powerful Big Mac right along and settled the hash of some of his best gunmen.

It looked like Big Mac would pretty soon be in the market for another Number One and his little back-watcher. Foyle swung around unhurriedly, leaned his back on the edge of the bar, and while he searched for possibilities he murmured to Gano, "It's a first-class job you're doin' to help me stay alive!"

Gano yawned cavernously again.

Atchley flapped a beefy paw. "I'll do the talking!" he told everybody. His type was not rare—a man who mistook a show of bad temper for toughness, and got away with it by the benefit of his age and a certain amount of prestige. He stamped forward and bawled, "In case some-body's deef here, I'll ask once more! Who wants to know about Ebb Grimm and the V Bar?"

Before Foyle could frame a retort, Gano piped up, "My fliend likee, please! Likee me, too!" He bobbed his head and grinned ingratiatingly. "My fliend is name Mr. Jason. Velly good man! Me— Doctah Sling Bool Hi—velly good man, too! Doctah of entomology. Also anthropology, ornithology, herpetology. You got bugs, please?"

After an astounded moment, a snicker broke out. A lean young cowpuncher choked. "Hey, Atchley, answer the question! You got bugs?"

Atchley, bewildered, batted his eyes. Redder than ever, he made a disastrous attempt to recover dominance by bellowing, "Who wants to know—"

The crowd roared. For the moment the general mood slid into hilarity. Gano grinned like an amiable imbecile and wanted to shake hands with everybody. Men pushed forward, including those at the door, to get a close look at the gibbering little coot. The young cowpuncher shook him playfully by the back of his neck, and rode his joke further.

"What kind o' bugs d'you want, Chink? We got all kinds! Ask Atchley—haw!"

"I show! Likee bugs on window, see?" Gano twisted himself loose. "On window, outside. Bugs, yes. Entomological!" He trotted across the barroom, followed by guffaws.

When near the door, he spun around. All laughter ceased abruptly.

His inane grin was gone. In its place was the faint, false smile that he had worn when he introduced himself to Foyle. In his pale eyes was a glitter of wicked mischief that made some of the cowmen nearest him draw their breaths in sharply. He held a gun in each hand, one from his holster, the other plucked out from under his yellow silk shirt. He seemed suddenly to have grown about a foot taller. The monkey had transformed himself into a menacing, malignant gorilla, aching to commit a killing.

"Entomology entails anatomical dissection!" he said softly, dropping all trace of the halting singsong. "I've had considerable experience in taking insects apart! If any specimen here doubts my dexterity, let him give me now a cause to display it! Just one tiny cause, that's all!"

He was deadly and evil. His face was the incarnation of malice, of cold hatred for them all. He had played the clown to them, at bitter cost to his ego.

Foyle stepped around the spellbound crowd, saying, "The joke's on you, insects!" It was on him, too. Seldom had he seen a jackpot tipped over so neatly—and without any help from him. The thought recurred to him that perhaps he was losing his edge, was slipping. That fatal time was bound to come, if a man stayed with the game.

Gano, swinging his guns, was inquiring, "What—no doubters? Not one?" He clucked his tongue. It had the sound of a handclap. "Mr. Jason, the sportive spirit here appears to be diminished! Shall we seek a more congenial clime? A cheerier atmosphere? Shall we, in short, get the hell out?"

"Let's go, Sing Hi!"

"Please, Mr. Jason, mangle not the noble name of Sling Bool Hi! Sing Hi, indeed! I may be a bug chaser, but I am not a bird!"

They backed together to the swing doors, two outcast gun fighters seeking the breeze, making the dry remarks to sustain their arrogance. In the dead hush the younger men in the barroom

164

breathed deeply, nostrils pinching and swelling, mouth muscles bunched. Some of the older men kept darting half-expectant glances toward Atchley. By those glances Atchley's standing could be estimated. He was the hothead most likely to start a blow-off, but only within narrow limits was he a leader. Nobody had command here. It was not a signal they waited for from him, but only for some kind of crazy play that might open up a chance for them to act. But Atchley did nothing, and nobody moved.

That fact made it clear that Ebb Grimm was not in this crowd. He would have been the one they watched, for a commanding signal. He was kingpin of the Pronghorn.

Most of this crowd must have ridden in from the roundup camps for Saturday night in town. They looked it. It was the time of year in this high country for the work to be heading along full swing. Ebb Grimm, by his name alone, somehow sounded like the kind of a man who kept his crew sweating eighteen hours every day and wouldn't abide any high jinks and Saturday-night caperings. If he wasn't out with his crew, tonight he'd most likely be home at the V Bar ranch house nosing through his tally books and ledger. Foyle decided it would be a good bet, if he could locate the V Bar. It would have to be done fast. He and Gano needed a load of luck.

The luck arrived right then. All bad.

It began with a floor board. Many hard-heeled boots for many years had clumped in and out of the Union Bar, and under the long punishment one of the floor boards at the entrance had loosened and warped. It rocked when trod on. In all likelihood the regular customers had gained a semiconscious awareness of it, and stepped over it without giving it a thought. Gano had no knowledge of it, and he was stepping backward. His right boot came down on the faulty floorboard. It rocked. So did Gano. And in recovering his balance he caught his left spur in the tipped-up edge.

Mr. Fellowstone Gano, alias Dr. Sling Bool Hi, teetered, and vanished from Foyle's side. He took a backward header, knocking the doors wide, and tumbled surprisedly down three wooden steps to the boardwalk.

"What the hell now?" Foyle muttered, thinking it another of Gano's little tricks, although he couldn't see much reason for it. He halted, keeping the crowd covered. The two-way doors flapped back smartly, hit both his elbows a crack, and his cocked guns went off. The bullets split the top shelf of the backbar.

The Pronghorn cowmen jumped to the conclusion that he had gone trigger-crazy. There was no percentage in standing still for him to shoot at. They stampeded at him in a wild rush. He dived out, missing the steps and colliding with Gano on the boardwalk.

Bounding to his feet, swearing, Gano chopped two shots and punched a hole accurately in the center of each swaying door of the saloon. His face was savage. He waved a smoking gun. "Our horses!" he snarled, and one look told Foyle what he meant.

Their two horses were gone from the hitchrack of the general store where they had left them. Not only that, but there wasn't a horse left at any hitchrack along the street. Somebody had gathered them up and taken them off, just in case the two Banner pilgrims staged a break. The town was out to get them, and didn't mind going to some trouble to make it a certainty.

A voice rapped from a doorway, "Put 'em up, you sons! This is the sheriff!" Without further notice or pause a rifle cut loose. That sheriff craved lightning service. He got it.

Foyle dropped twistingly down on one knee, threw up a gun, and fired. He saw the sheriff heave into sight and reel back into his doorway. The saloon crowd remained inside for the time being, steadied by the bullet holes in the doors, and hoping for the bold sheriff to get in his lick with the rifle. Foyle made a lurching run into the alley across from the Union Bar. The wounded sheriff got off another hasty shot at him, shouting hoarsely, "Dammit, fellers, come out an' give me a hand!"

Already in the alley, Gano was shooting at the

saloon, keeping the crowd to cover. His savage rage had passed as swiftly as it came. A dispassionate calmness smoothed his tawny face. His eyes shone like half-moons.

"Are you hit bad?" he inquired lightly, in much the same tone that he might have asked Foyle if he had a match.

"Leg. That damn sheriff's rifle!"

The sun had gone down. The dusk was deepening. "That makes it awkward," Gano commented, keeping his eyes on the saloon doors.

"Makes *me* awkward!" said Foyle. "Say, I saw a corral as we came in. Back o' the freight warehouse. Bunch o' mules in there. Ever ride a mule bareback?"

"Allah forbid!"

"He's not on our side. Look, this caper's a bust, no maybe. You better sneak round to that mule corral while you can. These jiggers won't hang back much longer. They'll bust out in a minute an' then it'll be all over. You know it."

Gano shifted his eyes. He scanned Foyle's drawn face curiously. "We might both try for the corral," he suggested, but his voice lacked conviction. He raised his gun and slung another shot at the saloon.

Foyle's short laugh was harshly derisive. "Me try to ride a bareback mule—like this? Get out o' here an' don't argue!"

Gano grinned eerily. It was a tortured grimace

that twitched one cheek and stretched his mouth all aslant. A smoky veil darkened his eyes. He put out a hand to Foyle, then quickly drew it back without touching him.

His grin turned shallow and false. The eyes mirrored once more the pale mockery. In mimic falsetto he singsonged cynically, "Me velly obedient servant! Me get! Goo'by!" He vanished soundlessly down the alley, hugging the wall.

Foyle hoped he'd make it. Only pure fools stuck uselessly to the finish, and they didn't work for Big Mac. Gano had stood up fine in the Union Bar jackpot. He had showed his stuff there, all right. But you couldn't look for such a man to be sentimental when it came down to a last chance at a getaway.

Foyle thought of Big Mac and cursed him. It crossed his mind that for Big Mac he was about to meet his end in a dirty alley, shooting it out with men he didn't know and who didn't know him. Bain Foyle—just another Banner badman, the fourth or fifth one to be sent up to the Pronghorn who never got back.

"Me?" he growled. "Hell!" He smashed three bullets into the Union Bar and dragged himself down the alley. His leg was like rubber. He was bleeding pretty bad. The sheriff's bullet had got him above the knee. He guessed the bone was broken there.

Gano had prowled left from the end of the alley,

to work around to the mule corral. There was no sign or sound of him now. Foyle crawled to the right. The livery stable was along there, across from the general store. It was closed, but cracks of light showed from inside. If he could get at the liveryman. Hold a gun on him. Make him saddle a horse. He might manage to stay in a saddle long enough to get out of this town and find hiding. If the horse was gentle. If he roped himself on. If they didn't come after him too soon. He knew he was leaving a trail of blood.

Chapter Four: **RENEGADE'S RODEO**

FOYLE REACHED the rear of the livery after scraping through the pole fence into the yard. The tall doors that opened onto the yard were shut. They sagged on their hinges and met unevenly, and through the crack he could see that the bar was up on the inside. The liveryman had shut up shop and cautiously barred himself in until the disturbance was settled. Somebody was with him. They were talking, arguing over something.

He was about to insert a gun barrel into the crack and try lifting the bar, when he caught the sounds of a stamping hoof, a snort, and the faint creak of leather. The sounds came from close by. He moved on past the livery doors. He peered around the corner, and checked a deep sigh of relief.

In the lane leading into the livery yard stood a buckboard and team that had evidently been backed in off the street for safety. The two horses had their heads bent in his direction, sniffing uneasily, ears cocked, aware of his presence before he appeared. The smell of his blood made them nervous. His crawling advance scandalized them. The near horse crowded over against its mate.

He couldn't give them a friendly cussing to lull their mistrust. The men in the livery would certainly hear and raise the alarm. The horses sidled off toward the street, conferring in agitated snorts, wanting nothing to do with a blood-smelly hobgoblin that didn't walk upright and swear out loud. A noisy racket broke out in the street and switched their aroused fright in that direction. They paused to consider.

Foyle rose, hopped forward on his good leg, and floundered into the buckboard. He snatched up the lines, and the horses stood shivering but passive, recognizing the authority of human hands.

The racket in the street grew louder, concentrated somewhere down past the Union Bar. Men were running about, yelling. Some shots blared, and hoofs pounded a boardwalk like a drum. It could have been a merry Saturday-night rodeo— somebody having trouble with his mount, and everybody pulling for the horse. Foyle coaxed the buckboard team forward and took a look. He had to get out by way of the street, anyhow. The lane was too narrow to turn in, and it ended in the livery yard, at that.

It wasn't a fractious horse that was raising the riot. It was a Satan-striped Spanish mule, ornery by nature and no saddle to handicap him. Gano was riding; staying on top, anyway, toes clamped in, taking the bumps. He couldn't afford to let go, and there was always a wild chance that his long-eared steed might take a fit to leave town with him. He had got hold of a mule, but whatever had since transpired between them was obviously all the mule's enterprise. The crowd complicated his dilemma, surging about, shouting, trying to box in the scampering, kicking mule and at the same time keep clear of its hoofs.

A determined cowpuncher ran out at it, twirling a rope. The mule, knowing what that thing was, skidded half a turn in a boil of dust and flashed its hind hoofs at his face. The cowpuncher dodged them by a hair, but got tangled in his loop and down he went. Exasperated, he sat up, dragging out his gun, and blazed impartially at the animal and the figure clinging to its back.

The mule took two jumps that landed it on the boardwalk near the Union Bar. Startled at the loud and hollow drumming under its hoofs, it leaped off, threw a high roller, and came down stiff-legged.

Gano's bobbing face dropped so low he kissed the mule's neck. But he still hung on.

Thoroughly mad, the mule uncorked a series of weaving bucks, shaking itself like a leaping fish. It tightened them up into a rapid display of acrobatics in which the object seemed to be to bite its own tail. Nobody could stay on the back of a Spanish mule without its permission, and not always then. Gano had picked the wrong mule; or perhaps there weren't any right ones. It wound up the business by swapping ends faster than a cat quitting an occupied kennel. That did the trick.

Tossed wide, Gano struck the Union Bar hitchrack and bounced off. He crouched in the dust, smothered in dirt and his nose running blood, a trapped target for the mob to blast to rags. The mule scooted back and forth, seeking an opening in the closing circle of men.

Foyle hit the excited team and let out an ear-splitting squawl. The team took off, snapping his head back. As the buckboard shot into the street both horses tried to swing north away from the roaring, frightening crowd. He hauled their heads around, lashing them. It was a fast and cramped turn. The buckboard yawed over on two wheels, the others spinning free. Banging into a porch post of the general store righted it, at the cost of the post, and Foyle sent the team full at the crowd.

Barely holding his balance on the bumping seat while whacking the horses, he got only a rapid impression of faces whirling aside, a confused jumble of bodies, arms and legs flying, and thuds against the buckboard. The team burst through into the open space before the Union Bar where the mule pranced and Gano crouched.

"Up an' jump, partner!"

If Gano heard the shout above the din, he didn't need the advice. It was that or be run over. He upped and jumped in one nimble motion. There wasn't much room for him between the Union Bar hitchrack and the buckboard. Rocking past, Foyle took a hurried look back and could see nothing of him in the kicked-up dust. He guessed Gano had missed and gone under, if he wasn't hanging to the rear axle and dragging. He couldn't stop to find out. He charged on at the other half of the crowd, the mule seesawing ahead, thinking it was pursued.

Breaking through this bunch was a livelier proposition. The others, their backs toward him, had been caught by surprise and followed their first impulse to scramble out of the path of a runaway team. These, though, had time to see what had happened and who was coming at them, and they didn't propose to scatter.

Stopping a panicked pair of strong horses, however, wasn't any casual pastime for men on foot in high-heeled boots. Particularly when the horses followed hard on the heels of a belligerent mule. And the driver laying about him furiously with the whip. Again came the mad turmoil of faces and bodies—but this time with hands clawing at the team, and the faces were lighted spasmodically by gun flashes.

The mule's progress loosened a hole in the crowd. The animal had gone frantic. It barged on through, and so again did the team, one man clinging stubbornly to the near horse and grabbing at its rein. Foyle reached far over and hit the man with the butt end of the whip. The man dropped off, rolling over and over on the ground. The raging cowmen hammered a flurry of shots after the jouncing buckboard.

An explosion of pain blinded Foyle. He rode upright on the seat, shuddering, every muscle taut, glaring into a dazzling white nothingness. Words formed in his mouth. He thought he spoke them aloud, but his lips were clamped shut.

Damn him to hell!

His curse wasn't aimed at the man whose bullet had found him, whoever he was, but at Big Mac, for in that instant the dazzling white fire brought with it a stark clarity. Had Big Mac deliberately sent him to his death? There had been those other Banner men, gun fighters of the old bunch, who became restless, unable to conceal a rebellious contempt of Big Mac after learning too much about him. They had gone, one by one, sent on mysterious missions—one-way trails, no return. And now he, Bain Foyle, last of that hard, reckless, but straight-shooting bunch, the top man—

The white flare clouded, darkened swiftly to black. He was falling a great distance. He was falling alone, yet in his ear was Gano's voice: "My fliend, you velly good man!"

When Foyle rose painfully back to the surface of consciousness, he thought cloudily that his body was being forced up through layers of barbwire. It was the hurting that clawed and nagged him out of a dream. In the dream he had just shot a hawk with his father's old percussion rifle. His father, in one of the rare sober periods since his mother's death, was bawling the devil out of him for it in the grave, troubled way he had when he wasn't drunk.

"Never did you any harm, did it?" demanded his father. He had read a good deal in the happier days, and he said, looking down at the dead hawk, "God creates the living. He created this wild bird. And along comes you, a fool boy with a gun, and—and—" he looked away, sunken eyes hopelessly drowned in memory of the loved woman lost—"slits the thin-spun life!" he finished in a whisper.

Bain, too, looked away, but only to hide his young intolerance. His father was getting queer in the head. Wouldn't kill anything, not even the thieving chipmunks that, grown bold in their immunity, scuttled and chattered under the floors of the house and raided the kitchen in broad daylight. Yet it was said that the old man had been considerable of a curly wolf in his time, and hung up a high reputation among shooters.

His father that night, drunk, staggered in and slapped him clear across the room. "Too cussed handy wi' guns!" he shouted. "I ever catch you again—"

Light penetrated Foyle's eyelids. His will fought sluggishly against the impulse to open his eyes. He wanted urgently to go back to the ranch on the Nueces and tell his father that he understood him now. But the dream had dissipated in the waking throb of pain, and he remembered with a dull regret that his father was long dead. He was a man, not a boy any more. He was Bain Foyle, top gunman of Banner.

Memory raced on, disclosing Van Gaughn, the Union Bar, the hostile Pronghorn cowmen. The fight. The getaway. There, against a wall of blinding white, memory faltered and came to a stop. Nothing more existed for him beyond that.

Shocked to full pitch, consciousness swept away the cloudy lassitude and freed his mind to leaping speculation. A bullet had caught him in the head—yes—as he careened south out of town in the stolen buckboard. What had happened after that? Where was he now? He tested his injured leg by flexing the tendons. It was bandaged and it hurt. Cautiously he slid a hand up to his head. It, too, was bandaged, and it throbbed sickeningly.

"Doctor!" exclaimed a clear, low voice. "He's—"

"Coming to, eh? Splendid!" said another voice. It was briskly professional, yet familiar. "Miss Reynolds, do you have any kind of stimulants in the house? Mr. Jason and I do not drink," the voice lied smoothly, "but there are occasions when a medicinal measure of whisky—"

"I'll get some at once, doctor."

A door closed quietly.

Foyle opened his eyes. He was lying on a bed in a lighted room, and Gano's ugly face was grinning down at him. He had a string of questions to ask and he began pouring them out.

"Where are we? How did we get here? Who's that woman? What happened after—"

"Shut up!" interrupted Gano superiorly. "I'm the doctor and I'll do the talking!" He darted to the closed door, put an ear to it, and returned to the bed. "Haven't much time. Won't take her long to fetch the whisky. I only asked for it to get her out of the room, when I saw you were coming to. Now get this! You are Mr. Jason. I am Doctor Sling. I am engaged in doing some very important research, and you are my co-worker and guide. We met with a misunderstanding in Van Gaughn. We were persecuted and attacked by ruffians! Stripped of our dignity, and robbed of our horses! We escaped—martyrs of the noble cause of science!"

"I could cry," Foyle grunted. "Say, last I saw of you there, you'd missed the jump and gone under."

Gano shook his head. "I caught hold of the back of the buckboard. Climbed on in time to keep you from falling off. How we smashed through that pack! You, the horses, the mule, and me—hanging on by one hand and shooting with the other! An effective combination. I must keep it in mind. Still, I wouldn't try riding that mule again to skip out of hell. The brute nearly wrecked my chaste beauty."

He stroked his nose, which was swollen. "They got their horses and came howling after us," he mentioned. "It was a bit difficult, driving the team and holding you on as well. I was tempted to let you go. You know—like that old story of the Russian who tossed his family out of the sleigh to the pursuing wolves. Very sensible of him. Lightened the load, delayed the wolves, and saved his life. As a boy, it was one of my favorite stories."

"How come you didn't?" asked Foyle.

Gano gestured airily. "Oh—I happened to recall Big Mac's order to help you stay alive until you did the job. So I drove off the trail and hid in the brush. They tore past in the dark, all terribly fierce, and for all I know they're still scouring the south for us. I then drove wide around the town and headed north. By the way, did you chance to notice the brand painted on that buckboard?"

"No."

"I did, and it interested me. When I reached the main road, northbound, I slacked off the lines and left it to the horses to choose the route. Naturally, with their minds on their supper, they trotted homeward. The brand on the buckboard was—V Bar!"

Foyle heaved a breath. "What? You mean—"

Gano nodded, his eyes glittering, the lips of his

huge mouth curled in silent mirth. "Yes—this is the V Bar outfit! We are in Ebb Grimm's house, uninvited but not unwelcomed guests!"

He raised a finger, listening, head cocked. His batlike ears seemed to quiver. "Sssh! Here she comes! Be ready for another surprise. You'll get one, if you're half the man I think you are, Foyle—Mr. Jason, I mean!"

Chapter Five: MISTRESS OF V BAR

THE FIRST SIGHT of the girl who entered the room jerked Foyle's scattered thoughts up short. He stared at her. At once a gnawing, like hunger, clutched at him inside and overrode the heartbeat throbbing of his pains.

Few women had ever had that instantaneous effect on him; none as strongly as this. In his kind of life there were no high pedestals for women, no rigidly observed laws of prim decorum. They took their social standing according to the flame of their attraction, and no degree was untouchable. The other kind, the kind he rarely met, caused him always to become more stiffly reticent than usual. *They* were untouchable, and for that reason he guarded himself against having any feeling about them. From that rule of conduct sprang a blunt and urgent question: Who and what was this girl?

She had a mass of brown hair with reddish undertones. Her skin had a kind of silvery, satin aura that, combined with her full warm lips, summed a voluptuous quality that the most popular dance-hall queen would have envied. Nothing short of an iron smock could have concealed the sleek curves of her body. Her eyes contained some of the color of the undertone of her hair. They were like molten copper, transparent around the deeper irises, but not empty. They were utterly feminine eyes.

There was something else, something more, invisible, not easy to define, yet immediately recognizable to masculine senses. It belonged in the realm of womanhood where, behind the vulnerable ramparts of passion and compassion, idolatry breathlessly waited with a boundless capacity to love the invader.

Gano, on his best behavior, relieved her of her tray and set it down. "Our patient is doing very well." He bowed, and flipped a hand toward Foyle. "Miss Reynolds—Mr. Jason."

Their eyes met and they spoke words that meant nothing. Foyle went on looking, feeling nothing of the pain, only the gnawing. Among the girls whom he entered in his private tally as "nice" he had never met one like this. But then, he had never met or seen a girl such as this anywhere.

Under his straight gaze her lips parted slightly, revealing the line of her even white teeth. She pinked. The color flushed from beneath her hair and spread until it crept under the neckline of her dress. Then her eyelashes screened her eyes. He knew that his eyes were saying too much, too candidly, but he couldn't remove them from her.

It was Gano who broke that up. "I have been telling Mr. Jason of my tribulations after I saved him from those ruffians in town," he said, coughing modestly. His eyes were saying a lot, too, fastened on the girl, but he stood partly behind her and she couldn't see them. "That was a dastardly outrage, Miss Reynolds! Quite unprovoked. Had it not been for me, Mr. Jason would surely have been murdered! Fortunately I was able to secure a mule and dash to his rescue!"

"A mule?" She regarded him dubiously. "But, doctor, it was a buckboard you brought him here in."

Gano smiled brightly at her. "Mr. Jason doesn't know very much about riding a mule," he murmured confidentially, and let that subject drop. "It's late, Miss Reynolds. I'm sure we are keeping you up. Ah, what a blessed angel of mercy you are in our sore distress! But you must not wear yourself out for us. You must have your sleep, my dear. To paraphrase the immortal Bard of Avon—"

The Bard went unparaphrased. The door opened abruptly and a man stood there. He was a short, neat man, up in his forties. His eyes were small and sharp. Chronic impatience and irritable severity could be seen at a glance in his brown, knotty face. His movements were curt and direct. He looked to be the type of cowman who drove himself and everybody around him hard, resented pleasure as a waste of time, and suffered dyspepsia from eating too fast. He looked as humorless as a snapping turtle.

His intolerant eyes stabbed at Foyle, at Gano,

184

and finally to the girl. "What the devil's this?" he rasped in a voice clipped tight from anger. "Did they come in the buckboard? It's down in the yard. They stole it off me!"

The girl lifted a restraining hand. "This is Ira Hamp, our range boss," she explained to Foyle and Gano. To the range boss she said, "Mr. Jason and Doctor Sling borrowed it. They were attacked in town and their horses taken, and they had to get away as best they could. Is everybody in Van Gaughn going crazy? Any stranger who comes in, they accuse of being a Banner gunman! It's outrageous! They could at least—"

"That don't concern me!" Ira Hamp broke in, while Gano was making clucking sounds of sympathy for himself and Foyle. "My business is to run this outfit. I'm runnin' the roundup on a mighty close schedule. I drove in town late for new rope. A ruckus was goin' on when I got there. It don't concern me. My concern is keepin' the crew at work, an' I'll do it long's I'm foreman!"

His use of that term—foreman—indicated that he was from somewhere up north. Southwestern cowmen didn't use it. The man who ran the outfit was the range boss, top screw, high-cock-a-doodle, or something casually disrespectful.

"I backed in by the livery," Ira Hamp went on, his voice getting tighter. The taking of the buckboard was a personal affront and a bitter offense. It had cost him time. "I went in an' asked

Harrison to water the horses. He wouldn't. He barred the doors. While I argued with the ol' fool, them two—" he speared his finger at Foyle and Gano—"stole the buckboard! I had to run around town an' borrow a broken-down ol' nag to get home! I didn't even get the new rope! They stole that buckboard, I say!"

"Well," Foyle put in mildly, "somebody stole our horses, so I reckon it's an even standoff."

The range boss took a step toward the bed. "I got nothin' to do with your horses!"

"Your buckboard is there in the yard, isn't it?" queried Gano. "Our apologies and thanks should be sufficient. After all, you only work here, so you don't own it!"

Ira Hamp thrust out his chin. He failed to detect the glint in the pale, slanted eyes. "Shut your trap, Chink—I'm just sore enough to shut it for you!"

Foyle, half rising from the bed, said swiftly to Gano, "Hold it, man, hold it!" Only he knew the lethal significance of the Mongoloid man's baleful grimace, the stillness of the hands, and the soft hiss of an expelled breath.

The girl stepped up to the range boss. "I think we had better go downstairs and talk this over, Mr. Hamp," she told him. "You can apologize later to Doctor Sling."

"I got no time for talk," he grunted, preceding her out of the room. "Not about this, anyhow. An' I sure don't apologize to no Chink!"

"Easy, Gano!" Foyle whispered. "Easy!"

Ira Hamp evidently didn't have a high opinion of feminine intelligence. They heard him, going downstairs with the girl, say roughly, "I wish Grimm was here! He'd know what to do with the likes o' them two thieves! He sure wouldn't put 'em up in the best bedroom, an' act the fool, treatin' 'em like—"

"That's my privilege, Mr. Hamp!"

"All right, Miss Donna, all right! So 'tis—till Grimm gets back. Then you'll see! He won't like it, I tell you now! You ain't been here long enough to know—"

The voices faded away. Foyle lay back in the bed and gazed up at the ceiling.

"Her name is Donna," he said reflectively. He repeated it. "Donna. Nice name. Donna Reynolds." It sparked a thought. He frowned, puzzled. "Who is she? Where does she fit in here on Grimm's V Bar outfit? D'you know, Gano? You had a good chance to talk with her before I woke up, didn't you?"

Gano didn't reply for a spell. He sat down and built a cigarette, using Foyle's makings. A tiny tremble shook his fingers. He licked his lips before he ran the tip of his tongue along the edge of the brown paper. He lighted the cigarette and smoked jerkily, hunched over in the chair. His eyelids were lowered, heavy and sullen.

"Yes, I had a good chance," he assented, "before

you woke up. To—talk with her. Then you opened your eyes. You looked at her. And she—that was all you had to do."

He flung the cigarette to the floor. Its burning end burst into a shower of sparks. He ground them out under his heel. He was unpredictable, by turns cynically gay and darkly brooding. The dark mood was on him. His voice was low and grating.

"All I know is what we both heard. Her name is Donna Reynolds. She is beautiful, she lives here in Grimm's house, and she hasn't been here long. And you ask where she fits in! There's the answer!"

Foyle scowled at him. "What's bitin' you? I know Hamp riled you, but that's no cause for you to blackguard the girl behind her back! Cut it out!"

Gano continued talking as though he hadn't heard. "What the hell does it matter what she is? It doesn't to me." A spasm of harried agony ravaged his tawny, uncouth face. "It's what *I* am that matters!"

He glared down at the floor. "Life has cheated me since the day I was born! And it could have been so glorious. Mongolism, they say, is an accident that can occur in the finest and proudest families. How well I know that! Mine was a fine, proud family. They bred great soldiers, diplomats, rulers. Their name is known throughout Europe. What a hideous shock to them was my birth! What a disgrace! My family was famous for its tall, handsome men, its elegantly beautiful women. I was a shameful little monster among them! They never quite regarded me as human, although I had their brains—their aristocratic manners—pride! The very sight of me remained a constant horror to them! The throwback! Alien monkey!"

Before such a stark revelation of concentrated bitterness, Foyle could find nothing to say. Sweat twinkled in the ridges and seams of Gano's low forehead. He passed a hand over it, smearing it. He sat there, huddled, glaring down the spent years into the faraway past. His voice fell to a sneering monotone.

"Oh, they didn't disown me. They couldn't! They packed me off to expensive schools—far off! They gave me an allowance, generous amounts, hoping I'd quickly drink myself to death. And they rushed me out of the country, when I killed a colonel in a cabaret for making a certain remark about my appearance. How glad they were to be rid of me at last!"

He cackled horribly. "A touching farewell, that! I changed my name. When the money they gave me was gone, I lived on my wits. Gambling and cheating. Trickery and theft. Murder and robbery. You think you've gone bad, Foyle? Hah! You've barely scraped the surface of sin! What else was there for me? All men have been my prey, all my life since!"

Foyle wished he'd shut up. This naked exposure of tragedy and crime embarrassed him. He sensed in Gano a compulsive urge to confession that was self-revulsion rather than a soul-cleansing. Some burning emotion had caught up with Gano, and fired a reaction that he could not throttle down. But he, Bain Foyle, was not his confessor, and he drew back from hearing more.

"I've changed my name frequently," Gano said. He fisted his knee. "Never could I change myself! Men are repelled by me. Women recoil. In their eyes I see that unreasoning distrust, dislike, animosity, shrinking repugnance! Or, worse, the unforgivable insult of secret, scornful laughter! I am a man!"

He struck his knee again in futile rage. "A man! Yet, because of this cursed half-Mongol face and half-dwarfed body, I am forever an outcast, a pariah! That girl downstairs. Donna Reynolds. She was civil to me. Friendly, even. I could have given her my blood for that! I am a man, I say! Then you looked at her. She was glad not to look at me again! The comparison was—too excessive! Damn you, Foyle! Damn your tall body, long legs, straight eyes, your skin—"

"Okay, *amigo*!" Foyle cut in. This was more comfortable ground. This abusive tangent offered a welcome return to normal talk. He said hurriedly, "Is she alone here, you reckon?"

Gano shrugged and straightened up. A grin, at

first wry and ghostly, then full and false, lightened his face. He spoke with almost his old tone of mocking insolence.

"What a discerning question! The ranch crew is out on roundup. And that, if I judge the Hamp creature right, means every last man who is able to move, including the cook. Ebb Grimm is off somewhere. He's probably lining up fighting men to oppose Big Mac. Of course she is alone! That is, except for us. And that, as Hamp warned her, would not please Mr. Ebb Grimm! It certainly would not please me, in his place!"

The pointed inference brought Foyle's scowl back. "They say Grimm's been a widower a long time. He must be getting along in years."

"What of it?" Gano scoffed. "He's well-to-do. He's the biggest rancher in this part of the country. Men of his age and wealth often become the—er—protectors of lovely but penniless women! He can give her security, comfort. Did you see the bracelet on her wrist? Real diamonds! A valuable bauble, not the sort of trinket that a ranch girl wears. Believe me, if Grimm gets word that there's some youngish male company dawdling around his prize possession, we can expect him home in a hurry! I hope it works out that way, so we can wind up this job."

Foyle released a sigh. The hard mask settled over his face, etched with lines that had come too soon for his years. Life, he reflected saturninely, was a string of mirages, like a lonely desert trail, each shimmering illusion crumbling as it was reached. Even he, for all his experience, could still be gulled, wishful to believe, his faith captured, until his cup dipped dry sand.

And yet—*Whatever she is,* ran an unbidden thread of thought, *I'm a gone duck! This time I can't go on!*

He brushed the private confession aside, refusing to accept it. "What shape am I in, Gano?" he asked.

"The sheriff's bullet," Gano answered, "seems to have grazed the bone as well as a tendon in your lower thigh. That accounts for the numbness. The other one could easily have knocked the parietal bone askew in your cranium—but happily you're quite as thick-skulled as I suspected! It fluked, and parted your hair rather prettily on the side. Donna Reynolds thinks I'm a surgeon. She's a darling. I put on an impressive show for her benefit. There's no reason why you shouldn't get up when the stiffness leaves your leg. You'll be limpy and sore for a while, but on the whole you got off lucky."

"Soon's I can," Foyle stated, "I'm getting out o' here, Grimm or no Grimm! Tomorrow! Today! Past midnight, isn't it?"

Gano took a walk up and down the room, fingering his lips and shooting glances at Foyle. "No, you won't!"

"Who says?"

"I do! You're my patient, remember! I forbid it!"

"Go to blazes! You just now said—"

Gano made a dismissing hand pass. "I've held a professional consultation with myself and reversed my opinion. You stay there. Your guns are hanging up there on the wall, out of your reach. All I have to do is give you a tap on the skull with one of mine, and you'll have a sudden relapse."

"Why, damn your nerve!"

"Listen, Foyle!" Gano halted at the foot of the bed. "For your own good as well as mine, listen! Whatever it is that's weighing on your mind, you had better forget it. We've got a job to do here, and we can't back out. Big Mac gave his orders. You know what it means to go against him! I can see you going in and telling him, 'We got inside Grimm's house, but we decided not to wait for him!' I can see Big Mac's face! 'Yes, we walked right out again. Because Grimm had a pretty girl, and I—'"

"Shut up about her, will you?" Foyle snapped.

Gano laughed soundlessly. "So solly—no can do! She's too important to us, apart from her charms. If you were thinking straight you'd see that. Now, look! Grimm will be back sometime. It'll be soon, too, if he hears about us being here! I suppose he keeps in touch, wherever he is, seeing he's the big chief. We will be here, waiting for him!"

"What about that town crowd? They're bound to find out where we are."

"True. Hamp will spill it out sooner or later, and they'll come for us. But if darling Donna stands up for us, they're not going to drag us out! She's mistress of this house. She's our ace! Our only card, in fact!"

"Hide behind a girl's skirts?"

"Lovely skirts, too!" Gano nodded, unabashed. "I imagine she has a lot of spirit. She would go all out for someone she—er—liked. We must win her trust, respect, loyalty. In a woman, those excellent qualities and virtues can usually be aroused, I have observed, by one dominant emotion—love. I don't possess the qualifications to handle that, so it's your job. Right?"

"Wrong!" snarled Foyle.

Thoughtfully, Gano helped himself to a stiff drink from the bottle on the tray. "It's a poor doctor who can't swallow his own prescription! Foyle, you can be the most thickheaded fool! That girl is already half gone on you. God knows you're gone on her! What could be more natural? She's lonely. Her protector is old and away from home. Along you come—a tall, passably good looking man in a rough way, reasonably young and obviously virile. Hurt, and needing her gentle care! You open your eyes and see her. You're a lonely sort of cuss, yourself. She, beautiful. Gorgeous! She's passion and fire and affection

194

and— Oh, hell!" He swung away, restlessly finger-combing his coarse yellow hair.

When he spoke next he pitched his voice low and flat. "All right, Foyle, walk out! Go back to Banner! Tell Big Mac that Fellowstone Gano is sticking to the job! I'll get it done, I swear, somehow. There's big money in it. Damn anything else!"

He looked suddenly aged, wearily satanic, a man saturated in all the blackest depths of crime. "Money is everything!" he muttered, leaving the room.

Chapter Six: THE NIGHT MARAUDERS

ABSENT MOST OF THE TIME, the following day Gano came into the bedroom and found Foyle staring at a blank wall. Donna Reynolds had brought Foyle his meals and later removed the dishes, and her visits had released a turgid flood of feelings in him.

He could recall her every word, every inflection of her voice, every motion. He could see her. The sunlight through the window brought out the undertones of her hair so that they glimmered, alive, like the deep fires recessed in polished quartz. It struck further fires in the transparent copper of her eyes, and placed a faintly blue shadow under the curve of her throat.

When she arranged the tray on the bed, her nearness had forced him to draw back, amazed and dismayed at what it did to him. It was useless to remind himself that she belonged to another man. His senses ignored it. This time the mirage persisted and he couldn't shrug it off and go on. Cynical reason promised that it would disintegrate and vanish like the rest in barren disillusion, while in his heart he wished fervently to stay hoodwinked.

"How's the patient?" inquired Gano, flicking ash from an expensive cigar that he had purloined from somewhere on the premises. "Decided to wait for Grimm after all, eh? Too bad! I anticipated earning twenty thousand dollars all for myself—plus whatever else I could get away with from here."

Foyle forsook his visions. He eyed Gano bleakly. "I'd about as soon leave her to that pack o' Russian wolves you spoke of!"

"Oho!" Gano clicked his tongue. "The protective-male instinct, eh? Methinks I caught a rapt expression on your countenance as I came in! I observe also that you've taken your guns down off the wall." He leered like a bronze satyr. "And the eyes of darling Donna softly glow with a pensive light that only a blind man could miss seeing. Congratulations, Mr. Jason—I do hope you'll both be very happy!"

Resisting a temptation to hurl something at him, Foyle changed the talk by asking, "Where did you pick up that name for me, by the way? Off a wanted bill, I bet!"

Gano waggled a hand reassuringly. "Your ignorance of classic mythology astounds me. Jason, son of Aeson, was that enterprising bucko who hied forth to win the Golden Fleece. A fitting name for you, say I. He won the damned thing, too, come to think of it, and carried off a lovely princess as a bonus. Those were the days! But let's get to business. My plans call for speed."

"Are you trying to take charge, Gano?" Foyle's tone was gently dangerous.

He was conscious of a subtle altering in the relationship between himself and Gano since last night. Where Gano's insolence had been lightly impersonal, it now had a core of steely malice. There had been something approaching a friendly give-and-take understanding between them, normal to their hazardous situation. Today it existed largely in form, little in content. Perhaps Gano regretted having gone that far toward friendship. He was solitary and friendless by choice, avoiding personal entanglements, letting nothing interfere in his credo of self-interest.

At Foyle's blunt question Gano let his one-sided grin fade. His oblique eyes stilled, drained of the slightest trace of humor.

"Not at all," he replied. "I know my place." A muscle quivered on a prominent cheekbone. "I am—the obedient servant. Far be it from me to intend any offense to the master!"

Foyle said uncomfortably, "Forget it! What's on your mind?"

Gano's face was an impassive mask overlying a sneer. "Ira Hamp came to the house again today for something," he related tonelessly. "He talked with Donna—excuse me—with Miss Reynolds. I listened. Our guess about Grimm is correct. He's in Texas, in the Panhandle, gathering ex-Rangers, discharged soldiers, and the like. It's more than a posse he's recruiting, although it's to be known as the Pronghorn Posse to give it a touch of legal color. It's a whole company! Over a hundred fighting men, fully armed and equipped—that's the number I heard Hamp mention! A lot of money is being raised to pay for it. Grimm was once a cavalry officer, and he knows what he's doing."

Foyle whistled softly. "Man! Big Mac better move fast!"

"I thought," Gano drawled, "that was what we were here for!" He was being deliberately disagreeable. "With such an army behind him, Grimm could ride down into Banner and settle Big Mac once and for all. It would be the finish for us—especially you! Territory law is thin and spotty. Not even the governor would bother to look too closely into the hanging of Big Mac's top gunman and a few others, after Big Mac got kicked out. Big Mac has plenty of political enemies and rivals. They'd thank Grimm for breaking him. They'd protect Grimm and his men, after it was done, and get them appointed special deputies or something of the kind. In cutthroat politics, justice is on the side of the winner, as we all know. I say *we* had better move fast! We've got to stop it, to save our own skins besides Big Mac's!"

Foyle granted the accuracy of Gano's statement of the case. Territory politics, tangled up in elective offices, government appointments, and military controls, was a jungle of intrigue. Once a man slipped, the rest pounced on him.

It had been so ever since the Mexican Governor Armijo fled, chased by General Kearney's U.S. troops, leaving his mantle of authority behind to be squabbled over. About the size of all New England, there was plenty of room in the Territory for private wars and feuds, and its politics occasionally got clouded in powdersmoke here and there. The old Spanish and Mexican land-grants problem had never been settled. There was dissatisfaction among erstwhile grand *dons* and *hacendados*, who supported for office any candidate promising restitution of their million-acre estates. The same candidates also promised the new homesteaders more land and free titles, at the same time vowing to the American cattlemen that the range would be kept open for them. Only a politician could reconcile those three burning problems.

"Two of us to stop an army!" Foyle reflected aloud. "This job gets tougher right along!"

Gano gave his sombrero an up-thrust and folded his arms. "Before Hamp left, he went into the ranch office with Miss Reynolds. The ranch office is a small building set apart from the main house, on the east side, the opposite side to the bunkhouse. It's kept locked. There's a steel safe in there. I had a good look at it through the window. Very likely that is where the money is cached for the Pronghorn Posse—the war chest. The girl has a key to it. She opened the safe for Hamp to put away a used-up tally book and take out a new one."

"You 'pear to have done considerable spying," Foyle remarked.

"I have made some use of my time," retorted Gano coldly. "I have learned that Grimm is gathering his recruits at a camp on the Muleshoe, just over the Texas line. When he gets them organized and leads them in, practically every Pronghorn cowman will join them. They are determined to force a quick showdown on Big Mac, that's plain. But nothing will be done until Grimm gets the posse ready. That may take a few more days."

Foyle nodded. "Old army officers gen'rally want everything set just right before they jump, yeah. Maybe Grimm will make a trip home first, though, for the money to pay 'em with. If the money is still being raised, then he sure couldn't have taken it with him."

Gano put his finger tips together and made a steeple of them. "Remove the head. Blunt the spear. Yes." His fingers curled inward. "But can we depend on it that he'll do that—and alone? No! Another way to stop them is to remove the war chest. At least it would delay them until they could raise more money. By then Big Mac would have warning, and he'd make the first move. We would be the ones who'd lead a posse here into the Pronghorn! Yes, if they lost their war chest—"

"I don't go in for robbing a place where I—uh—where I'm a guest," Foyle said shortly.

"Is that so?" Gano shrugged. "Well, there's no guarantee that we'd find it in the safe, so that's another chance we can't depend on. I have still another way, the simplest and quickest. Grimm prizes the girl. He'd be a fool if he didn't! He does, or he wouldn't leave her here as mistress of the place while he's away, with a key to his safe. If *she* were removed—and held as hostage—"

"That's out! Not for a million!"

"Why? She'll be alone here in the house with us the rest of the day! I overheard Hamp telling her that he'd try to drop in late tonight or early tomorrow morning, depending on how the roundup work was going. There are good horses in one of the corrals, and spare saddles under the wagon shed. It wouldn't be much trouble to take her off when it gets dark! We can be well on the way back to Banner by morning! Big Mac would pay as much for her as for Grimm, I think." Gano peaked his heavy brows thoughtfully. "Perhaps more! What's to stop us?"

Foyle got his legs out of the bed and sat up. "Me!"

"But you're able to ride, if we take it easy. You might bleed some, but Big Mac's money will make it up!"

"That's not what I mean, Gano." Foyle's left hand came out from under the blankets, dragging his gun belts. "What I mean is, I'd kill any man who tried it! *Any* man! Is that plain enough for you?"

They stared unblinkingly at each other. In his sinister mood Gano seemed to be pondering on whether or not to call the bet. Reaching a decision, he picked up his half-smoked cigar from the tray and relighted it. He took another drink, filling the glass to the brim and downing it in one gulp.

"You'll never live to see the day—" he began, and stopped as if the phrase was one that conveyed more than he meant to say. His smile came, more shallow and false than ever, not diminishing the chill of his pale eyes.

"All right, Mr. Jason. Then that's out—as far as you are concerned." He was either relieved at having brought about an open clash, or was cloaking his true feelings. "I shall be satisfied if we can get hold of Grimm or the money. Preferably both! The longer we have to wait here, however, the more risk we run. I never trust to luck, and I have a feeling that trouble is coming! If things go bad I'll not be surprised, but I'll not be caught if I can help it! You may get killed. After all, you're not in top shape to pull a shoot-out getaway if it comes to it. In that—er—sad event, I shall be left, of course, to my own resources. I'll use my own ways to get this job done!"

He moved to the door. "Is that plain enough

for *you?*" he purred, and minced out, quietly whistling a cheerful little dirge.

Foyle narrowed his eyes. The words and manner carried clear warning that his "obedient servant" was prepared to take matters into his own hands if the chance came his way. He was no longer to be trusted, and he hadn't the shadow of a scruple left in his sin-steeped soul. He could stand and challenge an armed mob, or slip up and knife a man in the back, whichever the occasion called for, equally without a qualm.

Some words that Gano had uttered, leaving the sentence unfinished, stirred up a hazy recollection, a dim and dreamlike figment that Foyle strove to capture and examine. He connected it with the buckboard, his head wound, with the blinding white flash in his eyes. It had to do with Big Mac.

For an instant he almost caught it. It was so close he knew it as a thought that he'd had at that time. An icy bit of truth. About Big Mac. But he was trying too hard. It eluded him. All he could remember was the white flash, and Gano's voice.

He shook his head, shoving the guns back under the blanket. He knew all there was to know about Big Mac. The lost thought couldn't have been important. The important thing was that Gano obviously was itchy, out of patience, eager to do the job and get away before all the risks piled up and exploded. That thought—of Gano carrying off Donna, in his present satanic mood, and handing her over to Big Mac in his guarded mansion of infamy—conjured up a shuddery vision that Foyle thrust away. He knew Big Mac. And he knew Gano, now.

He would have to get hold of Ebb Grimm soon. Or the money in the Pronghorn war chest. Or kill Gano.

Chapter Seven: WAR CHEST

IT WAS LATE NIGHT. A full moon poured steady light outside and the window caught it and bleached out the room's darkness to a gloom in which all objects were visible. The door swung inward, noiseless, casting a blurred oblong of shadow on the side wall. The shadow bulged. Gano slipped in and looked at the bed. It was empty.

Foyle, dressed and wearing his gun belts, stepped out from behind the opened door. "Don't you ever sleep?" he inquired. He dipped a glance at Gano's hands, half expecting to see a knife. When his trust ran out it ran out all the way.

Gano saw the glance. A slight tightening, barely perceptible, thinned his lips. A flare started in his eyes, and died. To the query he responded, "Yes, but I'm a light sleeper."

"So am I," Foyle said. He nodded in the general direction of the front of the house. "I heard a couple o' riders pull in. You seen 'em?"

"Yes. Two men." It was Gano's turn to inspect Foyle's hands, and he did it deliberately. "I've seen them before. So have you. In the Union Bar. One is the red-faced fool they called Atchley. The other is that lanky one who spoke up. Scanlon, Miss Reynolds called him. They've gone into the ranch office with her and shut the door and pulled a drape over the window. Must be something serious. Thought I'd better tell you. I'll go back now and try to hear what they're—"

"I'll take it this time," Foyle said. "Leg's a lot better. No reason you should do it all." It wasn't his intention to speak the words as curt commands, but because of his distrust his voice was crisp, hard.

Gano inclined his head, hiding whatever was in his eyes.

"I shall wait here. With abated breath!"

The room opened onto a hallway. There were stairs at one end. No lights showed anywhere, except from the slit under the door of a downstairs room, evidently the front room. It was an unusually large house. Foyle descended the stairs into the main hallway, limped through it, and opened the front door. There was no raised porch, but a Mexican-style *portico*, flagstoned, at ground level. Beyond the flagstones, the customary hitchrack. Two saddled horses.

On the east side of the house, Gano had said, was the ranch office. Foyle turned that way, came to the end of the *portico*, and there it was. A small building, shaded by cottonwoods, subdued lamplight yellowing the window. Probably the original ranch house, before prosperity erected the big house now overlording the yard.

He trod carefully under the cottonwoods to the closed door and stood motionless, listening to the voices in the office. The act of eavesdropping provoked a twinge of shame. He reminded himself that if he didn't do it, Gano would. The talk was muffled. He crept closer until he could distinguish the words. It was easy to pick out Atchley's heavy, rasping tone.

"Takes a pile o' money!" Atchley was saying grumblingly. "Mind you, everybody's chipping in. No holdouts. They wouldn't do it for anybody else but Grimm, though. That goes for me, too, I'll admit. We're gambling an awful lot on him! We sure can't afford to lose!"

A more modulated voice, that of Scanlon, queried, "Can any of us afford not to gamble, John? We've got to back Grimm. If we don't, this'll be another corner added to Big Mac's bailiwick. You know what that would mean. New laws, high taxes, graft, and payoffs! Gangs of gunmen flashing badges, serving warrants for murders they did themselves on Big Mac's orders! Crooked sheriffs, bought judges, and rigged juries! I had a cousin ranching down below Banner. When he objected to 'em selling him out for delinquent taxes, one o' Big Mac's pals shot him dead and bought the place for a dollar, nobody else daring to bid. Person'ly, I'll gamble all I've got to keep Big Mac out o' the Pronghorn!"

"Now, Frank, I'm not griping," asserted Atchley. "I know what we're up against. Haven't I chipped in more'n my share, there? Like to know how

Grimm's doing, is all. You heard from him lately, Donna?"

There was an affirmative murmur from Donna Reynolds. Foyle bent over sidewise nearer to the door, forgetting that his injured leg wouldn't yet take much strain, and caught the girl's closing words: ". . . coming for it any time now."

"Glad to know it," Atchley said. "Lot o' cash, that, to be keeping here. Makes close to thirty thousand dollars, all told. I guess that's a good safe, though."

"Take ten men to budge it," commented Scanlon dryly. "Grimm bought it from a bank that went bust up in Raton. Some boogers went to work on it with sledge hammers up there one night. Couldn't dent it. That's a safe an' a half! No, I wouldn't worry none about the money, not even if— Huh?"

Foyle's injured leg, held braced too long under his bent position, had got a cramp in it. In straightening up quickly to remedy it by kicking out, Foyle was forced to increase his weight on it. His knee buckled. He lurched off balance, and his elbow brushed the door.

"Huh?" Scanlon muttered again. "Was that you, John?"

"It sure wasn't!" A chair scraped and hard heels hit the floor. "Somebody outside!"

Any chance of darting off was hopeless. Foyle stooped over, holding his aching knee in his hands and working the cramp out of it. The door jerked open and there he was, the lamplight shining on him.

"Evenin'," he said without glancing up. "Got coffee on?"

Full of the intention to charge forth in pursuit of a prowler, Atchley hauled up short, blinking down at the stooping figure before him. All Foyle saw of the cowman was his thick legs, and he hoped he wasn't going to have to see more.

"What the blazes are you doing?"

"Getting a sore kink out o' my leg."

Atchley had a single-track mind, narrow-gauge. "Oh," he said, not entirely unsympathetic. Rough horses could wear down the gristle in any man's joints. But further consideration found the answer inadequate to his question. "What're you doing *here,* I mean?"

"Looking for the cookshack. This it?"

"Oh," said Atchley, satisfied. "No, it's back o' the house. Doubt if there's any coffee on. Hamp put the cook on the roundup wagon."

"Okay." Foyle made to move off, still rubbing his knee.

Scanlon said sharply, "Wait a minute!" His legs scissored up alongside Atchley's. "Wait—a minute! Who are you, that you don't know your way around here? Mister, let's see your face!"

Foyle paused, letting his hands dangle. Slowly, he lifted his eyes to the two cowmen's waists, their chests. He looked into the muzzle of a .44 six-gun, leveled in Scanlon's fist.

Scanlon breathed incredulously, "Well, by—" Shock threw harsh volume into his voice. "Don't move! Not a blink! Know him, John! Durn right you do!"

Atchley gulped, grabbed hipward, and then Foyle was looking into the muzzles of two guns. The second one was held by Atchley, and Atchley's florid skin had gone a paler hue. The gun clicked to full cock, finger tightening on the trigger. Foyle guessed the hammer was about to fall. There wasn't a thing he could do to stop it.

"Don't shoot!" It was Donna Reynolds who cried out. "He's Ben Jason—a friend!" Foyle had given her his first name as Ben, the nearest to Bain he could think of. "He's hurt!"

"Friend?" Scanlon kept an unwavering stare on Foyle. "Him! Donna, are you out o' your head? He and a Chinese bug doctor like to've wrecked the town a couple nights back!"

"Banner men!" blurted Atchley. He looked beyond Foyle, searching fearfully for a glaring-eyed yellow face in the dark. "Banner gunmen, or I'm crazy!"

"You're both crazy—as crazy as all the rest!" the girl accused them hotly. "He and Doctor Sling are from the north! From Denver! They came here for help, after you all attacked them in town like a lot of madmen! They brought back the buckboard

211

that they borrowed," she added, in proof of their honesty. "I think even Hamp realizes the mistake, only he's too angry to admit it."

Atchley burst out, "Lord Almighty, girl, look at him! His face! His eyes! What was he up to, prowling at the door?"

Foyle didn't say anything. Under the challenge of the drawn guns, it was difficult for him to disguise the dark hardness of his face, the tough recklessness in his eyes. The best he could do was to keep his mouth shut.

"He has already told you," the girl answered Atchley. "He wanted some coffee. What's wrong about that? It's the first time he has been downstairs. How was he to know this isn't the cookshack? He saw the light in the window, and came here. What could be more natural? There's no earthly reason to disbelieve him!"

"B-But—" Atchley spluttered, and Scanlon broke out with, "Now, look, Donna—"

It was as far as they got before she interrupted them both. "Prowling! Is that what you call it, when a man—a wounded man—comes up and knocks on the door? You heard him knock! Would he have knocked if he was prowling? It's ridiculous!"

Scanlon muttered, "Hell!" and twisted his ear. "It wasn't a knock, exactly. More like—"

"Oh—talk, talk, talk!" Donna Reynolds stepped between him and Atchley. "You talk yourselves into believing any crazy thing!" She pushed their guns down. "Men!" She sighed resignedly—and softly, looking at Foyle.

Seeing that he might move now and not get shot for it, Foyle lifted his hat to her. Ignoring the two glowering men, he said, "Whatever all this is about, I'm sure sorry I banged the wrong door." He guessed he could leave the two for her to handle. She did all right. "I better get back to bed. G'night—" he hesitated—"Donna."

Her color deepened. She smiled, and her eyes were glad.

"Good night—Ben!"

And that was how it was. Her eyes said so. Her eyes said that Scanlon and Atchley didn't have a chance of breaking through that. Their suspicions were weak reeds against her impregnable conviction and confident young faith. She would end up persuading them that they owed apologies to Mr. Ben Jason and Dr. Sling Bool Hi, of Denver, researchers in entomology, anthropology, ornithology. Past masters of triggenometry.

Gano was waiting in the upstairs room. "Learn anything?" he asked, deceptively diffident. "I heard voices. Did they catch you at work? Sounded like it to me."

Foyle slumped onto the bed. He wasn't sorry that the moonlight on the window had dimmed with the high ascent of the moon. He knew that his face, showing the reaction from Donna's look, would have betrayed him to Gano in a better light. The intense and feverish excitement had to be shielded behind a screen of cool calculation.

"The money," he said; "the Pronghorn Pool—the war chest—is in the safe, all right. I learned that! Grimm will be coming any time now to get it. I don't know if he'll come alone."

Gano scratched a match, lit a cigar. "How much?"

"Close to thirty thousand dollars."

"A-aah!" Gano blew a smoke ball and a ring. "In the safe! And she has a key!"

"We don't touch her!"

"Very well. So you said before. It is agreed." Gano crossed his short legs. His eyes glimmered amusedly in the semidarkness. "That safe! So heavy and forbidding. Foyle, I'll bet I can crack it in six minutes! Want to bet?"

"Ten dollars. No—twenty."

Gano chuckled. He was in high spirits. "Done! As soon as the visitors leave and darling Donna retires to bed. That's an old Whitehead box. I've cracked a hundred. Like to show you some night."

"I'll learn tonight what I can, watchin' you."

"H'm. You're coming with me? H'm!"

"Damn right I am!"

But Scanlon and Atchley stayed the night. Nor did they show any intention of leaving the next morning, but sat out on the *portico*, smoking and fidgeting, uncertain of themselves. Ira Hamp rode in soon after breakfast, and they walked with him down to the corrals for a private talk. Judging from the range boss's stubborn gesticulations, he was reviving all their distrust of Foyle and Gano. They began nodding vigorously, glancing toward the house, only too ready to align their superior male sagacity against a mere girl's opinion.

"They won't leave as long as we're here," Foyle told Gano. "More likely they'll send out the call for help to stand watch on us till Grimm comes for the money. There's nothing we can do. They're too cagey. We might as well pull out now while we can."

Gano nodded agreement. "I'm sure they'd be happy to see us depart! They're busy men, and it would leave them free to return to their work with easier minds. Tonight we could slip back for— er—something we left behind, and be well out of the country with it ahead of the hullabaloo in the morning, eh?"

"Leave it to you to think o' that!" said Foyle dourly.

Gano flashed a cynical grin. "I followed your thought!"

Frank dismay clouded Donna's eyes when Foyle made his announcement to her. "You're leaving? Oh, no! Your wounds!"

"I'm well enough to travel, going easy. It's

best." He tore his eyes from hers, his mouth hard-set, white around the lips. He stuck a thumb at Gano. "Can't do any good here, the way things are. Folks think—well, they've made it plain what they think of us, and nothing will change their minds. Makes it uncomfortable for you, too, us being here."

Scanlon, Atchley, and Hamp moved within hearing, looking pleased and relieved. Foyle raised his voice.

"If you could spare a couple o' horses, Hamp—"

Making no bones about his eagerness to be rid of the unwelcome guests, Hamp said, "Sure thing! We'll take yours in trade when I find who's holdin' 'em. Where you headin' for?"

"Denver."

"Well, well, that's a right long way!"

"Well, well, we hope it's far enough to suit you, as it does us!" put in Gano genially. He bowed to Donna. "Dear lady, it is impossible to express my gratitude, my deep appreciation, my most sincere and heart-felt—"

She didn't hear. She was gazing up into Foyle's face. "You'll come back—won't you—Ben?"

"Yes," he said. "Yes—I'll be back."

"Promise?"

He almost retched in shame. "I promise."

Chapter Eight: **ROBBERS' RETURN**

THEY RODE NORTHEAST over the range, as if short-cutting toward the river trail to Santa Rosa and on north. At the last minute Atchley and Scanlon had allowed awkwardly that maybe it was all a mistake, their being taken for Banner men, but nobody could afford to take extra chances these days. They didn't offer to shake hands, and Ira Hamp eyed grudgingly the two good horses Foyle and Gano picked.

Foyle rode looking straight forward, his face stonily controlled, his thoughts in battle. He had the wish to be riding away forever from the V Bar ranch. Opposing it was the wish to go back, and the knowledge that he would. There was nothing on top of the world that could alter that decision.

He would go back—to rob the one girl he had ever really loved. It was the least evil to which he was committed. He tried to believe that it would add just another regret to the growing pile, but he knew it wasn't so. It would rush him down the last stretch into the private hell of a harrowed conscience that refused to die.

Gano, regarding him sidelong, said, "If Grimm is anything like Scanlon and Atchley, he hasn't a chance. Big Mac will easily outwit him and get the jump on this Pronghorn crowd, and then— God help them! I think he's bound to win in the

217

end, no matter what happens." He was silent for a moment, then added in a changed tone, "When the smash comes, I'll do what I can to take care of Donna."

It had the sound of a grave vow, but Foyle countered crisply, "Maybe I'll be around to 'tend to that!"

Gano turned his face away, smiling faintly. "Maybe," he murmured, without conviction.

They drew in beyond the first high line of hills, scanned the surrounding country, and off-saddled. Nobody was following. Nobody was spying on them. It was another indication that the Pronghorn cowmen, for all their ready suspicions and violence, lacked wary persistence. That was the usual weakness found in honest men. The virtue of vigilance, constant and unwearying, held its most honored place in the armory of rascals. Simple men soon tired of elaborate precautions, and shifted their reliance to the risky faith that right was might.

Gano climbed the nearest hill and flattened out behind a stunted piñon to hold watch. At that distance the buildings of the V Bar ranch were square specks, but he had telescope eyesight, unaffected by the sun's glare. The hot day dragged by, and he lay patiently, never asking Foyle to relieve him. They had brought along no food. The water in their canteens had to be shared with the horses.

In midafternoon Gano called down to Foyle, "Scanlon and Atchley are leaving now. Hamp left hours ago. Let's hope there'll be no more callers today!" He rolled over and lighted a cigar. To Foyle, below, he looked like a boy sneaking a forbidden smoke.

A cool wind sprang up with sundown. The early moon rose, remote, gradually supplanting the sun. A tiny light shone from the ranch. Foyle went up the hill, and he and Gano watched the light. At last it winked out, leaving only the dark horizon and long streaks of moonlight on east-faced folds of ground.

They descended the hill, not uttering a word, and laid the saddles on their horses. They rode around the hill and lined out toward the spot where the light had been.

The buildings of the V Bar loomed up. Foyle and Gano circled around to the corrals, tied the horses, and paced soundlessly up to the yard. They knew their bearings and went directly to the little ranch office. The shadows of the cottonwoods hid them. The door was locked. Gano passed it up and stepped to the window. A slender blade flashed briefly.

"All right, Foyle, I'm going in."

"Go ahead; I'm right behind you."

They slid through the opened window into the office. Here it was dark. Foyle lost sight of Gano, but he heard a metallic jingle and traced it to the safe. It as a large safe, its top as high as his chin, the door massively hinged. He couldn't see what Gano was doing, except that he was on his knees, studiously fingering the lock-plate and making tests with what was evidently a handy little pocket kit of tools and skeleton keys.

It took less than five minutes. Gano, master of devious dark arts, whispered, "Foyle, you owe me twenty dollars! That was our bet, wasn't it?" He drew open the heavy door of the safe and ransacked inside, spilling out papers. "Ah! Here we are!" He stepped back with a cash box, wrenching off its lid. "Bank notes! How I love them! So easy to carry!"

Foyle said, "Here's your twenty."

It brought a low chuckle. "Small change! Keep it! I've got real money here!" Possession of the money had created a new man of Gano. The feel of the packets of crisp bank notes exalted him. His chill secretiveness had given way to a feverish joy that sparkled his eyes.

Foyle said, "Not so fast!" It was best to have the showdown now, if there had to be one. He got a hand on the cash box. "I'm in charge of this!"

Their faces were only inches apart. "You? You'll never live to see—" Gano began the worn phrase, and then Foyle's eyes flickered swift recognition of a rush of memory.

Sounds outside jerked their heads up, nerves taut. The sounds grew louder, resolving into footsteps and the growl of men's muttering. There had been no noises of horses, and there was none now. Only men on foot, treading by the little office. While he listened, Foyle stared in recollection into a blinding white flash and examined the thought that came with it. The thought was a sinister one, but he guessed it was true. He guessed he knew why Big Mac had sent Gano to join him.

Gano swung his stocky body, yanking free the cash box and whispering thinly, "Time to go!" His right arm moved, quick and sure. Foyle hit him before his hand reached the holstered gun. It was an uppercut to the chin and stood him on his toes. The next bowed him over backward. Foyle caught him and let him down easy without thumping the floor too loudly.

The cash box fell among the spilled papers. Foyle gathered up the packets of bank notes, stuffing them inside his shirt. Time to go, as Gano had said. Gano, however, was slated to be out cold for a while. He would know not to rely so much on a fast gun next time, if the Pronghorn crowd didn't catch him first and string him up. A good thing if they did, Foyle told himself. Still, he looked down at Gano, oddly reluctant to leave him lying there helpless.

A crash splintered the furtive hush in the yard. The footsteps stamped on into the house. Loud now, the men's talk mingled in a medley of profanity. The voice of Donna Reynolds called out an alarmed query. Some laughter boomed. A man answered in an excited, staccato tone.

"Honey, we're a-callin' for Ebb Grimm! If he ain't here, maybe you'll do to talk to till he comes! Eh, Red?"

"We-ell, I'd say so from here!"

The boots clattered on stairs. The girl's scream slashed through the night, then was drowned by the racket and laughter of the men.

Foyle dived out through the window of the office. He raced limpingly across the yard to the *portico*. The front door of the house, smashed in with a log, hung askew on its bottom hinge. The stairs directly before him, held seven men. Donna stood at the top of the stairs, dressed in a white night robe, holding a lighted lamp in her right hand.

A man had hold of Donna's left wrist. His hat was off. His head was a flaming red shock of hair joined to a shaggy beard. He was grinningly aping to kiss her hand, to the hilarity of the others. The laughter of the seven men sounded drunken. They were ragged, dirty, heavily armed. Three of them carried rifles. They all looked and behaved as if they had recently emerged from a long hide-out in an outlaw camp, and hadn't yet shed their brush manners.

Foresight played no part in Foyle's reaction. Fury flooded out the icily impersonal calmness that was the foundation of his gun training.

"Red!" he said. His voice grated through the laughter. "Red Murrell! Get back to your horse-thief camp on Pintada Canyon an' take your scummy buzzards with you!"

The seven men whirled around. Long hiding in the clay caves and rabbit-brush thickets of Pintada Canyon had sharpened them to an animal wildness. They glared truculently at Foyle's leveled and cocked guns. The guns were smooth and polished from use. The men were not scared, but watchful.

Because of his bandaged head Foyle wore his black sombrero tipped forward. His face was in dark shadow. The light from Donna's lamp at the top of the stairs made only the line of his jaw visible. But he had a clear view of Red Murrell, the man who, according to Big Mac, for months had tried and failed to earn the Banner bounty offered for Ebb Grimm's capture.

Red Murrell kept hold of Donna's wrist. His bloodshot, sunken eyes rested appraisingly on Foyle's guns. He had been a notorious hotshot until drink fogged the front of his brain. Neither whisky nor wounds had hurt his bull nerve, though, and he could still coolly size up an unexpected situation. His big fault was that he couldn't see very far ahead any more, and it had dulled his trust in his own judgment. He had lasted too long.

He asked Foyle thoughtfully, "Now, who in hell would you be?"

"You heard what I said!" The flat drone of menace in Foyle's voice caused the men with rifles to still their restlessness.

Red Murrell lifted Donna's hand and wagged it playfully. "I'd say from here, now, you're—"

Foyle fired. He shot Red Murrell in the forearm, knocking it loose from Donna, and an instant later slapped an up-lifted rifle with a bullet that wrecked the breech and that man's fingers.

Donna trembled startledly at the shots. The flame of the lamp in her hand guttered and smoked. The fear remained in her eyes, although she was now looking at Foyle. Foyle's eyes glimmered deadly cold in the dark malevolence of his face. He looked tougher than Red Murrell.

"You heard me!" he said.

Murrell pushed back his sleeve and studied his blood-wet forearm. He heaved his thick shoulders forward, then slowly relaxed. Eyeing Foyle, he said, "You're a leetle quick on the shoot! I oughta know who you are, but blast me if I can place you."

The unsteady flickering of the lamp got his attention. Donna raised the lamp higher, like a weapon, in an instinctive gesture of defense.

Red Murrell, flinching, exclaimed, "Don't you chuck that at me, gal!" His hairy head and beard left him too readily vulnerable to fire, and he betrayed more uneasiness over that than of Foyle's guns.

"All right, bad *hombre*!" He moved down a step, watching the lamp warily, but speaking to Foyle. "Yeah, we heard you. Pull your hackles down, we're goin'! Boys, take a good look at him, will you? I sure do want to know who he is!"

Foyle put his back to the wall and let them file past. Each man stared venomously at him, trying to discern his features under the shadow of the broad hatbrim. Three of them he had seen at odd times in the past, and he had met Red Murrell at a poker table. The rest were unknown to him.

Red Murrell, last to leave, sent Foyle a nod. "Here on, I'll be lookin' for you, a limpin' larrikin with a rag round his noggin!" he promised, and lumbered out after his men, casually shaking a trickle of blood from his hand.

Foyle followed him part way to the shattered door, motioning up at Donna to shield the lamp so that it wouldn't shine down on him. He heard the men troop off. They walked unhurriedly, knowing that the ranch hands were away on roundup. Red Murrell rumbled a few words and they hastened a trifle. The sounds of their footsteps faded out as they tramped on to wherever they had left their horses.

He became aware of Donna descending the stairs. At the bottom she sent him a questioning look, and he nodded and said, "They're gone."

She glided swiftly past him, the hem of her night robe skimming the floor. He watched her go out

225

through the front door and turn left toward the little office building. The Pronghorn war chest was her first concern. He followed, guilt and reluctance dragging at him, wanting to hurry to his waiting horse and ride away, but unable to do it.

With a key she unlocked the door of the office. Holding the lamp up, she passed inside. Her cry of dismay cut through Foyle like the whimper of a hurt child. He entered after her. Under the light of the lamp he saw all that she saw—the gaping safe, the spilled papers, the looted cash box. The brutal disorder left by plunderers in the night.

Gano lay on the floor, propping himself up on one elbow, dabbing at his bruised and cut chin and gazing vacantly at the traces of blood that it left on his hand. The light hastened the rise of his consciousness. Into his slanted eyes began creeping a glint of animosity. He stopped shaking his head, to run a stare up Foyle from feet to face. Foyle kept a gun out and met Gano's eyes stonily.

"Our money! Gone!" Donna spun around to Foyle. The rush of air flared the lamp. Her words came in a stammer of despair. "Gone! The safe— look—robbed!"

He said nothing. His deepset eyes, trained to an opaque blankness, met her paled and stricken face. Here was his test. He had to go through with this and not take a single weak or hesitant step.

Conscience would not survive this deed, and success meant freedom at last from its futile nagging. Failure meant downfall, the inevitable coming of the catastrophe that overtook men of his kind when they indulged in the fatal luxury of indecision.

Strange and warring expressions crossed Donna's face. There was incredulous wonder, then shrinking doubt, a heartbreaking suspicion.

"The window was—was forced open." The girl spoke haltingly, as if in shame. "It must have been done very quietly, or I would have heard. And— and this safe was opened quietly, too!"

She turned the lamp up brighter, fumbling with it. "Those men—the Murrell gang. *They* didn't come quietly, did they? No. They're horse thieves. And rustlers. But they're not—not expert lock pickers. They had to break down the door with a log!"

She gazed down at Gano on the floor. Almost in pleading, she asked him, "Why are you in here? You broke in, didn't you? Do you have the money?"

Gano, his eyes fixed unwaveringly on her since her first word, moved his head slightly in negation that carried more conviction than a thousand vehement denials. He straightened a forefinger at Foyle, and didn't speak.

Like someone in the unnatural composure of sleepwalking, Donna faced Foyle. "Were you in here tonight? Was it from here that you came into the house?" Her shoulders drooped. She set the lamp on the desk, tiredly, as if lacking the strength to hold it any longer.

Hushedly, she said, "Yes. It's in your face—in your eyes. I can see it. *You* have the money! *You!*"

Chapter Nine: **TRIGGER TERMS**

SOMBER APATHY dissolved suddenly under a storm of emotion. Frenzied wrath flamed in the girl's eyes. Her forlornly drooping body came erect and taut, the rich mass of hair tossed back, the faint blue veins throbbing in her white throat. She stood like an angry young goddess condemning the idol whose crumbling clay had destroyed her faith and sacrificed her pride on a false altar.

"Thief!" Her voice did not go loud and shrill. It was hardly above a whisper, yet penetrating, as audible as the crack of a whiplash. "They warned me. I wouldn't listen. They were right! Thief! Hypocrite! You would come back, you said—and you did! In the dark! To rob the house that gave you shelter and help when you desperately needed it! The lowest pickpocket would have more honor!"

Sitting up, Gano wagged his head in sad disapproval at Foyle, and sighed. "Evil companions in his youth corrupted him, no doubt!" He glanced into the cash box, saw it was empty, and his disapproval became more acute.

Foyle's face was gray and drawn, distorted by muscles bunched over clenched teeth. Gone was the stony stare. Donna made to speak again. He had to stop her. His endurance had reached its limit. He glowered down at her and commanded harshly, "Shut up!"

She met his eyes squarely. "Go, thief, with the money! I can't prevent you! Go, you lying, cheating—"

"Shut up!" he thundered, and now his eyes were crazed.

She thought he would hit her, for he drew back his right arm, and she stood unflinching to receive it. But he ripped at his shirt. He thrust wads of bank notes at her, tumbling them out, letting them fall anywhere, as if they burned him.

Gano let out a moan of anguish at the sight of a fortune treated so disrespectfully. He scuttled forward, hands outstretched to help gather the precious harvest.

Foyle, savagely glad of an object to vent some of his feelings on, stuck a gun at him and snarled, "Hands off! You ever touch that money again, I'll blast you down! Back up!"

One look at Foyle's face, and Gano backed up, worry in his eyes. "You're crazy!" he muttered.

Foyle drove him into a corner. Over his shoulder he told Donna, "Pick up your money an' get back to the house!" To Gano he said, "Turn round an' face the wall! You hear? This gun's ready to go off!"

"I believe you," Gano admitted, and obeyed.

Foyle plucked Gano's guns out and pitched them through the window. He said, "When you find 'em, keep going an' don't come back! It's time we parted company!"

"Time separates the best of friends," Gano concurred. "And so does money, come to think of it."

Leaving him standing there like a culprit schoolboy in the corner, Foyle paced out. Beyond the shading cottonwoods a white-robed figure waited, hair glossy in the moonlight. The storm in him had subsided some, but he snapped roughly, "Get into the house, I said! Hide that money before—"

"Wait, Ben!" she broke in. Her eyes were shining wet. "P-Please don't tell me to shut up, b-because I won't! Oh, Ben, I'm so horribly ashamed! I should have known!"

He walked toward her. "Known what?"

Her attempt to smile was a tremulous failure. "It's so clear to me now. It was he, of course—Doctor Sling—who robbed the safe. You caught him at it and knocked him down. Took the money away from him. But you wouldn't denounce him, because he had been your friend, even when I—You saved us all tonight—everybody in the Pronghorn." She hid her face. "And I called you a thief!"

A crack and a gun flash stabbed from the direction of the corrals. Foyle jumped at Donna and pulled her down with him. His first thought was of Gano. But there hadn't been time enough for Gano to retrieve his guns and slip off.

"Get into the house," Foyle said, "while I tend to that joker!"

He drew his guns and called, "You missed, Murrell! I'll be right with you!" He rocked up and made for the corrals at a weaving, limping sprint, spacing shots at the spot where the gun flash winked.

His guess was right. Red Murrell bellowed an oath of disgust as he mounted and took off. Shooting by moonlight was tricky business. When it came to tangling with a charging firecracker, a sensible man knew enough to quit.

Foyle turned back. Looking into the office, he saw that Gano was gone, and he went on into the main house. Lamps were lighted in the downstairs front room. There he found Donna. She had laid the money on a table.

An awkward silence lasted between them until Foyle said, "I guess we could put that back in the safe now. My bugarrooin' partner has pulled out, an' so has Murrell. I better stay the rest o' the night, though."

"I—I think you had better."

They carried the money back, and he helped her tidy up the office. When all was in place again she locked the safe. Foyle closed the window and drew over it the Navajo blanket that served as a drape. A scrap of paper fell from a fold of the blanket. He picked it up. It was a scribbled note and he read:

For reasons affecting our mutual health I find it advisable to resign my position as your obedient servant—G.

He grinned faintly, crumpling the note. There were few things to the credit of that ugly little sinner, but one of them was a sardonic sense of humor.

"I'll sit out the night here," he told Donna.

"I'll get some coffee." She smiled, and he recalled his excuse to Atchley and Scanlon when they had discovered him outside the door. He guessed nothing would ever shake her belief that he liked a midnight pot of coffee. Her every look and gesture betrayed her wish to please him and make up for what she thought was a hideous mistake. He would leave as soon as it was safe for her, he promised himself.

The tray she brought from the kitchen bore coffee and sandwiches for two. And she had snatched time to get dressed, abandoning all idea of retiring for the remainder of the night. "I'm much too wrought up and excited to sleep," she confessed, and he nodded. So was he.

"You see, I haven't been here very long," she went on, setting out the tray's contents on the desk. "Less than a year. From the time my mother died, I lived with relatives in a quiet town where nothing ever happened. Then they lost their money, and I gave them what my mother had left me—jewels, mostly—and, well, then things began happening."

She talked easily and naturally, her clear eyes candid. Foyle thought of the time in his own life when things began happening, and he wished with an impotent intensity that those things could have been different for them both.

Donna wore a full-skirted dress of flowered dimity, small at the waist, and she had put on a light woolen jacket against the night air. From a loose pocket of the jacket she took out her key to the safe.

"Please keep this for me, will you?" she asked. "Men have better pockets."

With his eyes on her face, Foyle slowly held out a hand to receive it. This, he knew, was not purposely a graceful means of expressing her trust in him. It was simply a normal action, quite guileless and unconsidered. And the more sincere because of it.

And because he wasn't paying the key any attention, his eyes being on her face, it slipped through his fingers when she passed it to him. They both stooped to pick it up, and her hair and his nose met.

Her hair was soft and his nose was hard, so they came to no harm, but mental composure collapsed. Donna raised her head, laughing over the small accident. Foyle looked into her eyes, so close to his that he could see the pupils expanding under his gaze. She ceased laughing, but her lips stayed parted.

His ruling thought was, *Whatever she is—whatever she has been—I can't go on without her.* He took her in his arms and kissed her.

The coffee cooled in the cups.

When he remembered to pick up the key Foyle saw that his hands were not steady. He said huskily, "There must be some way to work things out! There's got to be! If only it was possible to—to change everything—make life different!"

Donna, shyly radiant, answered warmly, "But it *is* possible, Ben! My mother did it. She was a successful actress, and a very beautiful woman, but after her second marriage she changed herself over into a capable ranch wife and made my stepfather very happy. He—my stepfather—hated the stage. He always feared that my mother would want to go back to it some day, but she was happy with him and never gave it a thought."

Reflecting on it, Foyle asked, "Were you on the stage, Donna, before—uh—you came here?"

"For a little while, yes. It didn't last long." She smiled, affectionate amusement in her eyes. "When the Captain learned that I was singing in a theater—well! There was really nothing at all wrong about it, but"—she flushed a little—"nobody could ever convince the Captain there wouldn't be! He came up and packed me off home with him. I'm glad now he did. I love this country."

Foyle knitted his brows. "But who," he asked, puzzled, "is the Captain? Ebb Grimm?"

She nodded. "My stepfather, yes. I call him Captain because that's what he was, once, and I think he likes—Ben, is something wrong? You look—strange."

"No," Foyle said. His voice sounded dead and hollow in his own ears. His face felt stiff. "No, Donna, nothing's wrong. An' there isn't going to be," he added gently, and she couldn't know that he meant to make sure of it by leaving tomorrow. The scales were too out of balance, so much guilt on his side and so little on hers.

The steady trotting of two horses beat a muted tattoo. They listened tensely. The horses came on up the trail into the yard. A whistle shrilled a single curt note.

Donna flew to the door. She gave back the whistle like a boy. "Hi, Captain! Welcome home!"

Ebb Grimm was tall, thin, and razor-edge straight. As soon as he stamped into the office he leveled a penetrating pair of eyes at Foyle and rasped, "Gr-hum!" What that signified could have been anything, but it closely resembled an old campaigner's grunt at the sight of hostile Indians.

He had a hatchet face, barbed with a beak nose jutting above dangling cavalry mustaches as long and pointed as daggers. Old army was his stamp. He was around seventy, and looked as if he would never die, except possibly by violence. But for the powdering of dust, his severely neat clothes might have been fitted on him by an orderly fifteen minutes ago. He wore bleached buckskin gloves with ten-inch gauntlets, and when he tugged them off, his hands showed as white and well-kept as those of a town girl of courting age.

Gravely affectionate, he bent and kissed his stepdaughter on her forehead, meanwhile keeping his piercing eyes on Foyle. "What's been going on, my dear?" he inquired crisply. "I met Hamp coming in. He's putting up my horse. Says he thinks he heard some shots. Who's this—hah—gentleman?"

"Ben Jason," answered Donna. "The Murrell men came tonight. The safe was robbed. They broke into the house. I was alone. Ben got here just in time. He saved the money and drove them off. There are some more things to tell you, but they can wait. I suppose Hamp has spoken to you about Ben, hasn't he?"

Ebb Grimm's snort shook his fierce mustaches. "Hamp's a fool! He never should have left you here alone, under any conditions. All that matters to him is getting the work done in record time, expecting I'll pay him extra wages. Atchley and some of the others aren't much better, either. Cow business and profits come first with them, and they can't get it through their heads that they won't have much business left to worry about if M'Cavan has his way. Gr-hum! It's like counting the cost of powder when the camp is surrounded and under attack!"

He dropped his irascible manner, shaking hands with Foyle. "Happy indeed to know you, Mr. Jason. Extremely grateful." He was a gentlemanly old war dog who asked no probing questions. "No higher recommendation is possible than the praise of my stepdaughter," he assured Foyle, with somewhat floridly old-fashioned courtliness. "Your inestimable service to her places me equally in your debt. Besides being deeply fond of Donna, I am responsible for her safety and welfare. The money, too, is of—hah—some importance. I trust that you will remain with us, Mr. Jason. We have a need of good lively fighting men."

Foyle said briefly, "Thanks, but I must leave in the morning."

Grimm thumbed his mustaches. He shot a keen glance at Donna, and frowned musingly. He drew out two long black cheroots, gave Foyle one, and struck a match for them both.

"I'm bound to induce you to change your mind, Mr. Jason," he vowed. "You're a Southwestern man, born and bred, I take it. I'm not. But I like this country, sir. Fine country. This here is one of the best parts of it. Why leave? No reason at all."

"I must leave—" Foyle began.

"No reason at all!" repeated Grimm firmly. "Fine country. Only politically rotten. Part of it, anyway. The part ruled by that scoundrelly Big Mac M'Cavan! You've surely heard of him." He sighted his cheroot at Foyle. "M'Cavan is more than just a rotten apple in the barrel, take my word for it! He has big plans. He has powerful backing. If you have any feeling for this country, sir, you owe it to your conscience to do your share toward stopping that blackguard! I certainly shall do mine!"

He inhaled the strong smoke, expelled it in a forceful gust, and continued. "At first inspection M'Cavan's plans appear to be preposterous—the dream of a madman. Federal authorities would laugh it off, yes. Until too late. Those fools!"

There seemed to exist a prevalence of fools, in Grimm's opinion. He said, "I shan't go into details now, but I swear that M'Cavan's schemes involve outright treason! Revolution! War! I know what war is. It's not to be laughed off. We've had our Civil War, and mighty uncivil it was. The fact that we don't want another, sir, is no guarantee that we couldn't have one! M'Cavan's plan is *not* preposterous! He expects to have the Mexican border states on his side. It could lead to war with Mexico."

"Could he win?" Foyle asked.

Grimm shrugged. "I've been a soldier. I've seen some strange victories and defeats. At the least, armed revolution means bloodshed. This one would be sheer horror! Think of it! Mexican bandits and renegade Yaquis, American outlaws, badmen, shabby adventurers—all swarming through the country, killing, looting, burning! That may be M'Cavan's purpose—a gigantic raid to take over the country long enough to plunder it to the bone. He and his backers can always escape down into Mexico and disappear with their loot. Or perhaps that's the second choice, in case the main plan fails. They wouldn't lose, either way, you see. Some few of us hope to stop them in time. Will you join us? A man like you surely can't stand aside and—"

Outside, Ira Hamp uttered a surprised shout, and Grimm broke off to point his beak nose at the open door. The shout was followed by a chilling laugh. A gun spat one solid report, and somebody grumbled an oath.

Unsteady footsteps scraped the gravel. Hamp entered at a staggering run. He hung a toe on the doorstep and fell headlong into the office.

"The Chink!" he gasped, laboriously rolling over onto his back. "Laughed—an' shot me! Laughed!" It was like him to condemn the laugh along with the shot.

Grimm bent over him. The whole front of the range boss's shirt was stained dark and wet. He had been shot in the chest. He tried to sit up, pushing Grimm away.

"Damn—your fight—Grimm! It don't—concern me any!" Then he choked and fell back, and his head hit the floor. He would never earn his extra pay for attending strictly to business.

Hamp hadn't thought to mention the presence of Red Murrell and his men, and it was a moment more before they opened fire with a volley that brought echoes rattling back from the far foothills. Ebb Grimm dragged a long Dragoon .44 out from under his coat, took a fresh bite on his cheroot, and cast an expertly disparaging glance around the office. As a place to fort up in it wasn't much. He kicked the door shut and bushed an eyebrow at Foyle.

"Gr-hum! Bad situation, Mr. Jason!"

Foyle met his old eyes and said, "Yeah." He meant, as Grimm did, that it couldn't be worse. By luck or design, the marauders had crept back and struck at just the right time for them. Foyle cursed himself for being caught off guard. He had been listening to Grimm's talk of danger, while the nearer peril closed in.

A gun blatted five times through the door, punching the lock into a twisted mass and sending splinters and bits of metal flying across the office.

A shallow laugh rippled, and Gano said in mock reproval, "Do be careful, Red! Might hit Mr. Grimm, you know, and Big Mac wants him alive! And we certainly don't want to hurt the young lady, do we?"

"We gotta git 'em!" rumbled Red Murrell. "An' quick! Don't you try stallin' me tonight, Gano! I know you from the ol' days. Always some cussed trick up your sleeve!"

"But my tricks work, you'll admit," Gano chided him. "Stop shooting, *compadre*, and listen—all of you. I want the occupants of this little edifice to hear me, too. We will now proceed to gather dry brush. That is, some of you will. Pile it up here around the walls. I, dear friends, shall then strike a match. Yes, yes! Proceed, jolly minions! Our entrenched hosts shall very soon be untrenched! They shall exit forth—laden with money, I urge, for I'm not sure about the fire-resistant qualities of that so-called safe!

"Am I heard and understood by all interested parties?" he ended politely.

There was no misunderstanding, outside or inside the office. His words were not too clear, some of them, but his meaning was lucid and lethal.

Foyle, guns in his hands, cocked an eye bleakly at the door, then at Grimm. No kind of defense was possible here. The little building would take fire, burn rapidly, and they would have to jump out and take whatever trigger terms were waiting for them.

He looked last at Donna, and then he took his eyes off her and said in a dead, flat tone, "Grimm, drop your gun!"

Ebb Grimm reared his hawklike old head. "What?" He saw Foyle's guns trained on him. He saw the face above them, dark and lean, somberly saturnine. "What, Mr. Jason?"

Foyle slapped out with a gun barrel. He knocked the big old Dragoon .44 from Grimm's hand to the floor. He called, "Gano, come in here! And you, Murrell! Don't fool with me, or I'll be out there to show you some shootin'! Who the hell d'you think's in charge here, anyhow? Me, damn you— *Bain Foyle of Banner!*"

Chapter Ten: **FOYLE'S FOLLY**

GANO ENTERED FIRST, saying, "It's all right, Red. Yes, he's Foyle. I thought it best not to mention that to you. Might have rattled you a bit. Nice fellow, really, as long as you don't cross him. I got along well with him for a while."

He strolled into the office, self-possessed, cool, giving Foyle his brightest false smile. "Devilish neat work," he complimented blandly. "You tossed back the money, and promptly won the whole jackpot! What a gambler! Now we have the money *and* Mr. Grimm! I take off my hat to you!" He took off his hat.

Foyle said coldly, "We? You resigned, Gano— remember?"

He hadn't looked at Donna since divulging his dread identity, nor at Grimm. He didn't want to have to look at them. Not ever again.

He heard Donna whisper stunnedly, "Foyle? Oh, God—no, no!" Then she was sobbing in Grimm's arms, and Grimm was making incoherent sounds deep in his throat, the raging, broken sounds of an old soldier betrayed and defeated.

Gano grinned slyly at Foyle. "I resigned as your obedient servant. I did not resign from the Grimm game! You and I now work on equal terms, share and share alike. I think my efforts have not been negligible in bringing about this triumphant

244

conclusion. I say, therefore, *we* have the money and Mr. Grimm!"

Red Murrell, glowering, demanded, "How 'bout me? I'm in it, too, an' I want my cut! Where's that money you spoke of, Gano? I'll take that, an' you can have Grimm."

"The blazes you will!" Foyle barked. "That's mine! Furthermore, I contracted to catch an' deliver Grimm—an' no two-bit badman turns me off! Your shootin' don't impress me, Murrell! *Sabe?*"

He couldn't make it all stick, he knew. The best he could do was to aim high, then strike a deal. In this argument over the spoils he stood alone against eight men.

To sway Gano back over onto his side was good trading policy, and he said, "Gano an' I got this job done. We didn't get much help from you, an' we didn't need any. Fact is, you nearly queered it."

"Right!" agreed Gano, but added, "Still, we'll take care of you, Red, don't worry."

Red Murrell moved his injured arm, looking speculatively at Foyle's guns. "I don't fall much for that talk," he objected. His eyes were attracted by the shimmer of Donna's diamond bracelet in the lamplight. "That's mine, anyhow! I'm puttin' my claim on it right now!" He grabbed at it. "Turn it loose, gal!"

"I can't!" Donna cried, shrinking from him. She

was chalky-white from fear and the bitter pain of broken illusions. "My mother had it fitted on there long ago. It won't come off now."

That frustration was the last straw for Red Murrell. It was obvious to him that the girl told the truth. The solid-gold bracelet fitted her wrist like a band. He cursed, relinquishing it, and swung a glare at Foyle.

"All right!" he roared. "You're Foyle—yeah, I know you now! Mister, you could be the ring-tailed king o' hell, but you don't rook ol' Red! I got six *hombres* there outside. They ain't school-marms! Nor me! All right!"

"Nobody's trying to rook you," said Gano.

"Nobody's goin' to!" Murrell swore. "We take this Grimm an' the money down to Banner—all of us! We take the gal, too, an' her di'mond bangle. Leave her here, she'd raise the alarm too soon. Let Big Mac figger our shares. I'll 'bide by what he says. That's fair an' it's my last word, an' be damned to you! I ain't never yet been skeered to fight, any time, any place, an' I don't know how to bluff! Not ol' Red!"

Gano murmured soothingly, "Fair enough, Red. We need you and the boys to help us get out fast before daylight, anyway. We may run into trouble, and you know the country. There's no fight. Your deal is okay. Eh, Foyle?"

"It'll do," Foyle said shortly. It had to be that way. The deal wasn't as good as he wished, but

Gano had cut the bargaining ground out from under him. This was no place for a blazing gun-smoke argument, one against eight, and Donna in the midst of it. Murrell's mood was recklessly stubborn and ugly. His six brush-prowlers would fight, no question of that. And Gano, playing his own game, would pitch in with the winning side.

Foyle went to the safe. "You still watchin' my back for Big Mac, Gano?" he asked, unlocking it with the key Donna had given him.

"That's another task I haven't yet resigned," said Gano.

Foyle took out the cash box. He tucked it under his left arm, and said to Donna and Grimm, without looking at their faces, "Bear in mind you're in my charge. Mine. Nobody else's. Do as I tell you. You can trust me not to—"

"I would sooner trust a—a ravening wolf!" breathed Donna.

Her stepfather gripped her arm. "Foyle, I'm not afraid of Big Mac M'Cavan or of anything he can do to me. But Donna is a young girl, a young lady. Banner is a bad place for her!"

"I know," Foyle said tonelessly, motioning them out of the office ahead of himself and Gano. "Do as I tell you now."

Ebb Grimm stiffened his shoulders, tamped his cheroot out carefully, and offered an arm to Donna. "Come, my dear," he said gently.

They stepped out under the cottonwoods. Saddled horses were brought up to the yard. Last to mount, Foyle looked the party over. He was in charge, he had stated, and he meant to keep them reminded of it. Gun prestige was all that upheld his command. He knew their kind. In their chief traits they resembled a wild pack of savage dogs, snarlingly mutinous, ready to pounce on the self-elected leader at the first sign of weakness.

"They love you not!" murmured Gano beside him. "They don't forget how you drove them out of the house, nor forgive. Red's arm is getting inflamed where you shot him. He doesn't wash often!"

Foyle slid a glance at him. "How about you?"

Gano smiled innocently. "I have my orders from Big Mac. They are not affected by any petty resentment."

Foyle tied the cash box and hung it on his saddle horn. "Okay, if we're ready to go!" he announced, ranging a stare over the unfriendly faces in the moonlight. "String out. Let's not crowd together. Grimm an' the girl ride up front with me, out o' the dust—an' out o' the cuss-talk some o' you spill so free! Gano, I reckon you could—"

"Red knows a short route to the river trail," Gano casually interrupted. "He can guide us. I'll ride ahead with him and keep in touch with you, so you won't go astray in the dark. Come on, Red!"

They got moving in that order, Gano and Murrell leading the way, Foyle following with Donna and Grimm, and the gang bringing up the rear. That deal wasn't good, either, from Foyle's own viewpoint, but the arrangement was a natural one and hard to argue against. Gano had a gift of raising perfectly plausible suggestions.

Foyle looked back once at the house and outbuildings of the V Bar ranch, and noticed Donna doing likewise. Her lips were moving. She was praying, he guessed. Or maybe she was saying a farewell, like himself.

Morning sunlight found them traveling south, closely following the river. After some consultation it had been agreed that the open trail offered too much risk of their being sighted, and their horses were not fresh any more. They rode under cover by the high bank left by the river in one of the shiftings of its course, and for added protection the hills shelved upward beyond the bank. They were safe, making steadily for Banner, not a doubt left of getting there without any trouble.

The orderly pattern of travel was relaxed. Only a semblance of it remained. Gano and Murrell, leading, and from habit glancing back occasionally, had let their horses slacken down to a walk. Murrell's half-dozen men rode in a bunch, smoking and talking, yawning, slouched in their saddles. They were less than fifty yards behind Foyle and the two captives.

Gano began peering backward more often at Foyle. He acted restless. At last he reined his horse around, said something to Murrell, and came riding back. He nodded to Foyle in passing, and joined the men in the rear. After a short while he came up behind Foyle. He rode alongside for a moment, silent, then cleared his throat.

"Two more days should see us in Banner, eh? Maybe three."

"Yeah."

Gano frowned. "Well—plenty of time," he muttered, and heeled his horse and rejoined Murrell up forward. He seemed irritated.

Foyle watched him go, and let his eyes drift elsewhere. The false river bed stretched southward, its pale sand a long flash in the sunlight, the sky clean and blue above it. On his right the eroded bank and the hills passed gradually by, changing shapes, yet retaining their monotonous sameness. The hot sun climbed toward noon, eating away all shadows.

He laid a thorough regard on the arroyo that Gano and Murrell were riding past. It was, he judged, an *arroyo madre*, as the Mexicans would call it. A mother arroyo, fed by little ones. It made a big, deep gash in the bank, where in heavy rain time it spewed torrents, although now it was as dry as the sandy bed. Probably, almost certainly, it ran far back up into the hills.

He looked behind. The six men were discussing a joke, guffawing, enlarging on it with leering comments, making it do lengthy service in driving out their brainless boredom. Foyle looked forward again. He spoke to Donna and Grimm, quietly.

"Listen!" he said. "I've got something to say to you."

Donna scarcely moved her head. "Say it, Bain Foyle! We can't stop you, any more than we can stop you from—"

"Shut up!" Foyle said. "Grimm, you were caught tight there, last night. You didn't have a chance. I did what I had to do."

Ebb Grimm snorted derisively. "Why trouble yourself to make excuses? You are Bain Foyle! That name is familiar to all of us. You came up from Banner to get me, for a reward. Nothing you say can alter that! I'm not a fool!"

"Maybe," Foyle said, "I'm the fool. Take this cash box. See that arroyo we're coming to? There's where you and Donna turn off! Ride up that arroyo and keep going. Ready, now!"

"What? What do you mean?"

"Do as I tell you!"

Grimm and Donna looked at him. They saw the same lean face, dark and saturnine. The same hard mouth. If there was any difference, it was only that the underlying shade of sadness in the eyes was more pronounced.

Grimm exclaimed unbelievingly. "Are you—telling us to escape? It's impossible! Murrell—Gano—the others—"

"I reckon I can hold 'em off long enough for you and Donna to get a fair start," said Foyle, still quietly, almost tranquilly. "I'm Bain Foyle, remember! Here's the arroyo. Here's your cash box. Get going—and don't stop for anything!"

Donna cried, "Ben! You can't!"

"Dammit, do as I tell you! The hell I can't!"

He hauled his mount around, crowding them into the mouth of the arroyo, booting their horses. He watched them go plunging up the winding gravel bed of the arroyo, and he smiled and felt a joyous relief. He saw them look back. Donna's hair was flying, tumbled over her neck and shoulders. Her lips parted and she called to him, but it couldn't be heard above the rattle of slithering, climbing hoofs. He waved at her, and laughed for the first time in years. By heaven, there went a girl for a man to have.

A babble of shouting burst out. The six men dropped their paltry joke and spurred horses forward. Murrell and Gano whirled, digging at their holsters, swearing in tinny tones.

Bain Foyle, gun master of Banner, slid off his horse and slapped it farewell. He spread his wide shoulders. He took a deep breath, drew his guns, and looked up at the sky. Blue and serene, the sky, clear as a baby's conscience.

"What a day!" he said aloud, and he laughed again.

It wasn't so bad, to die this way. Better than a dirty alley.

Chapter Eleven: BACK TO BANNER

FOYLE FIRED TWICE and spilled two of the half-dozen. The remaining four whirled in close against the bank, piling out of their saddles, cautiously changing tactics. Two shots and two down.

Charging up from the right with Gano, Red Murrell shouted, "Get him, quick! We gotta catch them two!"

The blue sheen of Murrell's gun barrel shortened to a pinpoint, as Foyle swung his smoking guns, Murrell had the use of only one arm. His left arm was swollen and his eyes were fevered. He triggered hurriedly, hooked his reins, and wrenched his horse up rearing. His massive head hunched down, and the horse took Foyle's bullet. The horse floundered, crashing into Gano riding alongside. On the left, the four men slid around a shoulder of the old riverbank. The first of them got off a shot and sent Foyle's hat spinning.

Foyle backed up into the dry arroyo and stood fast, waiting. Nothing stirred at the mouth of it, and a baffling silence closed down. The sounds of the two horses, carrying Donna and Grimm away, grew fainter and died out. He speculated about the doings of Gano and Murrell and the four men, until he heard scrambling noises and grasped the ominous meaning.

They were climbing the riverbank to get above and shoot down at him. That was their best play, the winning card that would soon finish him. He was resigned to death, but he had to hold it off somehow until Donna and Grimm had a long start. With difficulty he clambered up the left side of the deep arroyo, clawing at the sandy strata, and got to where he could peer over the edge.

Two of the men had reached the high ground. They were running across it, angling toward the arroyo and motioning to somebody beyond it. One of them spied the white bandage on Foyle's head. He yipped a warning. They both dived to the ground, and Foyle's shot went wasted. A gun rapped somewhere behind Foyle, on the other side of the arroyo. Sand exploded near his face. His instinctive jerk cost him his grip and he tumbled to the bottom.

"I got him!" bellowed Murrell. "Close in on him, boys! Come on, Gano!"

"Go easy, Red!" Gano sang out. "He's hard to kill!"

"The hell he is!" A bearded face bobbed into sight above the arroyo. Foyle sliced a gun up and fired, Murrell pulled back.

"Right in the whiskers!" commented Gano. "Red, didn't I tell you he's hard to kill? He's a shooting wampus!"

Murrell could be heard cursing him. At the end of a string of lurid oaths he rasped, "Quit grinnin', you yaller-skinned monkey, an' do some shootin' y'self!"

Silence fell again. Foyle listened for the coming of the four men on the left. They were creeping to the arroyo, stalking him, and once they reached it he would be without cover, like a bear trapped in a pit. There was nothing for him to do but wait, using up the shrinking margin of his time, watching for them to show themselves.

Something moved stealthily along the left edge, where the four were. A hat rose an inch. Foyle slung a shot. The hat spun away. Four gun muzzles poked immediately into view at different points. He was tricked, trapped and located.

A gun cracked muffledly. Red Murrell uttered a harsh cry and there was another report. The four gun muzzles lining the left bank went motionless, as if their owners had received a shock. Then they snapped up, leveled out.

Gano appeared on the right bank in full sight, smiling his shallow smile over a pair of blaring, kicking guns.

Foyle, about to send a bullet at Gano, changed his mind at the last instant. Gano wasn't shooting at him down in the arroyo. He was firing straight across it. The four on the left bank were blazing back at him. It was a stand-up shoot-out at ten yards' range.

Gano came on. His short and stocky body jerked, the yellow silk shirt dotted, but it didn't stop him. He concentrated calmly on one after another of the four. The furious gun battle lasted only a brief moment. It ceased suddenly, all guns silenced, and while the echoes still grumbled in the hills Gano stepped blindly off the edge and fell headlong into the arroyo.

Foyle caught Gano and broke his fall. He laid him on the sandy floor. Gano couldn't focus his eyes, but he was able to pronounce distinctly, "Bain Foyle, I've never known a bigger fool than you!"

"You're another!" said Foyle gruffly.

Gano quirked his lips wryly. "True. But this is the first completely foolish thing I've ever done. And it's the last. Damn you, I suspected you'd be up to some crazy trick. I should have shot you in the back this morning. It was high time. My orders from Big Mac were—explicit! Instead, I've killed old Red and those four. And they've killed me."

"What got into you, *amigo*? I figured you were on their side."

"That's the foolish part of it. I was. Until Red blew up and called me—a yellow monkey." The slanted eyes closed wearily. "I've killed other men for less. It came to me right then, Foyle, that you—that you—no matter how mad you got, you never once spoke as if you knew I was—well, different. Or even looked at me in that way. Even when you shoved a gun in my face. That doesn't mean a thing to you, does it?"

"No."

"It does to me—although I swear I never would have thought it meant so much. I was supposed to kill you after you got the Grimm job done. Big Mac doesn't want you back. Good price—ten thousand. Just another killing. I had a dozen chances. I held back. I tried hating you—tried to prod you into saying something that would make hating you easy. Hatred has always been easy for me—but not this time. Why? Damned foolish!"

Gano moved his right hand, and Foyle clasped it, looking down into the flat, broad face of the Mongoloid gunman.

"And because of it, Foyle—because of that damned foolishness—I finally decided," Gano whispered, chuckling faintly, "that—I remain—your—obedient servant—"

After a while Foyle stood up. The crunch of his heels in the sand made the only sound in the quietness. He looked down again at Gano and said, "I'm pushing on down to Banner. To see Big Mac. I've got to. Got to go through with the damned foolishness and make it stand good, *amigo*."

He was talking to himself. Gano was dead. Foyle left the silent arroyo, taking Gano's guns with him.

The horses, left hastily ground-hitched, untied, had spooked at the outburst of gunfire. They were drifting north in a bunch. When he limped after them they halted to watch him, but a walleyed buckskin swiveled and ran, and they all tore off. To try catching them was hopeless, with his bad leg. They would drift back to the Pronghorn country and be picked up there.

He limped southward. Back to Banner, his mind commanded him. Back to where he had started from. To kill Big Mac. To smash the ruthless power that he had helped to build.

Bain Foyle, last of the old gun-fighting bunch of Banner, the man whose return was forbidden by Big Mac, held his mind's command before him like a holy obsession. It drew him on, alone and afoot, through the days of hunger, and pain, and exhaustion. He rested briefly where and when he fell, and dragged himself up and plodded on. He had no other thoughts to occupy him, to keep old ghosts out. He didn't need them.

Big Mac M'Cavan sat at his untidy desk, smiling affably, his manner conveying the impression that Foyle's arrival was expected and welcomed. He chose not to show any notice at first that Foyle was a worn-out man whose haggard face looked dead below the dirty head bandage, who rested shakily on one leg.

"Ah, there, Foyle."

"Ah, Mac."

"Sit down."

Foyle sat down. *This time*—he thought. *This time*—

This time his holsters were empty. Two guards at the main door of the brick mansion had lifted his guns before letting him in. He guessed dully that his stumbling approach had been seen and reported before he entered the town. The guards were ready. So was Big Mac.

The same strong-jowled face, noble forehead, leonine head crowned by its magnificent gray mane. The same ponderous dignity and throbbing voice, buttered with the professional charm of genial superiority.

Big Mac glanced over his desk at Foyle's ruined boots and inquired, "Been walking?"

"Five days," said Foyle. He rested back in the chair. A wave of weakness and nausea rose in him. He pressed his cracked lips and fought it down. It was stuffy in this room. He sweated. The sweat was clammy under his armpits. The nerves of his bad leg crawled and tightened. The leg was stiffening again because he was seated, but he hadn't the energy left to rise.

"From the Pronghorn?" Big Mac asked. "How did you make out up there, by the way?" He spoke indifferently, but the shine was hot in his eyes.

"*Bueno*," Foyle replied. "Some trouble, but we handled it, Gano and me. Red Murrell took a hand. We got Grimm. And the whole Pronghorn war chest. And his stepdaughter. Did you know of her?"

"*Bueno* is right!" breathed Big Mac. "The

stepdaughter? I knew her mother, back East a long time ago. Might have married her, in fact, but Grimm— Well, that's an old grudge. Grimm and the girl and the money, eh? *Bueno* to hell! Man, you did make out! But where are they? And—er— where's Gano?"

Foyle eased his leg. He wasn't sweating now. He said, "Gano went under, shooting it out with Red and his bunch—right after I gave Grimm the money back and turned him and the girl loose. Yeah, it was *bueno* to hell, Mac, how we made out up there!"

Thick silence ran for a full minute. Big Mac forgot to smoke. His mouth was round, his cigar held suspended. His eyes flared, then cooled to sharp awareness, fixed on Foyle's face.

A drumming rumble grew audible, like thunder. In the hushed room Big Mac's chair creaked. Putting down his cigar, Big Mac reached forward to the line of desk drawers.

"Have a smoke, Foyle."

"That's the wrong drawer, Mac!" said Foyle, starting up.

"It's the right one for this brand of smoke!" Big Mac plucked a gun from the drawer and fired through an open pigeonhole.

The short-range discharge and the bite of burned powder sent Foyle back into his chair. In the hollow of his starved stomach Gano's guns had escaped the attention of the guards. He ripped his shirt open in both hands, rooting them out. Their front sights gouged his bare stomach and he shot as soon as they cleared. Too fast. Both bullets whipped papers stacked in pigeonholes. One, deflected, caused Big Mac to jump and let his gun hammer slap at half-cock. Foyle got his spent muscles under control and worked his trigger fingers twice. The four reports crashed a reverberating chatter in the closed room.

The drumming undertone swelled loud, gathering further noises, becoming a confused uproar. All the town seemed swiftly drawn into it. Something was happening in Banner, outside of this stuffy room. Men were shouting. A crackle of exploding cartridges brought a high note of authority to the drumming.

Big Mac's chair groaned. His gun barrel scraped the desk, and vicious rage at last shrank his eyes and smeared the bogus nobility of his face. He mouthed the weak curses of a weak man, a small bean in a bloated pod, and as his eyes glazed he squeezed the trigger again in a final jet of temper.

Foyle thumped to the floor and rolled painfully over to train his guns on the door. The two guards and all the rest—why didn't they come rushing in? It was getting noisier outside. Everybody shouting. Shooting. Stampeding.

He was telling someone about his father, he thought.

"The old man had it right. He knew. This kind o'

life doesn't count for anything. If you live to man-size, the time's bound to come when you know you've had enough—maybe too much. Then you get careless. It doesn't matter any more, and you don't try so hard. Then you're through. The old man knew, all right."

He thought he said that. It was mumbled behind closed lips, and sounded like moaning.

It was no mumble, the clear voice that said urgently to him, "Ben! Open your eyes, Ben! You're not going to die, you hear? You mustn't! You can't do that to me!"

He got his eyes opened, shocked, knowing that voice. "You?" he asked. She was holding his head off the floor, crying into his thin, dirty, unshaven face. The room was full of men. "Donna," he said, "this is a bad town—for you to be in!"

He tried to get up, having a vague idea that it was up to him to see her safely home.

John Atchley hovered over him with a flask. Frank Scanlon was there, too, and several others whom Foyle had seen before in Van Gaughn, but most of the men were strangers to him.

"Could he have a drink, Ebb?" Atchley asked.

"A short one might pull him together a bit," Ebb Grimm said. He took the flask and bent down to Foyle. "Only a short one, mind! We've got to get you out of here. Some of the boys need care, too. I rode to the Muleshoe camp, fast as I could, and got the posse started. No time to lose, after what

263

happened. Donna swung through the Pronghorn and met us with the bunch. When we got to that arroyo it told us all anybody could read. It even convinced Atchley!"

"It sold me," Atchley admitted freely. "Sure had been a whale of a gun fight there!"

Foyle drank from the flask, and coughed, his parched throat gagging on the whisky. "Gano sided me. He was a good *hombre*. Wish you'd bury him decent on the way back. I wasn't able to."

Grimm nodded. "It'll be done. We expected to bury you there. And there was where Donna was supposed to turn back home. We found your tracks instead of your body. Your boot tracks, leading south, a couple of days old. And right there Donna proceeded to act mightily disobedient! Refused to turn back! Yes, and rode us hard to keep up with her! She's a dangerous girl with a mind of her own, like her mother—I'm warning you, Ben!"

Foyle said, "My name's Bain."

"My old ears," stated Grimm, "are too dull to detect any difference. But what's everybody standing flat-footed around here for? We've taken this town in right smart style, but I wouldn't swear how long we might hold it without some trouble—and durned if we want to keep the ratty place! Big Mac is dead, anyhow. We'd better go home and be quiet till it blows over. Boots and saddles, men! And don't forget to commandeer the best vehicles for our injured!"

They were all grinning. Foyle, helped to his feet, looked into Donna's eyes. He felt lifted by a lightheartedness, a new cleanness. But the score had to be plainly shown, once and for all, nothing hidden, nothing ever again secret and disguised.

He said, "Banner is where I came from."

Grimm drew himself up and lighted a cheroot. "Exactly! Banner is where you're coming from! If you'll recall, Hamp is no longer with us. I would like a Southwestern man as range boss, one who knows the country. One who regards as his business anything and everything that concerns me and the V Bar ranch. It's not easy to find the right man. I—h'm—may give you a trial. Think it over, Ben, eh?"

Donna said, holding Foyle's eyes, "He will, Captain!"

Foyle said, holding Donna's eyes, "I will, Captain!"

Ebb Grimm said pleasedly, "Gr-hum!"

The Mustang Trail

Chapter One: HELL'S HUNDRED

THE FOUR-HORSE WAGON came banging down the crooked street, wheels slewing crazily in and out of the dry ruts, scooping up storms of dust. It carried a load, canvas-covered and roped down. So did the driver carry a load, but less orderly. His filthy rags of buckskins showed him to be a buffalo tramp—one of the hideously depraved brush-thugs who, without trade, never recognized by any regular skinning crews at any time, called themselves buffalo hunters. His matted mane of coarse black hair proclaimed some Indian blood, most likely Tonkawa. Drink always thickened the heavy features of the Tonkawa strain.

He was just drunk enough to roar through town like that, using all the street, not caring if he crushed man or woman, stirring up a stamping flurry among horses tied to the hitchrails. A bevy of dance-hall girls, crossing from the Shackelford House to the Bee Hive, scattered, uttering screams and more, forceful equivalents. There were few children here below Fort Griffin, and no ladies to speak of.

Emerging from the Brazos Hotel, and also bound for the Bee Hive, Mr. Rogate Bishop glanced up from clipping the end of a fresh cigar with a razor-sharp clasp knife. The wagon rushed at him and he saw the tattered driver grinning like a madman.

Casually agile, Mr. Rogate Bishop jumped back, but not before stroking the knife in a reaching sweep and slicing the near lines clean through. Then, lighting his cigar, he calmly watched to see what would happen.

What happened was plenty, for the rambunctious driver. Being drunk and belligerent, he tried to haul in to fight over the matter. His off lines swerved the half-wild, racing team. His wagon sideswiped Murphy's Bar and crashed into the Star Hall at the bend, and he kited off headlong among the floundering horses. By the time he scrambled clear of that tangle, Murphy and the Star Hall proprietor were out demanding payment for damage—with sawed-off shotguns cocked for argument.

"That was neat!" one of the dance-hall girls called to Bishop, and the others sent him looks of warm approval.

But his mind was on poker. He touched the wide brim of his black Stetson to them and went on over into the Bee Hive. There, soon deep in the constructive enterprise of matching cards into profitable sequences, he forgot the matter.

It was only an incident. Should repercussions happen to follow, he would handle them as they came along. In a place like Fort Griffin it wasn't possible to avoid occasional trouble and still enjoy life, liberty, and the pursuit of fortune. Something was forever cropping up. All you had to do was be ready twenty-four hours of the day.

"One," Bishop murmured, dealing. He drew to three jacks and a kicker, and filled, not to his surprise.

This time, he mused, a loaded six might be needed to clinch the pot. The rusty-haired young Texan across the table, for one, was growing restless, running out of chips. And, come the six-gun debate, Rusty would have help on his side. Besides the three other ducks in the game, there were quite a few hard-faced boogers in the Bee Hive who bitterly resented Bishop's unbroken run of luck since his arrival some days back. And the local law, such as it was, definitely bent not in his favor.

Well, that was the way it generally ran. He had packed his winnings out of other tough towns.

The fort proper, and a big store, stood on a hill above the town and overlooked the West Fork Trail that ran up the Texas Panhandle and on through the Cherokee Strip to railhead. It had been built as an army outpost against reservation-shunning Indians. The town below had sprung up haphazardly as headquarters for the hunters engaged in exterminating the so-called Southern Herd of buffalo.

Since the wipe-out of the buffalo, the town had

become a hellhole of buckskin tramps out to murder any man for a dollar, wild trail hands stopping over for a fast whirl, cattlemen fighting for the buffalo-cleared range, soldiers swaggering on the prod. Freighters and teamsters, a knuckly crowd. And a dangerous sprinkling of badmen and outlaws, thieves and killers from everywhere. They had to drift and congregate wherever the law was loose, farther and farther down, staying a jump ahead of tracks scored on dark back trails.

Somebody once had named the town Hell's Hundred Acres. That soon was shortened to Hell's Hundred—meaning the number of dives and deadfalls. No man owning anything worth stealing went unarmed, or walked alone in the night.

To top it all, the fort on the hill now was buying horses, all it could get. There had been the lost battles of Powder River and the Rosebud, and the stunning disaster of the Little Big Horn. General Custer of the 7th Cavalry—George Armstrong Custer, the undefeatable Long Hair—was gone to glory with nigh three hundred troopers. The proudly victorious Sioux and Cheyenne were on the rampage.

Remounts urgently needed for the increased army! Bring on your mustangs! If they're fit for cavalrymen to ride against the hostiles—bring them on! Fort Griffin and a dozen more army posts of the West are buying horses to remount the broken and vengeful 7th, the 5th, the army in urgent haste to take to the field on combat campaign.

Here was a new source of revenue, badly needed by penniless and desperate men. Who's got a horse that meets army requirements? The army demands a clear title and bill of sale. Okay, soldier; can do. Plenty furtive strangers around able to use a pen. First get the horse. Kill the owner. Go through his pockets for extras.

The West Fork, in less than half a year, was already known as the Mustang Trail, haunted and watched and waylaid by horse thieves who could tell at a glance if a horse would meet army specifications—sixteen hands and solid color, good build, sound wind, gentled so it at least wouldn't hit the moon at the flap of a saddle blanket.

"Raise ten," said Bishop.

The red-topped Texan had just ten white chips left. "Call!"

Bishop spread his hand and leaned back. The others, two boss freighters and an ambitious tinhorn, had dropped out. The Texan scraped his chair and stood up, reading Bishop's full house. He was young and tough, too shabby-dressed to be bucking a no-limit game. He hadn't started with much—four hundred dollars, all gone.

He said, "Where I grew up they shoot men for doin' that!"

Bishop returned moderately, "Where you grew up they should learn not to bet into a one-card draw." And then he, too, came to his feet.

He was tall and severe. His black coat, unbuttoned, allowed sight of two belts studded with rows of brass cartridges. That was for kindly warning. His black hat, fingered down on the right side of the broad brim, gave a rakish hint to his austere air. He had a muscled face, strong and dark, from which a pair of slate-gray eyes glimmered cold query at the world.

Right now his eyes pinned on the Texan, yet there was the impression that they were missing nothing of what else went on in the crowded barroom. A man could never let down, once he started this kind of life, and he had got started on it long ago and made enemies in many strange quarters.

The Texan finally jerked his lean shoulders and walked off. The game broke up then. Hungrily watched by hostile eyes, Bishop gathered his chips and cashed them in.

He was standing at the bar when the Texan ranged up alongside and admitted, "I didn't actually spot any flimflam there on your deal. It was too fast for me."

"Luck's a fast lady," observed Bishop. "Surprising how she comes through, with a little—hum—encouragement."

The Texan inclined his head in polite agreement.

"My name's Delaney. Friends call me Red, for some reason."

"Bishop, me. Rogate Bishop."

Red Delaney made a wry mouth. He turned away, and swung back again, sighing. "A town full o' poker tables—an' I buck 'Rogue' Bishop's game! What did I do to deserve that?"

"You only dropped four hundred," Bishop said. "If it hurts so bad, I'll loan it back to you."

"Mr. Bishop, those words are hard for me to swallow!"

"Wash 'em down with a drink."

"Thanks. You pay for it. As of now, I can't."

They drank together. Red Delaney set his emptied glass on the bar and said, "I've got a paying proposition for a man with some ready money."

Bishop nodded. "Hum!" These Texans—insulted by an offer of cash, but ready to trade you out of it!

"I'm dead broke," said Red, which to Bishop was needless and uninteresting information. "I started out from Refugio with horses to sell to the army, an' the first night out a gang o' stampeders got every one of 'em. I came on here to watch for 'em to show up. I had a few hundred dollars. Spent some. You cleaned up the rest."

"Offhand, I'd say you're in bad luck."

"Seems so, for a fact, this trip. But I don't put too much stock in luck, tell you the truth."

Neither did Bishop. Not too trustingly. Nerve and trained hands, plus a disregard for risky consequences, were more reliable, more faithfully productive of results. He had scuffed deep tracks, carelessly scored up a notorious reputation, and yet stayed always himself—a cool, remote kind of man with a private and peculiar sense of humor; essentially a lone wolf who bet straight on his own ability to boot fortune into line with his own desires.

Red asked him, "D'you happen to know of a place called the Sandhole, way down the trail at Guadalupe River? It's a low patch o' fine sand, hard-packed 'cept when the river rises an' flows over into it. Then the Sandhole becomes a quicksand. That's not often. A kind of mushroom-shaped rock sticks up on the far side. 'Bout ten years back some Indians—'Paches, I guess—used that for a trap."

Bishop motioned to a bartender to make free with the bottle, and paid for it. "What trap?" The subject didn't come near to touching his interest, but he had won money off this chump and guessed he owed him some slight consideration.

"Man trap," Red said. "An Indian girl would stand up on that rock, no clothes on, and entice a passing traveler to—uh—to sort of investigate. Well, a quicksand, you know how it is. Looks solid, till you step in it. When the man tried to struggle clear, these 'Paches came out an' slipped an arrow into him an' let him sink. They saved his horse an' saddle. Got several that way, before the Sandhole dried out again. The Indian girl was a *chisera*—a witchwoman. The rock's been called Crazy Chisera Butte ever since."

"She wasn't so crazy," remarked Bishop. "But you are, if you fancy you're pretty enough to stand naked upon a rock like a siren enticin' the weary—"

"Whoa!" Red protested. "Listen! My uncle got caught there. He was heading back home, after selling a beef herd up at Dodge, an' the *chisera* waved to him an' he—"

"Old goat!"

"Well, maybe he thought she needed help," Red argued, with faint conviction. "He was a gentleman, my Uncle Wesley. Anyhow, down he sank in that quicksand with all his money on him. All right, the Sandhole's dry as a bone now. All we do is hire a crew to dig—"

"We what?" Bishop interrupted. "Why, you sacrilegious son!"

Red worked his jaw for a moment, chewing down a cud of temper. He said, after taking a drink, "I'd see to it that my Uncle Wesley, and any other bodies we found, got decent Christian burial. We'd split the money, fifty-fifty. I don't see anything wrong in that."

"My eyesight's too good," murmured Bishop. He hadn't any desire to invest his money in a grave, wet or dry. "Digging for corpses—no, grave-robbing is out o' my line."

Swallowing again, Red remarked, "I'm surprised you're more fussy than I am, considerin' who you are!"

Bishop rolled a broad shoulder. "I draw the line at—hum—ghouls!"

"And I," said Red in the softest of Texas drawls, "draw the line at you callin' me that!" He lashed a terrific punch for Bishop's jaw.

Cat-quick, Rogue Bishop fended it off with his left forearm, followed through with a driving thrust, and swung around for business. He wasted no motion.

Shoved back onto his worn-over high heels, Red for that instant was wide open to receive what was coming. He got it—Bishop's right fist, wickedly accurate, full between the eyes. The Texan hurtled rearward, spilling men and drinks half the length of the bar. While he lay goggling, the Bee Hive buzzed into action.

Setting off a riot in Hell's Hundred never called for much special effort, day or night, and here in the crowded Bee Hive were sharp-edged men with tempers easily jarred. Texas trail hands and soldiers nursed a mutual antipathy. Freighters, thundering lords of the road, were touchy when caught afoot. Buffalo tramps and half-breed Tonkawas, despised for their debauched poverty, were always eager to jab a knife into anybody.

And the tinhorn sharks held a common grudge against Bishop.

Beginning with the upset customers, the free-for-all exploded, everybody savagely pitching in to knock off a score. Bishop got his back to the bar and struck out at all who charged within reach. It hadn't been any part of his intention to raise this frolic, but such spontaneous eruptions were too common to disconcert him. In a sardonic fashion he was appreciating the mad humor of it—until a tinhorn cheaply flung an empty bottle that just missed nailing him on the ear.

"Eh?" he growled, dodging another. "Bottles?" He had a thousand of them behind him, more or less. Full ones, at that.

Booting a bellowing muleskinner out of his way, he vaulted the bar. He helped himself from the tier of back shelves, and—while the bartender howled anguish—sent bottles flying to where they could do the most good. The crash of each bottle punctuated the uproar, and the swing doors began banging, tamer souls hurriedly seeking the sunny street. He could keep this up as long as the supply lasted.

A big-hatted cowman, taking matters too seriously, dug out a Dragoon .44 and cocked it in Bishop's direction. Bishop took him up on that. He brushed his coat back and a blue gun barrel flashed dully, spurted brightly, and the big hat flipped. The cowman grabbed for it, and a second bullet cut the brim, an inch from his fingers, and he let it go. He knew when to quit fooling with a gun master. So did several others.

The doors creaked busily. That big devil behind the bar was getting a little severe. He tipped a shot at the pool table. The cue ball went wild and englished all over the baize. When it rolled hobblingly to rest, badly chipped, the Bee Hive was occupied mainly by some Texans and a few unconditioned unfortunates on the floor, including Red Delaney.

An army major appeared from somewhere, stared sternly around, and marched out, snapping, "No more of that, now!" Nobody took notice of him.

Bishop asked the Texans, "What'll you have, gents? I'm in the position to serve anything you want as long as it's whisky."

"Make it whisky." They grinned, and peace and good will returned to the Bee Hive.

The bartender took over the job of serving. Bishop inquired the amount of his bill, and the bartender did some rapid accounting in his head.

"Fifteen hundred dollars squares the damage."

"Okay, thief." Bishop paid. "Somebody hoist Mr. Delaney up to the bar so's he can join us in the next round."

He noticed, through a front window, that the major had halted outside and appeared to be waiting for somebody to come out of the saloon.

The major fidgeted restlessly, darting impatient glances at the swing doors. Bishop saw no possible connection between that and the brawl, though. He had no reason to believe he was the awaited one, either—until the major came close to the window, caught his eye, and beckoned to him.

Bishop had one more drink and left the Bee Hive. The officer fell in step beside him.

"I am Major Jennisk," he stated in his thin, snapping voice.

"My name's Bishop."

"Yes." Major Jennisk nodded. He didn't offer his hand. "I am impressed by the way you handled that mob of ruffians in there. Considerably impressed. Let's go up the hill. I want to talk to you."

Bishop lighted a cigar and said nothing. At a glance he checked off Jennisk as a desk soldier. This soft-skinned man, with his pursy little mouth and piping voice, couldn't be imagined as a field officer leading hard-bitten cavalry, guidons proudly whipping, sabers aloft in the rush of a charge, bugle blaring. His polished boots were unmarked by any wear of stirrup straps. His blues and bright shoulder straps and campaign hat could not remove from him the look of a paunchy businessman.

No mistaking his kind. The Army of the West had a share of them and they ran to type.

Commissions won on the political field; fussy administrative jobs—while the rank and file fought to keep the trails open, fought the feathered tribesmen, trooped half-dead back to the post and rode doggedly out again, cleaned carbines loose in saddle boots.

When well out of Hell's Hundred and walking slowly up the hill toward the fort, Major Jennisk spoke again. "A man of your caliber, Bishop—you're wasting your talents. There are better things than gambling."

Bishop removed his cigar and spat out a flake of tobacco. "Such as?"

"Such as obtaining horses for the army," Jennisk responded promptly. "A worthy and—ah—patriotic occupation, particularly now. The army badly needs them. I have an order to buy up to a thousand head, for General Crook, and Mackenzie, and Miles. Provided, of course, the horses meet requirements. I haven't been able to fill half the order so far, and I am in receipt of—ah—pressing communications in reference to the subject. Hem!"

Again Bishop kept silent, inwardly speculating as to where this was leading.

Jennisk frowned irritably. In a moment he said, "A man came to me a few days ago, saying his crew was camped far down the trail with three hundred good horses. He had come on up to see into the selling prospects. From the way he went about it, I judged he didn't have a clear title to them. But in the light of the army's need, I—ah—decided to stretch a point."

He paused. His sharp round eyes swept sidelong over Bishop's impassively hard face. He cleared his throat and went on. "I offered to buy his horses. I offered him twenty-five dollars a head."

"What's the regular price for army remounts?" inquired Bishop. He knew the answer. His speculations were reaching to conclusions.

Hesitantly Jennisk replied, "Hundred and twenty-five."

Bishop did some mental figuring. He quirked a dark eyebrow at the result. "Hum! Three hundred horses, that price, cost the army thirty-seven thousand an' five hundred dollars. Right? But at twenty-five a head it comes to seven thousand five hundred. Who'd get the thirty thousand? You? Man, there *are* better things than poker! Graft, for one!"

Something distasteful puckered Jennisk's small, loose lips. "I call it business! The army would get its horses, paying no more than the regular price. That fellow would have done well to sell his stolen horses at twenty-five a head." His eyes narrowed. "Damned rascal cursed me and walked out! He'll pay for that!"

"Know his name?"

"Oh—Smith, he said. False, of course." Jennisk brought his eyes around again to Bishop. He declared with slow emphasis, "My offer is still open. Twenty-five dollars a head for those horses. And I don't care who delivers them!"

Bishop shook his head. "Not enough. I'd need to hire a fighting crew—"

"No," Jennisk broke in. "Your crew is already hired. At my expense. They're captained by a buffalo hunter named Hump. They're camped near a place called the Sandhole. Hump is a tough dog, but crazy like most of his breed. I can't rely on him. But I'll have to, unless you go down there and take charge. The job calls for a good man, a man who can handle a bad mob." He gnawed his lower lip and said reluctantly, "Thirty a head."

Bishop reconsidered. Raiding a horse-thief camp didn't clash with his broad-minded principles, and his pockets were light since paying for the Bee Hive damage.

"Forty," he said. "I've got to take along some horse-wise jigger who knows that country down there. Got the right boy in mind, but he's a damned Texan an' I'll have to offer him more'n a few dimes."

"Thirty-five!"

"Major, you've bought three hundred horses for the Army of the United States of America—a worthy an' patriotic occupation!"

Chapter Two: CRAZED ALLIES

RIDING SOUTH down the last stretch of Plum Creek to the Guadalupe River, Red Delaney remarked to Bishop that they would soon be reaching the Sandhole. Red said it wistfully. He had not given up the idea of excavating Uncle Wesley and various other defuncts, and giving them all decent burial. With profit.

But the Sandhole held no interest for Bishop. Its corpses could forever lie undisturbed, as far as he was concerned. Their cash value was speculative, probably nil. He dealt as a rule in ventures more positive of results, such as drawing to three jacks and a kicker, himself dealing. Still, the Sandhole meant meeting up soon with the Hump gang. He allowed himself to become interested to that extent, meantime deploring his dwindling stock of cigars.

Along here the trail grooved an immensely wide and shallow ditch, a dry brown scar cut by north-bound Texas herds. Skulls and ribbed skeletons of cows and horses, toothed bare by coyotes, marked this road of march. At day's-travel spaces were the great bare patches of the bedding grounds with their broken monuments of abandoned wagons— where the Texas longhorn outfits had camped for a night.

"It wouldn't be much work," Red said, deep in his thoughts, "to get 'em out. Plain diggin', that's all. Uncle Wesley, I bet, was weighed down with all o' fifty thousand—"

"To hell with your uncle!" growled Bishop. Four days in the saddle and he had enough of this affair. He was cogitating ways to better it. Jennisk would go to forty. Fifty. Sixty? Jennisk had to fill his order. Jennisk was hungry for his graft. Seventy or eighty? Hell, no man owed any loyalty to a shifty jasper like Jennisk. That toad.

Red grinned and said, "Okay, friend! But I know what I'll do with this stake, if I get it." He broke that off. "Strangers ahead!" he warned—unnecessarily, Bishop having already noted, counted, and sized up the riders coming forth to meet them.

A down-at-heel crew, this. They wore blackened tatters of buckskins and rode rib-raw Indian ponies. But all carried a shining new Henry repeating rifle slung across the saddle, and a belted pistol and long skinning-knife. Frowzy and unwashed, most of them wore dirty head rags to hold back their unkempt hair.

"Phew!" Red breathed. "What hell's door did this pack o' wolves break out of?"

Bishop said, a cold detachment in his voice, "Hump's crew, I guess." And then in irony: "If that big duck in front is Hump, your luck's still out! I croppered him in Hell's Hundred, an' I doubt he's ready to overlook it."

"Your luck, too, Mr. Bishop, seems to have slipped!"

"On this deal, Mr. Delaney, I didn't shuffle the cards."

Bishop's tone carried no hint of worry, but his eyes glimmered like tarnished silver wiped across by a reflection of flame. This was a bad break. By their looks the oncoming rabble had been getting in some hard drinking lately.

They met on the cattle-carved trail and pulled to a stand, without a word or sign of greeting. Into Hump's gross face washed a look of recognition, swiftly followed by scowling rage. His right hand slid down, while he wrenched his pony broadside, and by that motion he made clear his intention. It was a drunken maneuver.

Bishop drawled harshly, "Wup-snub it!" And he brushed back his coat. He watched until that groping paw slowly came up empty, and he drew out a folded paper. "This is for you, if you're Hump. And if you can read."

Hump could read, after a fashion. His thick lips worked on the words of Jennisk's brief message. He raised a wildly bitter glare.

"Says you're cap'n!" Intolerable resentment gusted a curse from him. His cutthroat gang leaned forward, glowering, catching his temper, without comprehension of its cause. *"You!"*

"Right!" said Bishop, and he, too, leaned forward in his saddle. A startlingly satanic smile creased his dark face. "Me!" He knew the breed of badman he had to deal with, and was gambling for prompt dominance. Nothing less would do. "You don't like it? If that's the case, we'll iron your objections out right now!"

Red Delaney held his breath. Hump's gang numbered seventeen; well armed, made into savages by barbarous living and drink and natural bent. Brush-thugs. And there sat Rogue Bishop, smiling his devil's smile, throwing arrogant challenge at their leader. It was enough to make the imps of chance weep.

And yet, his crazed glare dimming, Hump sighed heavily and looked away from Bishop's eyes. The fury banked for the time, he muttered raggedly, "I don't like it, but if the major says so—"

Bishop demanded at once, "Where's the horse-thief outfit?"

Hump pointed his chin downriver. "This side, a rifle shot b'low Sandhole, 'bout. They don't know yet we're here."

"They'll know tonight!"

"What? Not till I git more men. That's a border outfit. Tough. They know their business."

"So do I," said Bishop. He stared out the black, bloodshot eyes. "I'm giving orders, Hump. First we'll take a look at their camp. Push on!"

Riding with Bishop behind the shabby desperadoes, Red exclaimed hushedly, "Man, oh, man! The pick of a thorny crop! An' we work with 'em? I'd as lief prance barefoot in a nest o' rattlers! Notice the new rifles?"

Bishop nodded, thinking of Hump's wagon rocking down through the street of Hell's Hundred. Without doubt, its canvas-covered load had been firearms and whisky, supplied by Jennisk, probably at government expense.

Hump's venom spread out and settled into the brute minds of his followers. They kept fiddling with those new .44 Henry rifles and peering back at Bishop and Red—behavior most impolite in Western country. Bishop began building up a definite dislike for Jennisk.

As for Red, he tugged his holster forward, yanked his battered Stetson down firmly, and mumbled something about if only Uncle Wesley could see him now. So they passed the Sandhole and the mushroom-shaped rock called Crazy Chisera Butte, and drifted carefully in under the cottonwoods along the Guadalupe River.

The Smith horse-thief outfit had picked a good site for a camp. It was a long clear meadow running up over a rise at the next bend of the river, flanked by thick brush. The men didn't need to spend much time keeping the band of horses from straying.

They appeared to be unhurriedly packing up, preparing to break camp. They were big-hatted, lean men, and moved with that languid agility of riders of the border country where heat imposed economy of action. They would hit the trail *mañana.* No rush. *Poco tiempo*—you lived longer.

Bishop watched for a minute from the cottonwoods, then told Hump, "Take your mob and circle wide around. Time it so you edge in at sundown. The moon will come up 'bout an hour later. In that hour, while it's dark, we get those horses. I'll fire twice, for signal. You all sing out like the law, and shoot high, but stay in cover. Those *hombres* are way off their home range, and it's a fair bet they'll scoot if they think you're Rangers or a posse o' deputies. So don't let 'em see you, or they won't be fooled worth a damn!"

Hump lifted a corner of his upper lip. "An' what'll you two be doin'?"

"We'll be way forward on the bottom slope o' that meadow," said Bishop, "ready to turn back any who might head north to give us trouble later on the trail. Now get goin'—an' don't botch the trick!"

His cool presumption, necessary and dangerous, lighted a repetition of the wild glare. Hump sucked in a noisy breath. His fingers spoked out and stiffly clawed air. Then he whirled around and grunted to the listening group, and he and they drifted off, Apache-quiet.

When they were gone, like malevolent ghosts, Red muttered, "And after this—then what? They'll knife us, first chance!"

"If we give 'em the chance," agreed Bishop. "We'll try not to do that."

There were hours to wait before dark. They rode part way back to the Sandhole, picketed their horses and aired the saddles, and ate scraps of dried beef. No coffee. A fire was out of the question. They sneaked a smoke, though, squatting on their heels tiredly after the long trek down from Fort Griffin. On that trek Red had come to know the gun fighter's long silences and to respect them, and he didn't speak.

At last Bishop crushed an inch of burning cigar into the earth thoroughly and murmured, "Let's go, Red."

That casually natural use of his nickname was quietly pleasing to Red. He realized the caliber of company he was in. It meant something to have this self-contained lone wolf of a man call him Red without thinking of it.

Red responded, rising, "Okay." Then, feeling that this was not enough: "I'm ready, Rogue."

They left their horses on picket and went afoot to the spot where Hump had parted from them, and from there crawled forward to the bottom of the sloping meadow. A patch of dwarf willows tempted them on farther, and they crept in, and waited. Voices came down to them, and they heard somebody breaking deadwood. Those sounds sank to comfortable murmuring around a cookfire torched against the graying sundown. The western glow faded swiftly toward the brief twilight that in twenty minutes would be blackness.

Twenty minutes to go. Red glanced at Bishop for some sign of strain, and saw only a calm meditation. Chewing on a fresh cigar, unlighted, Bishop was passing the time in trimming a broken fingernail with his clasp knife.

Red rolled his shoulders restlessly. Horses were his line. He could take care of himself, but trouble was not his trade, as it was with Bishop. This hawk-faced gun master simply accepted peril as a normal part of his life, a gambling hazard.

With the light yet a deep blue-gray, Bishop was still scraping his fingernail when mischief broke loose. At the first shuddering yell he sprang up—and saw disaster. It caught him unready; yet he could not blame himself for that. All logical prophecy had to be predicated upon sanity, and the keenest intelligence could not predict the actions of a whisky-sodden maniac.

Mounted men—Hump's ragged riders—dashed out at the horse herd. Yelling, waving blankets, they streamed against the sky line. For one moment they were howling demons bursting through the gloom, all the startled horses strained up and point-eared. Then abruptly the mad confusion— the whole horse herd thundering downhill in panic, men running from the cookfire. The horses smashed through the camp and came charging on, the roar of them drowning the yells, shouts, shots. They formed a hurtling mass calculated to trample to shreds any live thing in their path.

Bishop and Red turned and ran, their only thought to reach their picketed mounts ahead of the oncoming horde. It was a forlorn bet. They heard the hoofs crash through the dwarf willows behind them, and they both spun around. Red squalled, waving his arms, while Bishop blazed two guns empty over the bobbing wave of heads.

The stampeded band split and passed them, came together again, and boomed on. Their dust fouled the air. Half blinded, coughing and choking, the two men pushed on in the wake of it, knowing what to expect from this insane catastrophe. There was no hope of finding their horses waiting. Soon, Red's desperate laugh and flinging gesture put the final stamp on it.

Where they had picketed there was nothing but hoof-scuffed emptiness. Their mounts had snapped ropes and gone bolting off when the frenzied bunch came slamming through the dusk. Far up ahead the drumming fell to a splashing rattle. The horses had struck the river somewhere and were churning across, in nightmare fear of the howling spooks.

With the decline of that racket the descending night grew relatively quiet. Bishop and Red stood listening. Scattered shots carried the news that the border men had not fled far. The firing suddenly increased, and now there intruded the rocking thump of riders tearing down the open meadow.

Hump's rabble or the border men, it made little difference.

Bishop strode off fast. There were times when a man hunted cover, if he had any sense, and this was one of them. Red shared that unspoken opinion.

They hurried to the Sandhole and crunched across it to the big mushroomed finger of rock. The fringe of the horse herd had swerved this way and broken the surface crust. Boot tracks in the pounded sand would be hard to pick out in the near-darkness. They clambered up onto the top of Crazy Chisera Butte, lay flat with guns drawn, and Red whispered wryly that this would be a handy time for the river to overflow and sink those coming riders.

The riders were some of Hump's gang. They hauled in close to the rock, and one of them got down to examine the sand. But it was too dark now for him to read anything from the track, and he cursed and remounted. After some muttering indecision they rode back toward the sound of gunfire.

Red wiped his face on his sleeve. "Guess they'll wait for moonlight, eh? Or maybe till morning, if that Smith outfit keeps 'em busy tonight. Man, did those horses run! Just like they knew exactly where they were going. Well—it's farewell to *that* stake! You sure took on a sweet bargain, mah fren'! Don't you reckon, now, just between us, that diggin' sand might've been easier?"

Bishop's eyes glinted in the dark. "One more reference to your lamented uncle, an' you'll join him in peace everlasting!" The gun master wasn't in a good humor. This rampaging night wrecked the promise of profit. Worse, he was set afoot—a shameful bobble for a man with self-respect. "Let's get off this damn rock an' hunt our horses."

Red brought up a remark concerning the hunting of needles in a haystack. "They're miles off in any direction 'cept up, an' still going! Our saddles have slipped under their bellies, an'—"

"You got a brighter idea?" Bishop growled.

Red hadn't, so they climbed off the rock and headed in the direction taken by the runaway horse herd, saying no more because their tempers wouldn't stand anything like argument. The moon crept up and laid long shadows while they trudged, and at last they met the river where it bent the trail.

Here the low bank was freshly tramped to mud. On the far side reared a barrier of flat-topped cliffs sheering a plateau. In the slanted moonlight the curve of the river ran, a great silver bow, disciplined by the cliffs and the contour of the land. It spread wide, and for that reason could be judged shallow. The horses had forded it.

Bishop and Red unbuckled gun belts and neck-slung them and started wading. There was a chance that the horses had been brought to halt somewhere along the foot of the cliffs yonder.

Against the moon-silvered surface of the river the two men threshed blackly like bears in brittle-bush. A rifle spanged sharply down at them, twice. Two bullets sprayed water just before them. While the echoes of the shots rattled up and down the river, Red floundered back to the muddy bank, talking half aloud to himself. There, breathing hard, he looked around at Bishop.

Standing waist-deep in water, Bishop held the cliffs under dour inspection. He splashed onward a couple of steps. The rifle lashed a third shot that plonked narrowly to his left. He backed, joined Red in the mud. They exchanged stiff glances. They had to get hold of horses before morning.

Bishop said, "I got him spotted!" and his voice was low and wicked. "You keep him busy till I get him!"

He slipped off and vanished, leaving Red alone. A fresh outburst of gunfire crackled from the direction of the meadow. Hump and his raiders had stirred up hell there with their mad prank. Those soft-spoken men from the Rio Grande had elected to stick around and make a fight of it. The browned and sun-baked *vaqueros* didn't scare so easily, and had most likely managed to save some of the saddle mounts of their *remuda*. Tomorrow they or the buffalo tramps, whichever crew won out, would be hard on the trail of that runaway fortune in horses.

Chapter Three: CHISERA

BELOW THE BEND Bishop gave a minute to search the night around him with his eyes and ears. The gunfire was receding, falling to a muffled spatter, and he judged that the fight had shifted out of the open meadow and deep into the brush. One crew, then, was retreating south, the other in pursuit.

Red's gun blared, upriver, promptly answered by a rifle shot and the screech of a bullet. Satisfied that the sharpshooter had not changed position, Bishop eased into the river and worked quietly over toward the shadow-blackened wall of cliffs. The cliffs, he found, did not reach to the water's edge as had appeared from the other side, nor were they as sheer. Along here they shelved brokenly and were veined with narrow arroyos, and at the foot ran a beach of stony gravel so low that most of it was wet.

He tugged off his boots and up-ended them, and for a while he sat there on the wet gravel, letting them drain. Red paid out another shell, and right on time the rifle chipped in.

Soaked to the chest, Bishop began to grow chilled in the night's slow breeze. He wrung some water from his clothes and put his boots on. His discomfort hardened his intentions against that high-placed sharpshooter. Buckling on his gun belts, he straightway set out to tackle the cliff. No doubt there was somewhere a handier route, but he hadn't time to waste looking for it.

The arroyos were what made a possible task of scaling the cliff. They bent and angled, one into another, but always they webbed upward. At last he crawled out on top and considered taking off his boots again. Climbing in wet boots was brutal on a lifelong horseman. He scowled, predicting blisters. Dammit, Achilles, that jigger with only one vulnerable heel, didn't know when he was well off.

The plateau spread out before him, an immense grass-furred plain, its eastern limits lost in a moonlit mystery of space. These river-edged cliffs were an escarpment, a giant step onto a higher level of ground. Bishop sent a searching stare along the rim. He could pick out nothing worth special notice, and had to wait till Red got off a blind shot. Then he spied the flash of the answering rifle and he marked that spot.

He prowled a wide half-circle to bring him around to it. The sun-cured little seed stems of grama grass swished whisperingly on his boots, for he walked upright on the approach. So he stepped high and gently, and came up in silence behind a figure lying flat over a leveled rifle.

A small figure, this. But size meant nothing. Some of the deadliest killers were little men. Possession of a good gun, plus ability in using it, made them big. This one wore buckskins and beaded moccasins, and a cattleman's big hat. Likely a half-breed, brush-raised and snaky, hungering to kill somebody for the gloating satisfaction of it.

Bishop stooped noiselessly over the prone figure. With considerable satisfaction of his own he snapped a sinewy grip on an ankle. As if tailing a calf, he jerked upright and whirled the shooter upside-down. It fetched a terror-stricken yelp. The rifle went sliding over the edge of the cliff to a long drop down.

"Okay, runt!" he rasped, catching the other kicking foot. "Sing up when you hit the river—so I'll know you got there all right!" He started a swinging motion, his long legs braced.

His wriggling captive pealed an unmanly scream. The tone of it caused him to lessen the swinging. He took the trouble to tip his head and bend a frowning inspection to the screamer.

The big hat had fallen off and followed the rifle a thousand feet down. Long hair swept the ground, unusual only for its fair color. And, besides the face, there were a couple of other physical conformations indicating positively that this was not a man.

Bishop released both ankles on the back-swing, muttering irritably, "All that damn climbin' to catch a bit of a girl!"

The girl sort of rolled to a half-sitting position,

her arms stretched out behind her, staring up into his forbidding face. She began edging off, but froze motionless when he lowered a glance at her. He was annoyed. He showed it. His feet hurt—the only tender parts of his tough anatomy.

Red had heard and glimpsed something of that encounter on the cliff. He shouted, "Hey, Rogue, did you get the son of a gun?"

"It's no son!" Bishop called down shortly.

"What? Sun?" Red was confused. "Well, the moon's as bright as— Say, you all right? Seen anything o' the horses?"

"Just a filly! But it's a beginnin'!"

"Huh? Hey, I better come up! You sure you're all right?"

Ignoring the question, Bishop sat down. He got his boots off. He lighted a cigar. The girl looked on. She was pulling herself together. But she failed to respond when he—the wire of his temper relaxing under the soothing influence of foot comfort and strong tobacco—commented that moccasins maybe had their good points. He would wear moccasins if ever he made a habit of wading wet rivers and climbing cliffs, which Lord forbid.

About the time the cigar was a stub and the unlovely feet re-shod, Red showed up. Red came hurrying along the rim of the cliff, all wet and dirty and in a foul humor, and at once he snarled at the person who sat facing Bishop, "Durn you,

I'll whip your—" and then, seeing closer—
"H'm?"

The girl leaped up. In the moonlight she was a
sudden flare of color, her hair a flung-back stream
of polished bronze, her clear eyes blazing, taut
dignity in every line of her firmly rounded little
figure.

"You will *what?*" She actually advanced on
Red. "Why, you dirty horse thief—get off my
ranch!"

She hadn't talked like that to Bishop, who had
all but flung her into the river.

Taking upon himself the role of kindly umpire,
Bishop chided Red gravely, "Watch your
language, man! This young lady is—well—a lady.
Not the kind you're used to." To the girl he said
confidentially, "Just a roughneck. Doesn't know
any better. I give you my personal guarantee I
won't let him come near you."

Inasmuch as Red was now shying off like an
abashed stripling at his first box-lunch social, the
guarantee wasn't necessary; but it rang a
chivalrous note of fine old Southern gallantry.
Rogue Bishop was no more a Southern gentleman
than he was a Chinese, but he knew the rules.

Red gulped, "Sorry! Beg pardon, ma'am! I—I
sure didn't expect to find any lady around here!"

"You didn't, Red," Bishop assured him. "I did."

"B—But what's the lady doing here, Rogue?"

"That's an intimate question that I haven't been

so bold as to ask. But now you've brought it up"—Bishop bowed his head to the girl—"my name is Bishop. That busted mustanger calls himself Delaney, which may be his right name for all I know. We are looking for our horses, Miss—ah—Miss—"

"Donavon," she supplied. Something in the big man's tone, or his courtesy, brought her to add, "Sera Donavon."

"Sarah?" Red took it up brightly, anxious to redeem himself. "Well, now, that was the name of my Uncle Wesley's favorite wife. My favorite, I mean. His third wife. She was the cutest little button." He was about to splice that fact into a happy knot of mutual regard, but the girl cut him off.

"No," she said coldly. "Not Sarah. I don't like that name. My name is Sera. S-e-r-a. Can you spell? Mr. Bishop can, I'm sure. Please explain it to your man, Mr. Bishop, will you?"

"I don't know that I can get it through his thick head," said Bishop. "He's ignorant. He doesn't know Spanish names."

"My name isn't Spanish," she said. "Sera is short for Chisera."

"Uh?" Red blurted. "*Chisera!*"

The blank silence that followed was broken by Bishop. "My illiterate *segundo* is thinking you're up on the wrong rock," he explained tolerantly to the girl. "Also, you're not—uh—dressed according to specifications. He's got a single-track mind. Prob'ly takes after his uncle."

Sera Donavon evidently knew the lurid legend of Crazy Chisera Butte. Her face crimsoned. She said with great distinctness, "My parents didn't know the meaning of the name, when they gave it to me. They thought it a pretty name. I shortened it after I learned it was Indian for 'witch.'"

"And so," Bishop suggested, "that left you only a little bit of a witch!" The glint of humor in his eyes made the remark acceptable. He asked in the same moderate and slightly ironic tone, "Do you gen'rally shoot at folks you don't know? We're hunting our runaway horses, is all. Those were scare-off shots you banged off at us. Wouldn't surprise me if you could have hit us, if you'd tried."

"I can shoot," she agreed quietly. "My father taught me, after we settled here. I thought you were from an outlaw gang of buffalo tramps who passed by today. If your horses are with the others that came on over a while ago, they won't stray far. What was all that shooting I heard down the river? That was what brought me out on guard. Did Mr. Smith have trouble with that gang?"

Bishop said, "Some," and sent Red a rapid glance and changed the subject. "What kind o' ranch have you got here?"

"Didn't Mr. Smith tell you?" The girl showed some surprise.

"Mr. Smith didn't get much chance to talk with us before the stampede—and even less after it started."

"Oh. Why, this is a horse ranch. My father and I came here from Valverde, after my mother died. Almost any trail-herd outfit, by the time it has traveled up this far, will have a few sick horses in the *remuda*. Dad traded for them. Some he sold, after he got them into sound shape. But he kept the best. He worked very hard. Pretty soon, he said, there would be a high demand for army remounts."

"Smart head!" commended Red heartily. "What I did, though, I crossed good stock to picked broncs and got—"

"Snub it!" interrupted Bishop. To him a horse was a handy means of getting from here to yonder when such getting was called for. He wasn't a bit interested in the breeding and training of the beast. It required hard work and patience—two details of no compelling value in his fast life. He asked the girl, "Where's your dad?"

She answered, "Thieves ambushed him last fall when he was taking some horses up the trail to sell. They killed him. He was a good man."

Bishop inclined his head and touched his hat, generously willing to grant that the unlucky Mr. Donavon had been a good man within his scope. "So your folks have passed on to a better world," he observed, thinking of horses at $125 per head, delivered. "You got a crew?"

"I had five good Cherokee riders," Sera Donavon told him, "but there was no money to pay them, so I let them go." She added ruefully, "I'm not the horse trader my dad was. He could always raise some money." Then brightening. "But I have a fortune in fine horses, if I can get them up to Fort Griffin."

Red burst out, "Lord, girl! You mean you're all alone here?"

She looked at him. Crisply, she retorted, "Being alone is better than having unwelcome visitors!"

"An' that means you, son!" murmured Bishop to Red. "Button up your unwelcome mug, will you? I'll handle this!"

The expression on Red's face betrayed his burning indignation. Red was brought up on the Texas tradition of punctilious respect toward all women. It galled him to play bad dog-in-leash to a notorious hard case whose designs, he darkly suspected, were as sinister as those of a lobo stalking a lamb. There wasn't a thing he could do about it now, either. Rogue Bishop had won the inside track and was playing it for all it was worth.

Under Bishop's deceptively idle questioning Sera Donavon let it be known that the Donavon horse ranch was blessed with a perfect location. Down the river there was a passable road leading up onto the grassed plateau. The river there ran deep. You had to cross hereabouts at the ford, then follow down the strip of gravel bank, if you knew the way. The Donavon house stood at the top of that hidden road.

Sera's father had known what he wanted, and he had found it—dependable grass and water, the range so located that it could be easily guarded from the tramps and outlaws and brush-thugs who roamed the trail. About the only thing he had failed to provide against was his own sudden death.

"My man and I will see you safe home," Bishop told Sera courteously. "Those buffalo beauties are too busy to ford the river tonight. I'll appreciate, if you insist, some hot coffee and a fire to dry by. I'll take the coffee black. With a dash of whisky, please, for the sake of my chest."

Red wanted the same. But he would have waited for a proper invitation, if it meant shivering all night. Where he was raised men just didn't move in like that on a young lady. He eyed Bishop askance, searching him for nefarious intentions. Red could get along with a badman, and even get to liking him, but the presence of a girl—with horses—canceled out any such masculine friendship. He had no illusions about Rogue Bishop.

And Bishop, quite aware of the trend Red's mind was on, drew his wide lips straighter and said ever so gently, "Come on, Red, if you want."

Two meanings edged his offer. He, more blindingly sudden than Red, could revoke a

306

friendship as soon as it began to sour, and dissolve it in gun smoke if necessary. He recognized the challenge and distrust in Red's eyes, and it was his way to meet aggression head-on for prompt settlement.

Under the pale, cold stare, Red tightened up visibly. He glanced at Sera, to catch her reaction to the veteran long rider's cool presumption.

Evidently sensing the undercurrent of sharp discord, Sera murmured a hurried invitation and set off at once south along the rim of the cliff. The two men followed, pacing well apart, each in meditative silence.

As Sera had described, the Donavon house crowned the crest of a road that ran up a deep pass crookedly splitting the cliff. It was large and comfortable, log-built. As well as guarding the pass, it commanded a view of the high plateau. Farther back were some outbuildings—barn, bunkhouse, stables—and beyond them the horse corrals. The only difference between this and a going concern was the unnatural hush, like that of a ghost town not yet in decay.

Bishop built a roaring fire in the main room, and while he and Red spread out to steam, Sera busied herself in the kitchen. Moving over to peer in at the girl after a while, Bishop nodded approval. She was preparing not only coffee but a hot meal. She was okay. Strikingly pretty and attractive, too, although rather on the small side. A man could search long and do much worse. And she surely did need a good man to take her in hand and keep her out of trouble. A girl like that, foolishly trying to go it alone—damned shame. Time something was done about it.

Returning to the fire, Bishop found Red watching him. He grunted a blunt "Well?"

Red made no response. But from his look Bishop guessed that Red, too, was growing more than casually interested in Sera's present and future welfare. These Texans certainly did take an earnest stand on such matters. It might become desirable, Bishop mused, to toss Red down the cliff before this thing got really serious.

Then Sera came in from the kitchen to serve the food, and Bishop took his thoughts off trivialities.

Chapter Four: LOOT ON THE HOOF

THE MORNING BROUGHT a change of affairs. It started with Red's finding of a razor that had belonged to Mr. Donavon and scraping off his rusty bristle. The instant Bishop laid eyes on him, at breakfast, he knew that he had underestimated the Texan's crafty resourcefulness. He, master of bland guile, had been dirtily double-crossed by an amateur, while he slept.

Besides shaving practically to the bone, Red had washed and scrubbed himself pink. He had cleaned the mud from his clothes. He had combed his hair. In the morning's bright light he flaunted a slick freshness. Not handsome, the dog, but definitely clean and wholesome. Anything but a frowzy roughneck.

With darting energy and fine examples of Southern chivalry, Red swooped forward and drew out Sera's chair for her, and alertly helped her to coffee and everything else on the table before she knew she wanted it. Astonished, Sera thanked him and kept glancing at him all through breakfast.

Blasted caperings, Bishop thought dourly. By contrast, in the pure light of morning he looked what he was—a tough gun-slinging gambler seasoned with faithless cynicism and biting violence. Any day was wrong for him that didn't begin with a bracer compounded of black coffee fortified with 100-proof bourbon, followed by six inches of cigar, preferably Mexican.

This new day, bereft of bourbon, out of cigars, Rogue Bishop was not at his best. The insolent sunlight picked out pitilessly the furrows from beaked nostrils to mouth—the leather skin, deepset eyes, lean jaw—hard features that the moonlight last night had kindly softened.

He didn't eat much breakfast. It was nourishing food, he supposed, but who wanted to astound his innards this early? Finding a cigar butt in his breast pocket, he clamped it between strong teeth, heaved back his chair and growled a word, and stalked outside, leaving Sera and Red in an animated discussion that had something to do with horse-breeding and related subjects.

"Oh, but look, Red!" Already she was calling him Red—that busted horse nurse. "When you mate a Morgan to a mustang—"

Where in hell did a girl pick up such talk? This young upstart crop knew more than was good for them. Chewing on the cigar butt, Bishop inspected the outside scenery. He judged it inferior to most that he had known. Not one roadhouse saloon in sight. A forsaken stretch of wilderness, this, barren of anything in the way of decent civilized trappings except for this empty-handed Donavon ranch.

After some time Red came out of the house. He

went walking brightly around, finally heading over to the corrals. He didn't appear so spright and perk when he came back.

Confronting Bishop in the yard, Red muttered harriedly, "Hey, something's not right here!"

Something, Bishop agreed, wasn't. He eyed Red pointedly. Red, however, was not referring to himself.

"Rogue, they's a couple hundred horses grazing loose, beyond the corrals. They're all colors. Duns, bays, what-all. Our two are with 'em. Still got the saddles on."

"What's wrong with that?"

"It's awful strange how that stampeding bunch found the way straight here. But that's not all. In the corrals are about three hundred head more. All sorrels, those, with white stockings, and all the same brand—small D on the left flank."

Bishop shrugged. "The Donavon brand, I guess."

"No," Red said. "The Delaney brand—*my* brand! I told you how I was cleaned out by stampeders. I told you I was hanging round Fort Griffin watching for those stampeders to show up some day with my horses. Remember?"

Bishop remembered, and coupled it to another remembrance. He heard Red whisper dismally to himself, "Chisera! Could it be, after all, that she's really—"

"About the time your much-married uncle was allegedly lured to his grave by an undraped

311

woman," observed Bishop, "this girl was maybe ten years old. Still," he conceded after a moment of reflection, "she might now be sort of followin' the example o' that Indian witchwoman, in a big way. The witch only got a horse or two at a time. Maybe our Sera likes to get 'em by the bunch."

"No, it's not possible!" Red argued. He wasn't happy, for a man who had found his stolen horse herd. "She's straight, I could swear. Besides, she's Donavon's daughter, and—"

"So she says!" Bishop shook his head. "Where's the proof? For all you know, she might've come here an' stood up an' dazzled Donavon an' his crew into diving off the cliff!"

That, Red's bemused look conveyed, was not impossible.

"She's acquainted with that boss horse thief who calls himself Smith," Bishop pursued, privately enjoying a measure of sardonic amusement at Red's expense. "It was the mixed bunch of horses he was holding. Strange, all right, how they ran straight for this range. How d'you figure your stolen herd of sorrels got penned up here on a hidden ranch where strangers ain't welcome?"

"Don't know," Red admitted.

Neither did Bishop know, exactly. But he took a broad-minded view of the circumstance. They weren't his horses.

Sera came out to the front door and called, "Did you find your horses with Mr. Smith's?"

Transferring his regard to a lone cloud in the blue sky, Bishop left it to Red to grapple with that question and get himself in bad. It was remarkable what advantages a man often gained by simply keeping his trap shut at the right time. Out of a corner of his eye Bishop watched Red tramp slowly to the house.

There went a Texan whose plain-speaking tongue was about to land him in a stew. Any girl able to lie up on a cliff, alone, planting bullets accurately within splashing distance of unwelcome strangers, could certainly be counted on to light a fire under a man rash enough to try outtalking her. There went a cooked duck.

"Red! Is something wrong?" She could tell from Red's face that something was way out of kilter. Bishop couldn't credit her with any amazing feminine intuition on that score. Red's expression was a plain giveaway to a blind mule.

Red halted before her, at lower level than the doorstep—his first error. Right away he hung his foot in his mouth by demanding, "How did my stolen sorrels get penned up here on a hidden ranch where strangers ain't—uh—h'm?"

"H'm?" said Sera.

Letting the lone cloud go its way, Bishop scratched and touched a match to his cigar butt. This was a promising start. Now let the fireworks explode. Let sizzling hostility's smoke becloud the underhanded trick of shaving before breakfast.

313

Doggedly, Red said to Sera, "Our two horses are with the loose bunch, yes. The mixed bunch that stampeded last night and ran straight here. Yes, ma'am." He was trying painfully hard to strike a middle course, to be neutral, logical. And he wasn't succeeding, because his words lacked the trim of subtlety. "But what I want to know is, how did those D-brand sorrels get there?"

The girl stiffened immediately. Her small figure filled the soft buckskin shirt. "Those are my horses," she answered, quietly and distinctly. Red's question was out of line, one that could rouse trouble among men.

Red would have known better, had Sera been a man. He would have dropped a careful hint, kept his right hand dangling, and given room for compromise. Such rules of armed etiquette, however, did not apply to a girl. Rattled, Red stuck his foot in deeper.

"Where'd you get them, please?"

Sera's eyes gained a steady blaze. "I traded for them."

Somebody on horseback was ascending the steep road up from the river. The crooked pass hid him, but the quick-climbing hoofs rolled stones and a champed bridle bit clinked faintly. Bishop crossed to a patch of *chamiso* brush on the edge of the yard, fronting the house, and sank to his heels to wait for whoever might crop up. Red was too flustered to hear those slight sounds on the road,

314

and it seemed a pity to distract him from the splendid job he was doing of skinning himself.

"Who did you trade 'em off?" Red asked, after a miserable pause. "That Smith horse-thief outfit?" It was a sorry way to couch the query.

He began a stammering scramble for words that were less offensive, but Sera didn't allow him time to arrange them. The little mistress of the Donavon ranch was thoroughly angry, brutally stripped of her softened feeling for this busted Texas horse raiser.

From where she stood in the doorway of the house, Sera Donavon could see down into the pass. She gazed beyond Red at the man now riding into sight around the last bend, and said icily, "Mr. Smith will answer you for me!"

And behind the gold bloom of *chamiso* Bishop brushed a hand under his coat, muttering, "Well, by Jupiter—his name *is* Smith!"

He recognized that oncoming rider; knew him as one of the many half-forgotten ghosts of wild old days when youth flared a brilliant flame and reckless daring spat in the face of death. A frolicking time of fortune, that, till law and the army trooped in. The survivors still at large were now mostly bartenders, livery flunks, taciturn drunks, and drifters—here and there a hard-bitten gambler, a gunslinger too wise to trap, or an out-and-out badman not yet caught and hanged.

Of the old wild-bunch breed, few could lay

claim to a tougher record than Mr. Smith—
Angelito Smith. Below the Rio Grande his name
was pronounced *An-hell-eeto Smeet.* Above, it
was just Smith. On both sides, and his blood
came from both, the mention of "Little Angel"
identified him. It was the name that appeared on
most of the dodger bills, in bold print at the top.

Up the Donavon pass he rode, the neat little
man. He was slim, wiry, a dandy in dapper silk
shirt—white, with pearl buttons—tight pants of
fawn twill, black bony-skin jacket, and a tall
Mexican sombrero heavily brocaded in silver
scrolls. A pair of bone-handled guns, laced down
in a broad buscadero belt containing two rows of
looped shells, bobbed gently as he rode up to the
house. He was a dude from the original chip. Even
his boots bore the hand-stitched decoration of the
Mexican eagle and the Texas Lone Star.

"The son of a witch!" muttered Bishop behind
the *chamiso.* "Looks like he's doin' even better'n
me!"

Mr. Smith reined in his fine black horse before
the house. He swept off his sombrero and bowed
low in the saddle to Sera, his dark eyes meantime
measuring Red Delaney, the stranger.

"Good morning, Miss Donavon—and such a
beautiful morning!" he intoned. His voice was a
caress, deep and sincere, with a mere tinge of
accent. He lowered long lashes over glowing eyes,
in tribute to a loved princess.

He was the same as ever, Bishop thought. The same low-down, conniving coyote. The same whip-brained little cuss who could dazzle any woman and outwit most men. It was no wonder that Sera, so desperately alone, referred to him as though he represented shining virtue in a bad world. Mr. Smith had evidently not yet bared his claws, for some reason.

He asked her, holding his sombrero to his chest, "Did the horses come up here last night? I hope you were not too disturbed. We had some trouble at the camp."

"Yes, they're here, Mr. Smith," Sera told him. "They came running right back to their old range. But this—" she hesitated—"this gentleman is asking questions about the sorrels you traded to me for them."

"Questions? He insults you—*you,* Miss Donavon—with questions?" Smith bent a stern look at Red. "Who are you?"

Red said, "My name's Delaney an' I'm from Refugio. That mean anything to you?"

Smith shrugged. "It means nothing," he replied. But the shrug served a purpose, executed with the lightning deftness of a sleight-of-hand artist. The gun was gone from his right holster. It was in his hand, covered by the sombrero. Red didn't see it, nor did the girl. Bishop, behind the *chamiso* and rearward of Smith, did, and grinned in recollection of that border trick.

Unaware of blundering straight to suicide, Red said, "The sorrels carry my brand. I didn't sell or trade 'em off. They were stolen from me an' my crew, on a dark night, by some unknown gang of stampeders who all we saw of 'em was big Mexkin hats—like yours!"

Smith glanced down at his sombrero, held against his chest. His thumb was easing back the hammer of the hidden gun.

"For such a very serious charge," he stated, "you should produce proof, Mr.—ah—Delay!"

Red snorted, "I can! Everybody down in Refugio knows a Delaney horse. I bred up that strain. My brand's registered. In my pocket I've got the registry papers on every sorrel horse in those corrals! That's where you slipped, when you stole 'em!"

"In your pocket? Ah!" Smith's cough covered the final click of the hammer. He would not shoot a hole through the expensive sombrero. He was about to show his claws.

Bishop rose up from the *chamiso*, drawling, "What size hat do you wear these days, Smeet? That'n looks pretty big from here."

Smith twisted around swiftly in his saddle. His dark eyes stabbed at Bishop, strolling across the yard, coat thrown open and hands resting on his hips. With recognition of that tall figure, Smith exclaimed incredulously:

"*Por Dios*! Begod, it's you, Rogue!"

"Me it is," assented Bishop. "Long time no see, Smeet. Got a cigar on you?"

For a short spell Smith watched him coming forward. A dark anticipation rippled over his face, and vanished. To meet Bishop on even terms required reining his horse around; Bishop would not allow that, if the hands on hips meant anything. Smith juggled his gun back into its holster and flashed a smile. He and Bishop had not always got along too well, but it was best to wait for a likelier opportunity to dig up old scores.

"*Hola, amigo!* My hat? Big, yes, but it fits me fine. Cigar? Certainly! Here, take two."

"*Gracias,*" said Bishop, taking four from Smith's handful and a fifth to light up. "You a horse trader now?"

They didn't shake hands. Each valued his fingers too highly.

"Oh, I deal in horses once in a while, Rogue."

"How's business?"

Smith started a shrug, and stopped it. He carefully replaced the sombrero on his head. "Fair. Just fair. I make a living."

"You should do better," Bishop said meditatively, "considering you never paid cash for a horse in your life. Or for anything else, if you could help it. What's the deal here, Smitty?"

Red, for once, was smart enough to keep quiet and listen. Sera looked ready to spring loyally to the defense of the maligned Mr. Smith, the gentleman whose manners were so faultless and charming. The girl's wrathful eyes said that her fervent hope was that Mr. Smith could hold his own in this uncouth company.

Mr. Smith could. By guile and gun smoke he had got out of more fantastic jams than Sera dreamed existed. He chose guile now for a beginning.

"You insult me, my friend!" he protested painedly. "You judge me by yourself! In my past I have had to stoop to deal with ruffians like you, but I remain a man of honesty and honor and—"

"Snub it, Smeet!" Bishop interrupted rudely. "Hell, I know the deal. You stole horses you found you couldn't sell, an' traded 'em off for horses you *could* sell! The old switch!" He turned to Sera. "And you fell for it! Why?"

The girl blazed at him, "You don't know what you're talking about! I traded my two hundred horses for Mr. Smith's three hundred."

"Why?" Bishop repeated. "Why did he trade at a loss?"

"Because," retorted Sera, "his sorrels all have white stockings, and he's heard that the army will buy only solid-color horses."

Red spoke. "White stockings don't count against solid color, with the army. Any horse dealer knows that."

"I know it," Sera flung at him. "I told Mr. Smith.

320

But he was sure he was right, so we made the trade."

Bishop wagged his head. "Smeet, that's low. I'm ashamed to smoke your cigars!" He puffed contentedly. "You traded her three hundred horses, without title—or an awful flimsy title—for two hundred that you could sell on a good sale bill. The old switch! On a poor little lone gal, Smeet, that's cheating!"

Furiously, Smith spat. "Rogue, who are you to—"

"It's a shame!" continued Bishop. "You'd sell her horses. Then, if I know you, back you'd come for those sorrels—and for her! You border buzzard, you'll never learn that honesty is the best policy."

"Have you learned that?" Smith inquired surprisedly.

"We-ell, not so far," Bishop admitted. "But I've heard about it, an' I've been thinking of giving it a whirl. Kindly hold your horse still, will you?"

Chaper Five: BADMAN'S BID

SMITH TIGHT-REINED his restive black horse, and said to Sera, "Dear lady, I am sure your regard for me is not lessened by the foul accusation of low scoundrels." He had the gift of fluent speech, and his air of injured innocence matched that of a martyr at the stake. "Would I trade off horses to you that weren't honestly mine?"

"You sure would!" Bishop put in. "An' did! But the deal is hereby revoked! Those horses stay right where they are. Beat it! Don't come back, or you'll have a fight on your hands!"

"Right!" Red seconded. "Those sorrels are mine. The others belong to Miss Donavon. That's how it is, an' it stays that way!"

Smith split a thoughtful look between them. One of the few sins he had never been charged with was lack of nerve. But he wasn't in a winning position for a showdown with Bishop. And there was Red to consider.

"There is a connection, I think," Smith murmured, "between this and last night's stampede. Friend Rogue, I do not like you for sending those brush-thugs to raid my camp! You, too, are in the horse-trading game, eh? I might have known it! Wherever quick money can be made, there you'll find Rogue Bishop!"

"And Little Angel!" said Bishop.

Their eyes locked, and between them shuttled the same thought. Five hundred good horses at $125 a head, on this isolated ranch that was like a derelict ship without a crew. Owners—a slip of a girl and one penniless Texan, who had no means of getting the horses up to the Fort Griffin market. High stakes.

And more than that. Above all, there was the challenge, the hard pride of two gamblers, each out to beat the other. The steady stare between Bishop and Smith silently promised a cutthroat game to the last chip.

Red saw what was up and his face went gaunt, for he knew what happened to lesser players when lobos of the rawhide clan met and clashed. The prospect of a fight seemed to create a complete change in such men. They could be easygoing, soft-voiced men, comfortable to get along with—then, all of a sudden, smiling a cold, sinister savagery that was blind to everything but the consecration to kill a particular man who by some sign, unnoticed by others, had flashed a challenge.

Smith turned back to Sera. "Miss Donavon, am I to be robbed of my horses? This is your ranch. I appeal to you. Let me prove that the sorrels I traded to you were honestly mine."

And Sera, the unwitting umpire in a deadly game, said, "Of course, Mr. Smith! These two men—they don't belong here! They're strangers to me." She sent Red a scorching glance. "Insolent, insulting riffraff!"

Smith bowed his full agreement. He dismounted. "Then let us go to the corrals. May I offer you my horse? He's quite gentle."

"Thank you." She took the reins and let him help her into the silver-mounted saddle. Docile as a pet pony, the black horse circled around and high-stepped daintily under Sera's touch, Smith pacing alongside, Bishop and Red following.

At their approach, the sorrels pricked ears and stamped nervously. They were not yet accustomed to this place, and were penned in the corrals to keep them from straying off. Farther on, the mixed bunch grazed out loosely, although restlessly alert after last night's scare.

Bishop inquired of Smith, "What's your proof? I doubt if even you can talk these horses into signing an affidavit."

Smith climbed into the biggest corral. "Wait and see!" he retorted superiorly, yanking his sombrero down firmly and tightening the chin-strings. "My horses will always obey me and nobody else, friend Rogue, and that's proof enough!"

Bishop watched curiously. He remembered that Smith was a wizard with horses and could transform an outlaw bronc into an amiable pie-eater without breaking its spirit. There were men who possessed that uncanny power. Even Red, his eyes on Smith, grew professionally interested.

Sera, seated on the splendid black, simply displayed a smooth-browed belief in Mr. Smith's integrity.

As Smith stepped across the corral the sorrel horses crowded uneasily out of his way. They didn't appear to know him from any other two-legged freak. They split into two packs and danced around the corral, and came together near the gate, where they snuffed comments and inspected him suspiciously. So far, no good.

Smith pursed his lips and keened a thin whistle. The sorrels took no notice of that, except to spear their ears a little sharper.

It was the black that answered to the command. It lunged forward, cleared the gate effortlessly with inches to spare, and landed among the astounded sorrels. The black was a jumper, and a king among horses. It knew its royal rights, and shouldered the sorrels aside. The sorrels scampered off on a round-the-clock whirl, raising dust. The black, with Sera still hanging on, trotted to Smith, obedient as a well-trained hunting dog.

Smith whipped up into the saddle behind Sera. The dust of the running horses all but obscured him. He sang out blithely, "You see, friend Rogue?" Then the black jumped the far fence, with its light burden of Little Angel and little Sera.

As a clever stunt in horsemanship it was superb, but as a tactical trick it seemed merely mischievous. Sera, apparently more astonished than alarmed, didn't even cry out or attempt to struggle. Smith had reached around her and taken the reins.

The black swung sharply to the right and followed along the outside of the fence, on a course that would bring it back around the corrals. Red, swearing, ran to meet it. But the black passed behind the stables, then the barn. In full stride, it raced straight on across the yard.

Smith's intention became clear, and was made clearer by his mocking laugh at Red. This was no flashy, purposeless stunt. Running, Red dragged out his gun. Because of the fearful risk of hitting the girl, he fired high.

Smith's laugh rang out again. What Sera thought of the escapade grew plain when she began struggling. Her chances of breaking loose were slimmer than those of a dove in a hawk's talons. Smith had been known to out-wrestle big Indian bucks, on a bet. The black flashed by the house and went clattering down the pass. Red ran hopelessly on.

Bishop rejected the notion of entering himself in any footrace with a horse. His annoyance at Smith was considerable, but his feet had done enough work last night to last them a long time. There were plenty of horses here, and a catch-rope coiled over a post of the drop-pole gate. The loose ones, his and Red's among them, couldn't be handily caught afoot, but the sorrels were penned.

He took the rope and climbed into the corral, and after some tagging around with the sorrels he got the rope on one. The horse at once stood fast, showing good training, and let him lead it out of the corral and replace the drop-poles.

With the rope Bishop fashioned and fitted a hackamore. No doubt there were saddles somewhere on the benighted place. He considered searching the stables. On the other hand, urgent haste demanded precedence.

Red came sprinting back. "She screamed!" he gasped, out of breath. "I heard her!" He snatched the rope from Bishop, leaped onto the sorrel, and took off bareback without a word of by-your-leave. The headlong way he dashed down the pass, with only a single hackamore, raised 5-to-3 odds that he would break his neck.

"Why, cremate his gall!" Bishop scowled, picking rope fiber from his fingers. From where he stood he caught a glimpse of the black horse, far below, Smith and Sera still aboard, streaking southward down an open stretch of the trail. Smith had a sure-win start, and that black was a lot of horse.

No pushing rush, then. You broke yourself, barging bullheaded into the other man's play. Going after Smith called for wary care. Smith knew what he was doing, the slippery little cuss.

Bishop investigated the stables, and carried out a saddle and bridle and a rope. He caught another sorrel and laced the saddle on and hit the pass at an easy canter. Meantime, he heard what sounded like an angry shout far down the river, and a couple of shots. Then a faint scream, and silence.

Red, he guessed, must have caught up with Smith—and got the worst of it. Too bad. Kind of a middling-decent jigger, Red. No discretion, though, where a pretty girl was involved. He wasn't the first, and he came by it honestly; his Uncle Wesley—

Bishop forded the river and headed south, but shunned the open trail. Putting himself mentally into Smith's place, he foresaw that Smith—and his border riders—would be on watch for him. That shrewd half-pint had sized up the deal fairly close. The girl was the key, the queen bee. Carry her off, and the stingers came droning after her.

"That was smart, Smeet!" Bishop muttered, riding the sorrel fifty yards clear of the trail. "That was damn' smart. But I'll outsmart you, you short-size son!"

He passed the Sandhole, off to his right, and guided the sorrel gently on into the cottonwoods. Up ahead lay the long strip of grassed meadow, the empty remains of the destroyed camp where nothing moved.

He was not deceived by the silence. About here, he judged, Red had charged into a jackpot. Here were eager eyes probing for him. He could feel the stealing search of them, from the brush on both sides of the meadow.

He halted and considered the prospect. Most men were right-handed. On the right, then, most of them would be, rifles nestled in crotches of the brush. He reined the sorrel to the right, to skirt wide and come up behind them.

A furred cap bobbed up from behind a woodbine-wound dwarf oak; the cap of a buffalo tramp. And the round eye of a Springfield repeater. Bishop drew and fired. There was nothing else for it. The cap jumped, and immediately the thicket was full of brush-thugs. Up the meadow, rifles cracked and lashed the brush.

Bishop heeled the sorrel hard. He knew what he had got into—a creeping attack by Hump's renegade rangers. They weren't licked, by a long shot. Hump had gathered fresh recruits from the scavengers of the brush. Guns blammed from the tangled low barberry and currant bush, and the sorrel jumped.

The sorrel took it from there. Scared wild, it smashed through the brush and broke out onto the meadow. No hand on the reins, however strong, could stop it. Bishop bent low in the saddle and let the horse use its own best judgment. This was no time to argue, and often a horse knew best. Maybe the east side of the meadow was safer, at that.

He heard the solid thump of horses behind him, and he hipped around, gun in hand to cut down

any ambitious duck who thought to clip him. But
the riders were Smith's border men, getting out of
that ambush as fast as they could. Among them
was Red, lolling senseless, his head gashed,
supported by a horseman on each side. And Sera
on the black, Smith up behind her.

Bishop split the brush on the east side of the
meadow, and wrenched the sorrel to a shivering
halt. Smith crashed in near by, and Bishop sang
out to him, "Hell of a caper! Damn you, can't you
ever learn to watch your rear?"

"I thought we ran them out of the country last
night!" Smith snarled back at him. "They weren't
more than a dozen or so: Now—hell's initials—
forty of them! Aren't they your men? Why did
they shoot at you?"

"They shot at me," Bishop answered, "because
they're not my men. No, *amigo*—they're out to
get me as well as you!"

Smith stared at him. He murmured, "I *sabe*!
When rascals fall out—"

"Then," said Bishop, "honest men get their just
deserts. Yeah. It's a shame there's not an honest
man hereabouts."

"You never spoke a truer word!"

Gunfire from Hump's thugs on the far side of
the meadow hailed into the brush. There was
cover here, but no protection. One of the border
men, standing by his horse, bent over. His smile
was small and blighted as he fell on his face. His

horse snorted uneasily and another man caught its reins. Smith glanced without sentiment at the fallen man. He had seen death too many times to be deeply touched by it, but this threatened to become wholesale slaughter, catastrophe.

Bishop said to him, "We got to get out o' here, Smitty!"

The old friendly name brought a stiff grin to Smith's face. He and Bishop were now a pair of hard-pressed long riders caught in the same jam. Grudges were dropped by mutual consent, though only for the time being.

"The river, eh, Rogue?"

"Sure. And over to the ranch, quick, before they get the same idea. It's likely they don't know yet where the horses went, but it won't take 'em long to scout out. We can stand 'em off from up there."

"If we get there!" growled a leathery *Tejano* whose blood-soaked shirt gave the reason for his morose pessimism. "That long stretch 'tween the cottonwoods an' the river—ay *de mi*! They'll shoot into the bunch of us there an' wipe us out!"

"We won't be in a bunch," Bishop said. "Just a couple at a time, on a hard run. The rest blaze away an' cover for 'em. I'll start it, to see how it goes. Let the girl have that dead man's horse. I'll take her along."

"Now, Rogue, not so fast!" drawled Smith. His daredevil grin perked wickedly. "Miss Donavon is my responsibility. She will ride my good black, in charge of two men—you, Isidro, and you, Joe. Be sure she reaches the river safely! Two others will bring along Mr. Delaney. I take poor Nick's horse."

He slid off the black, leaving Sera in the saddle, and mounted the dead man's buckskin. Isidro and Joe nudged their horses up alongside the black. Isidro was all Mexican; he touched his hat to the girl and murmured a polite phrase. Joe, a solemn individual who didn't hold with any such fiddle-faddle, took the black's reins in his fist.

Smith's look at Bishop was brightly inquiring. "Ready, Rogue? Shall we start out and—as you said—see how it goes?"

What Bishop thought of that setup he didn't bother to say, and his expression showed nothing. But when, at his curt nod of assent, Smith chuckled, a baleful glint flickered in Rogue's eyes. Mr. Angelito Smith, backed by his tough border crew, was being too blasted smart for his fine britches.

Bent low, they forced their horses through the brush slowly to where it thinned out toward the cottonwoods. The trees afforded them some further cover. At the fringe, though, there before them lay the long stretch to the river. Much of it could be seen by Hump's crowd in the brush up along the high west side of the meadow, and those rifles had to be taken into account.

Bishop and Smith halted to look it over,

inspecting every rock, bush, and hollow for its possible value on their course.

"Looks like a better'n even chance to me," Bishop said. "I'm going to hit for that bed o' rocks way down yonder."

Smith nodded approval. "Once past there, we can keep out of sight till we're out of range."

"We?" Bishop frowned. "Pick your own route!"

"There's room for us both. I'll stay behind you." Smith chuckled again, tightening his chin strings. "Well—luck to us, eh?"

"To me, anyhow! Here goes!"

Chapter Six: **FALLEN ANGEL**

THEY PLUNGED out of the cottonwoods onto the open terrain, lashing their horses, Bishop first, Smith hard behind him. Within a few seconds a shouting uproar raised the signal that they were seen. The firing had not slackened, ripping back and forth across the meadow, and now it struck furiously from the thickets in a solid wall of sound.

A bullet smacked the dished cantle of Bishop's saddle and droned off. He heard the whispering screech of others, and he bent close over the sorrel's neck and swerved sharply, twice, to throw the shooters off their aim. Smith, following on the buckskin, sang out an oath. Bishop twisted to see what was his trouble. Smith had an eye cocked up at the bullet-torn brim of his fine sombrero; that was all.

As they drew close to the bed of rocks the buckskin took an extra spurt and came almost abreast of the sorrel, crowding it over, so that Bishop would have to swing wide around the rocks and give Smith the inside track.

Bishop rasped, "Stay back o' me!"

"I thought you could ride!" Smith jeered. "Watch where you're going!"

That did it. Bishop reined the sorrel hard over back onto its original course close by the rocks, banging broadside into the buckskin and knocking it offstride. Both horses stumbled, and Smith swore. A protruding shoulder of rock loomed up directly ahead.

Bishop, barely grazing by it, called out, "Watch where *you're* goin', Smeet!"

Either the buckskin was running too fast and disorganized, or Smith was too proud to pull back until too late. The horse did as well as it could. It clattered sort of sidewise up the sloping shoulder nearly to the top. There, on a slick spot, its hoofs abruptly shot out from under it. Momentum carried Smith on over the top while the buckskin rolled back to earth.

Bishop glanced rearward, mainly to make sure that he was out of sight of the shooters. He saw the buckskin go rocking off, empty stirrups slapping, in a westerly direction. He saw Smith tumbling down this side of the rock, and from the manner of the fall he judged that Smith had landed on his sombrero at the first bounce. His diagnosis proved correct. Reaching bottom, Smith lay spraddled, motionless.

"If his neck's broke," Bishop muttered, "he's swindled some hangman out o' forty bucks!"

Yet a tragic quality touched that sprawled, lifeless little figure. In its torn and rumpled finery it represented a gay elegance, a lawless scorn of dull conformity. It seemed a shame to leave it lying there for thieves to plunder and buzzards to pick, and coyotes to crunch the bones at night. It was easy to forgive rascality after the rascal was brought low.

Bishop circled back and reined in under cover of the rock. He reached down and grabbed Smith by his jacket, hoisted him up over the sorrel, and set off again for the river.

Smith hung limply, arms and legs dangling, like a dead man. Then he groaned an oath as his head bobbed in unison with the sorrel's swinging lope. He was only knocked out, and Bishop scowlingly contemplated heaving him off for fooling him.

By the time the ford was reached, Smith was making feeble attempts to ease his position. Bishop dumped him below the riverbank, in an agreeably soft couch of mud, and waited for Isidro and Joe to bring Sera along. That was a situation he intended to alter, promptly, to one more in line with his liking.

According to all the noises, two or three parties were staging their dash out of that hot spot in the brush. They weren't all following the same route. Isidro and Joe had orders to start as soon as Bishop and Smith tested the getaway.

First to arrive, though, were the two men with Red Delaney. They came slapping and slithering along the muddy bank, having hit the river farther down. Red gave them no trouble. He sat bowed, clutching the saddle horn with both hands, in a fog of slowly returning consciousness. At that, he was better off than Smith, who lay groaning in the mud. It took the two men a little while to recognize their dapper chief in that bedraggled blob. They asked questions while picking him up.

"He mishapped on a circumstance beyond his control," said Bishop. "How're the others doing?"

"They're comin'."

"H'm!"

They arrived two and three at a time, by various routes, till most of the crew were gathered at the ford. Here and there a bullet-tagged man cursed, binding up his wound. Talk ran sparely to those who hadn't made the getaway, who had got dropped.

"Cal got it soon's he quit them cottonwoods."

"My *primo*—Eloy—no get much more far."

"Hey! Them *ladinos* are comin'! Let's git!"

"Hold it!" Bishop said. One last rider was rounding in, on a stumbling horse whose head threshed low in dying protest.

It was Isidro. His mount floundered down the bank, and he fell clear, rolling helplessly in the mud. He wheezed, "They're comin'!" and caused a general move to cross the river.

Bishop got to him swiftly. "Where's the girl?"

Isidro's neck and chest ran blood. "Back there —some big rocks! That black horse got hit. Joe, damn fool, 'fore we start he tied her hands to the horn, see? Then Joe get kill'. I try go help her. No good! They shoot me pret' bad, huh?"

"I think they've finished you, *hombrecito*," Bishop told him straight.

"I t'ink so, too," said Isidro.

The men were splashing across the ford, taking Smith and Red with them. Two of them turned back and looked down at Isidro and then at Bishop, inquiringly.

Bishop said, "Yeah, you might's well," and they legged off and picked up Isidro.

Bishop vaulted aboard his sorrel. "When Little Angel gets his head to work," he said to them— and his eyes were chips of ice—"you tell him from me he's a stinkin' *ladrone* and I'll fix him some day for this bobble!"

He was gone then in a hoofed spatter of mud, not over the river, but away from it, pounding toward the bed of rocks.

He was alone, and that suited him best, as always. A lone wolf was hampered by company. He recalled, not for the first time, words heard or read somewhere along the scarred path of his life: *Down to Gehenna, or up to the Throne—he travels the fastest who travels alone.*

Hump's thugs were everywhere. They had broken from cover and were combing every bush and hollow, like hungry wolves sniffing out the dead and injured. They were advancing between Bishop and the bed of rocks. Those cursed rifles, so much more effective and authoritative than six-guns, in open country. And the tramps knew it, knew how to use them.

Bishop, his run blocked, angled off to skirt that ragged line of hunters. Somebody spied him, raised a whoop, and he heeled the sorrel to a dead run. No use; they were after him. From his course they would strain their brute brains for the answer to what it was that he was desperately seeking, and would find it first. Diversion, then, was the next card. He raced westward, leading the pursuers away from his goal.

The sorrel, breathing as though barbwire sawed its throat, blundered into soft footing and all but threw a header. This was the Sandhole. Bishop leaped off. He let the winded horse go and ran to the mushroom-shaped rock of Crazy Chisera Butte. He scrambled up the rock and lay panting atop it, his heavy guns drawn and ready.

A bunch of skin-clad riders swirled around the Sandhole. One of them yelled a word that was ignored, and turned in. That one was smarter than the rest. He got off his pony and nosed the ground. Following tracks, he came up under the overlapping lip of the lonely rock.

Bishop jumped him. It was about twenty feet down, but the thug was large and broke his fall. His boot heels hit at the nape of the inquisitive thug's neck.

The pony ran off. The brush-thug buried his face

in the sand and didn't breathe any more. Bishop stripped him of his rifle and bandoleer of cartridges, and carried him around the rock. He tossed the body into a patch of greasewood, and climbed back up Crazy Chisera Butte. He now had a rifle and about fifty rounds for it—enough to last out for a spell.

From up here he could look out over much of the land. He searched it carefully, located the bed of rocks, the black horse lying dead, a small figure huddled against it. The distance was within range of the rifle.

To her credit, Sera wasn't treating herself to any woman-foolish hysterics, as far as could be seen. Or perhaps the spill had knocked her out. Anyhow, she didn't tug and struggle to free her tied hands from the saddle horn. It would have attracted the eager attention of the buffalo tramps and won her a bullet or—if they detected it was a girl—capture. They would get around to her soon enough as it was, for the dead black's saddle and any other petty plunder worth the taking.

Fortunately, the horse had taken a dying leap in among the rocks, and it and the girl lay where they could be seen only from higher ground. Still, that was thin security. There was plenty of higher ground hereabouts, besides the butte and the cliffs across the river.

Most of Hump's gang were congregating at the

ford and exchanging a lively fire with the border men up on the cliffs. It was an undisciplined mob, for stragglers kept slouching by the Sandhole, some on foot, quarreling over bits of gear stripped from the dead.

One hairy scarecrow came limping along in frayed moccasins, from the meadow. Peering sharply around, he made directly for the bed of rocks at a shambling trot. He had spied out a prize and meant to keep it secret to himself.

Bishop tried out the rifle. It was satisfactory, one shot sufficient. With detached observation and no compunction he watched the limping man jerk up his head and hands and pitch forward.

Bishop nodded, blew the smoke away, and cocked on the next shell. There were bound to be others. Too bad the thug fell so straight, head to the rocks. It could provide a hint for an inquiring mind. The rifle was almost too good, and these blunt-nosed .44 slugs hit like a sledge hammer. Next time he would aim off-center.

He did, and had to do it fast, twice, on a pair who turned aside to inspect that body for possibles. They searched it, shrugged, and might have passed on unharmed if one of them hadn't paused to scan the dead man's tracks and position. He called to his partner and gestured, and so Bishop got off two shots.

The sound of the rifle couldn't fail to be heard. The salvation was that it would scarcely be noticed, much less located, as long as other rifles exactly like it kept thudding the same note along the river and raising echoes.

Trouble was, a harvest of defunct hoodlums could be expected to attract notice and some speculation. It might be thought they were corpsed by miraculous sharpshooting from up on the cliffs, but that left open the puzzle of why Smith's men should reach so far when so many other prospects were closer to hand, at the ford.

In an hour Bishop added two more to the gather, after which that spot became warily avoided for a long time. He guessed the word had gone out that the place was unlucky.

In the afternoon he detected Sera moving, straining to free her hands, and he supposed sympathetically that her nerve had cracked and let in panic. Then he saw a shaggy, rag-bound head edge up slowly above a rock, not more than ten feet beyond her, and that explained her wild struggling: she had heard that creeping prowler.

He took careful aim, waited, let the head rise another inch or two, and fired a shade low to make dead sure. A tiny puff of scored rock exploded. The shattered face lifted for an instant, gaping, and fell away.

Bishop thumbed up another shell, ready for the next, his mood cold and heavy. It was plain they had at last come to the suspicion that something or somebody in the rocks was under long-range protection; must therefore be of value. They had the craft and cunning of predatory beasts, more dangerous by far than true intelligence. The more guarded a thing, said cunning, the more valuable. Material and intrinsic worth was the only standard they knew. To the support of that shabby banner they could call up an animal courage fiercer than the deliberate bravery of intelligence.

During the down-sweep of the sun's great arc Bishop flayed the scalp of another crawler. The firing at the ford sank to occasional sniping. They had not been able to cross the river, and were holding their patience till darkness.

Sullen great thunderheads roiled the eastern sky, promising a black night, a cloaked moon. Now came the long waiting, the sun diving into the west.

Bishop's searching eyes kept reverting to Sera; he kept thinking of the good rifle in his hands and how one careful shot could sledge-hammer a person right out of existence, in a wink. No pain, probably, hit square.

His hard face was deeply lined as the sun met the horizon. He looked and felt very old, and he sighed like a tired old man as sundown streaked purple shadows and gold clefts across the land. Quickly the sun bowed out and left the brief after-blaze in the sky, the earth in deepening veils of jet, and then the rifle was useless.

He laid the rifle aside, and the bandoleer. He slid

down off the butte and Indian-crept toward the bed of rocks. Nothing like a set plan occupied his mind. The dominant objective was to reach Sera ahead of the prowlers, because leaving her there alone and alive—well, it wouldn't do. The memory of it wouldn't do to take along.

Chapter Seven: **A MATCH FOR SATAN**

ON THE DARKENING ground the dead thugs lay in curiously lifelike attitudes, as if relaxing around a nonexistent campfire at the end of a day's honest work. For a short spell Bishop relaxed among them, listening and getting his bearings. Their presence didn't bother him. Dead dogs couldn't bite.

What did bother him was the silence everywhere. No sound came from the ford. For some time now not a shot had echoed anywhere along the river, nor from the cliffs. Even an ear pressed to earth failed to pick up any rumor of horses moving about. He distrusted the silence, reading from it a calculated design and a creeping purpose. A trained instinct clanged warning of unseen danger closing in around him.

He slid on to the rocks, eased in among them, and paused to listen again. Dammit, they *were* coming near. Those faint, indefinite rustlings were not conjured up by oversharp senses too eager to corroborate intuition. He went forward, drawing a gun with slow care, hooking his thumb over the hammer.

Before him, a dozen yards off, bulked the rounded black shape of the dead horse. And Sera, a lighter shape beside it. She was working her bound hands, doggedly, like a man trying to saw through an iron bar with a two-inch file. She didn't at once see Bishop, and the length of his glance at her was no more than enough to assure him that she was alive. His eyes were caught by two rocks, close to his right, which he was positive did not belong in the mental picture he kept of this place from his day-long vigil.

Sera saw him then, a crouched shadow, motionless. She began a frantic struggle. The two rocks shifted, making a faint, dry rustling. Fearing the girl might scream, Bishop sent her a hushed murmur: "Keep still!"

She did. So did the two rocks. Bishop held his gun on them, till one whispered, "That you, Bishop? This is Red!"

"Who's that with you?"

"Smith!"

"Well, I'll be damned!"

They crawled forward, draped in mud-daubed tarpaulins. Their heads peeked out from under, giving them the arch appearance of shy turtles rather than two desperate men on a suicidal venture. Bishop wanted to know what made the rustling, and Red explained that the tarps were stuffed up with straw to accord them the rounded look of rocks.

Smith, coldly bitter, told Bishop he was fortunate. "You didn't have to crawl down a cliff like this and float across a river, and fool forty cutthroats! No! You got out of that, with your cursed trickery!"

He didn't mean it in that vein, and Bishop knew it and asked him, "Who made you turn into a rollin' stone?" He received no answer. He didn't need one. Nobody had made Smith do it.

From the far distance of the cliffs Smith and Red, with the border vaqueros, had watched thugs get bowled over when prowling near Sera, and knew it was Bishop's work. They weren't doing any good up there, so they started down as the time seemed right and they could cook up a chance to get there to Sera.

Bishop could guess at that picture, and he wasn't too surprised to find Smith here. Angelito was a no-account little catamount, slippery as they came, but he hadn't yet sloughed off the old code. A matter of personal pride, maybe. And the girl was young and pretty. That helped.

"Will you two quit scrappin'?" Red protested. "This sure ain't the time an' place for it!" He turtled on cumbrously and murmured to Sera. A hand and knife wiggled out weirdly from where his head had been and cut free her wrists.

Smith's poking head twisted, and he started after him. Red was not to be allowed to hog the credit. It had to be made clear to the girl that she was saved by virtue of the inspired gallantry and brilliant leadership of Angelito Smith—not by an inferior underling who, taking cheap advantage of a pause for discussion, got there first with a dollar pocketknife.

Above the rustle of Smith's straw-stuffed tarp Bishop caught a muted medley of other sounds. "Hang up, Smeet!" he muttered.

Smith's head came around, inquiring irritably, "What?"

"Shut up an' listen!"

When the straw was still the sounds came clearer, instantly recognizable. Now that it was dark Hump's hooligans evidently felt that the bed of rocks could be investigated without risk. They compromised with caution by taking long, creeping steps, and not talking above the pitch of a mountain lion's courting grumble. Their progress probably couldn't be detected from rifle-shot range, but from here they were within a stone's throw.

Red was an unmoving rock huddled protectingly beside Sera, who couldn't huddle closer to him than the mud on his masquerade.

Equally hampered, unable to dig out a gun for fear of rustling his straw, Smith hissed urgently to Bishop, "Do something! This cursed canvas—we had to tie them on! I can't get out without raising a noise! Do something!"

"What? Hell, here they come!" Bishop cocked his drawn gun and dug for the other. "Do what?"

Smith breathed a soft Spanish oath, which contained a strong statement regarding Bishop's parentage. "Do anything! You can match Satan when you have to! I know it! Quick—do something!"

"Match?" muttered Bishop. "Why, sure—sure!"

He fished out a match. He thrust it under Smith's tarp and scratched it alight with his thumbnail, and withdrew his hand. "You better ki-yi for the river pretty quick now," he advised Smith.

The results came fast. There was a sizzling crackle and a puff of flame. Smith let out an astounded yelp. He leaped up like a kerosened stallion and ran, a pillar of flame, the tarp flapping out behind him. Fire, the best friend and worst enemy of man, diligently torched the tar-soaked tarp and singed its wearer.

Smith kept on running, tearing at the burning embrace. There could exist nothing like fire to set a man's best foot forward. Smith simply bounded on a few high spots, smashed through brush that would have balked a burro, and sailed on.

At that moment Sera or Red, or both, leaned on the dead black horse to see what in hell had happened. The carcass vented a loud and sepulchral grunt.

It was amazing what darkness and the unknown could wreak among the ignorant. Bishop had often noted it in some Indians who were not too town-broke. These more or less white savages had been absent from town a long, long time. Living without law like wild animals had sharpened their muscular reactions and brute instincts, but dulled their thinking faculties. Confronted by anything unusual, their brains broncoed.

A fiery apparition, springing up out of the ground and darting through the night, was a novelty. Some of them ran howling after it. Others, of a more Indian cast, ran elsewhere. None dallied to cogitate on the meaning of that unearthly grunt. Pretty soon there came a splash, a hiss, and the fire went out.

Bishop banged into Red in the dark and yanked Sera to her feet. "Come on—quick!" He rushed her off, half carrying her along to keep up with his long-legged strides. Red tore loose from his trappings and overhauled them near the river.

"There's a better place to cross, where Smith and I floated over. More hidden. Deep in the middle, though. Can you swim, Sera?"

"Lead on, Red—never mind the questions!" Bishop told him. "We'll get across! Damwell got to!" As far as he could recall, Smith wasn't much shakes at swimming, in spite of all the times he had crossed the Rio Grande, usually in a hurry. Smith would be hunting a shallow place, if he could still get around. Well, that was his problem. "Step lively! There goes Hump singin' out!"

Upstream, Hump was loudly cursing and calling his mob together. Men were snarling at one another, each vowing he would have caught that blazing booger if only he'd had a little help.

Red said, "Here we are! Right over there's where Smith and I got down the cliff. It's not too tough. Sera, let me—"

Bishop tripped him and barged straightway into the river, with Sera in his arms. Toward midstream the footing dropped away, embarrassingly, and he had to use his arms for swimming.

Red splashed up alongside, anxiously reaching out to help Sera, and sinking himself every time he tried it. Like most riders of the Southwest, where a yard-wide trickle counts as a river, neither Red nor Bishop could dog-paddle six strokes without going down for a fresh start from bottom. They called it swimming.

Sera, a lithe fish, went down for Red and helped him ashore, and rippled back for Bishop, who had decided to hold his breath and walk. On the east bank both men sat down, spent and puffing, while Sera—not a bit out of breath— inquired concernedly, "Are you all right now?"

"Cert-huh-'nly!" gasped Red, and Bishop mentioned that he was glad to have been on hand to get Sera across. No trouble at all.

With a stout resurgence of energy Red led the way up the cliff. This, he explained, required knowledge, experience, and an excellent memory. Sera agreed that it was so; for she had taken this short cut many times and it was marvelous of Red to have discovered it. She stayed behind till Red clambered astray the fourth time, and then she scampered on ahead and led them up onto the cliff.

The border vaqueros, tightly on the alert,

informed them that the *ladrones* down there were up to something. Had they seen that strange streak of flame? Yes, they had. It was certainly most mysterious. Smith had not come back. Had they seen him? Yes; Smith was engaging himself in important matters, said Bishop, and would show up presently. Meantime, watch the river. Don't let those filthy *ladrones* come over, or surely they would find the hidden road and perhaps storm the ranch.

Verdad. This was true. Unfortunately, the thunderheads kept piling up, obscuring the moon, so that the river below the cliffs was a sleazy ribbon difficult to see. The brush-thugs could cross it tonight without a witness.

"We'll guard the road," Bishop ordered, "and watch for cliff climbers. Put spit on your gunsights."

And then Smith came along.

Smith presented a sad sight. He was scorched, nearly drowned, and exhausted from climbing. His rage sustained him. At sight of Bishop, he grated, "You hell-spawned traitor! You—you—"

"Now, *amigo*, what's bitin' you?" Bishop queried. "We all made it, didn't we? What's the beef?" His hands were thrust under his coat.

Smith saw that. He whipped a narrow stare to his men. "Watch him!" he snapped. "He's no friend of mine!" And in a brittle tone: "What's here?" He wanted to know who the devil Bishop thought he was, to be calmly usurping command, and he tongue-lashed his crew up and down for taking orders from anybody but himself.

Considering that he hadn't been around to give any orders lately, his recriminations were not entirely reasonable, and some of the border men told him so to his face, angrily. These men were a thorny lot, full of independence and self-esteem. Recent events had stretched their high tempers. It wasn't safe for anybody, even Smith, to cuss them out as if they were humble peons and sheep-herders.

It was a promising start for a bad row, a mutiny. Smith knew it. He turned it off, saying, "String out and watch the cliffs, some of you. The rest guard the road."

That, they informed him caustically, was what they had been about to do when he showed up. It made Smith madder than ever, but he had to hold the lid on or risk complete loss of control over them.

Bishop tried pouring more fuel on his fire by suggesting kindly, "You rest a spell, Smeet, an' let us handle it, huh? You look kind o' done up. You're not yourself."

He recognized Smith's trouble, and relished it. In the ordinary course Smith wasn't really a bad loser when a trick got turned against him. What he couldn't stand was being made to look ridiculous. It knocked away all his sense of humor. Also, being a confirmed dandy, he hated having his elegant garb ruined.

Ignoring Bishop's barbed suggestion, Smith nodded to his crew and spoke to them with forced friendliness. They moved off to take up their stations, saying no more. He had created a resentment among them, though, that would take some time to erase. Worse, there now existed a spark of doubt that might flare up and destroy all their confidence in him. It was difficult to retain complete respect for a leader who let himself be made a fool of and then pawed the hole deeper. He could not afford another mistake.

Red, passing up a chance to keep quiet, said, "Ought to turn my sorrels out an' let 'em graze with Sera's bunch. They're not much likely to drift."

Smith turned on him with savage joy. He needed badly an excuse to relieve his feelings, and here was one all set up for him.

"Your sorrels? And the others you call Sera's, eh?" He spoke almost caressingly. "That about takes care of all the horses on the place! How do you go about it?"

"She and I own 'em," Red answered simply. "The brands are in our names. We can both show the registry papers to prove it any time at Fort Griffin or anywhere else."

"Ah, yes! But the horses will be sold by me!"

"How do *you* go about it?"

"Like this!" A gun spiked from Smith's hand.

"Y'know, Smeet," casually put in Bishop, "it won't do much good to shoot him for his papers. They're in his name. They're no use to anybody else, without a bill of sale."

Smith frowned. He disliked all documents, regarding them as unnecessary, and his knowledge of them was hazy. Larceny was becoming complicated.

"Thanks for mentioning it," he acknowledged, sarcasm edging his tone. "All right—he'll write out a bill of sale to me."

Bishop wagged his head. "You could haul a wagonload of bills of sale, all signed over in your name—an' still you'd run into trouble trying to sell horses up in Fort Griffin! You cussed out Major Jennisk and got him sore. He's an unforgiving kind o' sour critter. He's posted you as a horse thief. He doesn't like you personally a little bit. No, you don't sell horses to Jennisk. Not you, Smeet!"

In his wrathful dismay Smith appeared tempted to go ahead and shoot Red and then take a crack at Bishop. Off-tracked by a new thought, he demanded, "How do you know all that? Do you have any connection with Jennisk?"

"Yeah." Bishop's nod was matter-of-fact. "I contracted with him to deliver some horses, on a kickback deal that would pay us both a profit. Your horses. That is, the horses you stole off Red. At the time I didn't know it was you, nor where the horses were stole. Country's full o' Smiths an' horses." He sucked a tooth reflectively. "Not that it would've made any difference."

"So!" grated Smith. "So! I knew it! These mangy buffalo tramps—"

"Don't pop your skull," Bishop advised him. "It'll get you in trouble some day. The point is, you can't sell horses to Jennisk at any price—but I can! Think it over! What's that scorched smell? Oh, sure—your clothes. Thought for a minute it was you."

He watched Smith go stamping off. He turned to pass a remark to Red, and decided it would be lost.

Red, staring hard at him, said, "I figger your game, Bishop! You're aiming to tie into a trade with that damned bandit, for a split in the loot! Well, I lost those sorrels once an' I can lose 'em again. But how about Sera's horses? How about Sera, herself?"

"The subject," responded Bishop, "has its place in my mind."

"That answer's not good enough!" Red said, and now a taut string of wildness rang in his voice. "I've watched Smith, how he looks at her! He's after her!"

Bishop nodded. "So are you."

"And you're after her, too! By the Lord, I'll kill—"

Then a man sang out that Hump's mob was coming up the road, and conversation broke off.

Chapter Eight: **TRICKERY TRADERS**

THE RABBLE PACK CAME UP like a sudden storm. They had left their skinny ponies and eeled across the river in the cloud-densed darkness, and found the pass and the road. Their attack was as simple as a wild bull's charge. A grunted word from Hump, and the pattering rush.

Yet it had the merit of surprise. Nobody on the high ground dreamed that they had already massed on the road and were creeping up it. What betrayed them was Hump's grunt, and the patter of moccasins. They must have forgotten that sound travels upward, especially up a deep pass. And they didn't know the bends of the road. Their minds clung hungrily to the thought of the dazzling prize—hundreds of saleable horses—and the thought left no room for cautious considerations.

There were so many of them. They outnumbered Smith's remaining crew four or five to one. The narrow pass was a funnel of gunfire, most of it blind shooting in the dark. An evening breeze cruised along on schedule and blew into the pass and rolled gun smoke up into the faces of the high-ground men, who sneezed, coughed, cursed, and fired blinder than ever.

The raiders slowly backed down, and the air cleared. Bishop discovered Smith beside him, when he took time out to wipe his eyes. The glance that ran between them was impersonal, professional.

"They'll take a real whack at the cliffs next, don't you reckon? This mesa is okay against riders, but those tramps don't mind crawlin'—an' they're good at it."

"Yes. They won't quit now. Damn it, wish I had more men! Men like the old San Carlos crowd."

"That was a crew, all right. I looked for you to come up governor o' Chihuahua, that time. What went bad?"

"Lost my temper and shot a general. He was a cousin of the *presidente*." Smith shrugged. "Time we strung back along the cliffs. You watch the road, eh?"

The assault up the arroyo-gashed bluffs was a silent affair, till Hump's bellow rang out, startlingly near, ordering his mob to the final scrambling dash. They had crept up the arroyos in the dark—not a hard trick for them. Smith's men knew they were coming, could hear their slight sounds, but couldn't catch a glimpse of them. Then the bellow, and suddenly dim figures bobbed up like a troop of clawing, clambering apes.

Thin spurts of flame lashed down from the rim. The attackers fired at the flashes, and for a minute it was a blazing battle at short range. Few as they were, the border men had the advantage of lying prone for steady aim and exposing only their heads. The climbers, when hit, had a long way to fall. Some of them screamed as they tumbled down.

Again the attack folded, more and more of the figures flopping back flat into arroyos and crevices, till the great bluffs became a black nothingness as before, yet alive with noise. The descent was harder to do, but they had no further need of silence.

After a while Smith returned to the road. With him were Red and Sera. They found Bishop enjoying a cigar, its lighted end shielded under his coat. Guarding the road was an essential job. The fact that it had turned out to be a soft snap, while Smith and his *valientes* banged away for their lives on the cliff, did not ruffle Bishop.

"Three more men killed," Smith told him, "and we're low on shells. We can't stand off another attack like that. So we're pulling out of here!"

"Where to?"

"East. I'm told—" Smith motioned at Sera— "it's a very bad route, no water, and that we'll never get the horses through. But it's either that, or sit here hoping those devils won't try us again. I think they will!"

"So do I," agreed Bishop. "That's no reason we should go off cockeyed into any hellacious desert, though, with five hundred horses. You been too busy to use your head, Smeet. I haven't. The thing to do is let three or four of your boys keep on the move, back and forth along the cliff, shooting. Hump's just bright enough to figure we expect another attack there. So he'll fool us. He'll rush the pass again. Most likely that's what he intends to do, anyhow, but we want to make sure of it."

Smith blinked rapidly. "Have you gone loco? Here we are, low on shells, three men dead, and you talk about—why, that mob will wipe us out! What are you thinking of, man?"

"I'm thinking of how they ran two hundred horses at me an' Red last night," Bishop said. "I'm thinking it's a fair shake to run horses right back at 'em tonight! An' five hundred horses should do a better job, h'm?"

He watched Smith's eyes change expression, and went on. "If we do it right—charge slam through 'em on a downhill start—then we're clear! They'll be too banged around an' disorganized to trail after us. Besides, their ponies can't be far off. The ruckus will spook 'em."

"And if we can keep the horses bunched," Smith put in, "we'll be far up the trail to Fort Griffin by morning. *Bueno*! I would have thought of this, of course, only—as you said—I've been too busy."

"Of course." Bishop trimmed the chewed end of his cigar. "Which reminds me. When we reach Fort Griffin you better lie low. I'll sell Jennisk the horses. As for how the money's to be split up— well, we can argue that out on the way."

Smith shook his head. "Let's not leave room for

argument," he urged gently. His eyes glinted. He laughed and half turned away as if to ponder on the matter. "I like your plan very well," he admitted. "That is, up to a point. And that point, friend Rogue, is where you speak of selling the horses. And of splitting the money! I've got a better idea."

He swung back, his left hand out in gesture, the way a man would when about to offer an explanation. But as he came fully around, a gun showed in his right hand; and Bishop bit down hard on his cigar and murmured, "What idea is this, Smeet?"

"No split!" said Smith. His eyes were brilliant now.

"No sale!" said Bishop, and raised his eyes from the gun. Its muzzle waved lazily between him and Red. "You'll get nothing."

Smith laughed again, a soft sound like bells of triumph muted by distance. "I get everything! May I tell you about my idea?"

"You've got the floor."

"*Gracias*! You are going to help drive the horses up to Fort Griffin, friend Rogue. Red and Sera will make out to you the bills of sale, and the rest of that paper nuisance. You will sell the horses to Jennisk and hand me the money—and *I* shall decide about any splitting of it!"

Bishop said reasonably, "It's a long time to hold a gun. I'll jump you long before that."

Smith let the muzzle droop. "You won't, and I won't need a gun, after I explain my idea. Friend Rogue, you think something of Sera. So does Red. So do I, for that matter." He shrugged. "But I'm in command here. These are my men. They know this thing has gone bad. If I tell them we've got to scamp out—they'll scamp, believe me! East to the desert! You could follow us or stay here."

Red spoke up, watching Smith's gun. "Do you mean you'd take Sera along on such a trip?" he asked, and Sera moved up closer to him and he put an arm around her shoulders.

"What a question!" Smith snapped impatiently. "You fool, do you think I would abandon her to those devils? Of course I'll take her along! And I'll gamble I can get through that desert with most of the horses, and sell them to ranchers down the Sabine, no questions asked! Well, friend Rogue, what d'you want to do?"

"Wring your neck! But it can wait." Bishop slanted a look at Sera, then at Red. "Better hit the pass, huh?"

And that was his admission that Smith had him up a stump. They nodded. The loss was theirs, but anything was better than Smith's alternative.

Bishop stabbed out his cigar, dourly thinking ahead. It seemed likely that a high price was to be paid for having made a flaming fool of Smith, and not entirely in money. Smith could be lavishly generous at times, but to his mind this thing was a

362

contest between himself and Bishop. Sera was an interesting side bet, and Red didn't count. The main objective was to beat Bishop, skin him mercilessly and salt him down and rub it in.

"All right, Smeet, let's get it goin'."

Smith's chuckle was high-throated, nasal, a dirty snicker. "First, please, let me have your guns!"

For a moment they only stared at each other. Then Smith said, with a slight catch in his voice, "It's that—or I shoot, and go east, with my crew, and the horses, and Sera! Be careful! If you pull on me, we'll both go under! Then what?"

Bishop remained utterly still. Smith said quietly, "Damn it, Rogue, don't look at me like that! I'll shoot, I tell you!"

At last, slowly, as if under tremendous effort, Bishop spread his coat and lifted out his pair of guns. He stooped, placed them on the ground, and straightened up.

Smith's small sigh of relief was audible. "Manuel—come here!" he sang out, and reaction from strain put a high lilt into his voice. "Pick up Mr. Bishop's guns and take care of them for him! Ah, good, good! Now we can start, eh, Rogue?"

Three men scuttled busily along the cliffs, sliding from one place to another and raising a hullabaloo of shooting. They set up a convincing performance that gave the effect of ten men nervously expecting another attack there at any minute, and suffering an epidemic of false alarms.

Another man won the job of cat-footing down the pass to listen for invaders. He took his boots off, for quietness and speed, and gave his solemn oath not to fall asleep down there.

Smith and the rest, including Bishop, Red, and Sera, hurried to the corrals. The first necessity was for everybody to get a good saddle mount under him, and for several of them that wasn't simple. There were spare saddles at hand, to be picked over and chosen, but catching horses for them in the dark was something else.

Bishop climbed in among the sorrels and roped a puff of wind. Sera generously offered him the horse she caught. He went on roping, so she turned it over to Red and dabbed another.

Eventually they were all respectably horsed. Then came the task of rounding in the mixed horses from pasture, soothing the disturbed sorrels out of corral, and introducing the two bunches together, praying that they wouldn't suddenly elect to take off into the wide world.

"Peter's Gates, don't let 'em run!" said a vaquero; and Red muttered, "Shut it off! Give 'em a chance to get acquainted, will you?"

Red knew horses. So did Sera. They circled slowly around the two horse herds, crooning nonsense to them, and everybody else drew off and let them work on it. Maybe they knew the language.

The horses mingled, snuffed one another curiously, and with one accord raised expectant heads and ears. "Well?" they seemed to be asking. "Where do we go?"

Red and Sera pushed in gently, urging them on, still talking gibberish to them. The riders closed in, helping, making no abrupt sound or movement. This wasn't a cattle herd. These were good horses, high-spirited, intelligent, faster on their feet than mounted men. They could dash off in a wink and flip their tails farewell, if they took the notion.

The riders coaxed them on to the yard, there held them bunched and temporarily contented in striking up snorting acquaintance. The sorrels appeared to have the edge in the social concourse; they formed cliques and sniffed at horses of different breeding. But on the whole they got along.

After a while the barefoot scout came sprinting up the road, whispering oaths at sand-spurs in his toes. "They come!" he gasped in Spanish. "*Ay*, a hundred! They come!"

Smith glanced at Bishop. "Now?"

Bishop sat stonily on his horse. "Wait!" his bleak growl commanded. "Let 'em come up!" In a minute he said, "Now!" And then his command harshly broke the subdued night. "Run the horses down the pass—pronto, you knotheaded buzzards! Now!"

It was a low trick on the horses, after wheedling their confidence, to shout roughly at them and smite them with quirts and rope ends. More indignant than scared, the whole herd curved in a ramming riot down the pass. Dust behind them was a choking fog and the roar boomed like a prolonged explosion. It was as if an avalanche crashed into the pass. There came a tiny, flatted popping of shots down below, and cracked shreds of howls; some whinnying squeals.

The riders hurtled through the blinding ruck of dust and the darkness, clamped hard in their saddles, their mounts shivering in every muscle from fear of the uproar, fear of the unseen road dropping steeply away under racing hoofs.

Then they were bursting out of the narrow funnel, wheeling sharply and gouging gravel; churning across the river and stringing out to bunch the horse herd and head it north. Some ribby Indian ponies slashed leanly across their path, and whirled about in wild confusion and dashed off.

Back in the pass a few voices cried out the dragging oaths of beaten and broken men, and somewhere on a faraway hill a coyote yapped an insistent summons to its pack.

Chapter Nine: A SALE OF HORSES

A HERD OF TRAIL HORSES, requiring much the same handling as a trail herd of cattle, soon fell into a daily routine. They covered less than twenty miles a day on the average, grazed along the way, and had to be bedded down at night—except that, unlike cows, horses didn't need to lie down very often. They grazed twice between midnight and sunup, usually, and if their noses were pointed in the right direction they made another mile or two, which was all to the good. In the morning, around four, there was the hasty breakfast, if any, and the catch-up with the herd. The wrangler followed closely with fresh mounts ready for instant notice—or he didn't hold his job long.

This was a horseback outfit. No wagons. No cook. They chewed jerky. Or shot a stray cow and roasted the beef on sticks, over a fire. Hardest on the dispositions of the vaqueros was the lack of coffee.

However, spirits perked up as they neared Fort Griffin, and grins of anticipation broke out when the fort loomed up distantly on its hill. Bishop remained bleakly taciturn. Red and Sera hadn't much to say, either.

The only one of the outfit who had kept in a good humor all the trip was Angelito Smith. He rode jauntily along, his ruined sombrero cocked at a dashing angle. By means of extravagantly elegant manners he rose superior to his scorched garb, which had split here and there, and when he wasn't whistling he was making irritatingly cheerful remarks. Whenever he looked at Bishop's dour face he chuckled. His attitude toward Sera was that of a knight to a captive princess, scrupulously courteous—and proprietary, Bishop noticed.

Although it was still morning, Smith called a halt on the Clear Fork and issued crisp commands. "You will go on alone to the fort, friend Rogue, and talk horses with that crooked major! If all seems well, tell him to send out a troop to meet the herd and take it in. That way, he won't see me. And my men are shy about going to the fort. Their appearance is against them, and—er—they're all on the wanted list!"

"They look it!" said Bishop. "How 'bout Sera? An' Red?"

For reply Smith called out four names. "You," he told the four men, "will camp here with Miss Donavon and Mr. Delaney, while the rest drift the horses on up the trail. Keep a sharp lookout! If you see the slightest sign of this thing going bad, shoot Mr. Delaney at once! Then make for the old Sabine hangout, with Miss Donavon!" He spoke to the others. "As soon as you turn the horses over to the soldiers, come straight back here. Well, Rogue?"

Bishop said, "How 'bout my guns? Plenty ducks in Hell's Hundred don't like me!"

Smith sadly shrugged. "Sorry. I can't take that chance, now all the chips are in. You see, Rogue, I'll be right on hand when you come out of the fort with the money, and I wouldn't want a row over it! I don't think you'd hold out on the money, because of Sera. But you're a tricky devil, and I've got to make sure!"

Without another word Bishop swung aboard his horse and set off for the fort. There was nothing else for it. Smith had the game figured out to the last move, like a master chess player, and nothing could prevent the ultimate checkmate, outside of kicking the board over.

Because of his vulnerable gunless state, Bishop skirted around Hell's Hundred. His empty holsters were hidden under his severely respectable long black coat, but men of violence—and tinhorn gamblers—often possessed a kind of sixth sense about such things; they smelled out in a minute whether you were armed or not.

Bishop's roundabout course brought him up north of the hill and the fort. The gates of the fort faced south, but he came to a door on the north side, and, being in a satanic mood, he booted on it.

A large woman opened the door and bellowed at him, "This is Laundress Row, no callers 'thout post commander's p'mission an' who d'you think ye are, ye civilian?"

She was Irish and army from way back and probably knew trumpet calls better than the trumpeters. Being on Laundress Row, she would naturally be the wife of a sergeant.

Immediately, Bishop doffed his broad-brimmed hat. He bowed in the saddle. "Forgive me, Madam—or Miss? I banged for a soldier, I having an interview due with the major, and it's private. How could I know that I knocked on the door of sweet femininity? It was unbeknownst to me, I swear. Still, I'm not now regrettin' me error, for at its worst, which is best, I have seen a fair face. Now slam the door on me, dear lady, an' I go my lonesome way with memories to last me for many nights to come!"

The broad, sunburned face of the large woman softened. "Yer talk don't kid me, but the words are nice," she sighed, and threw open the door. "Come in, ye big black rascal! I think ye're nothin' but a gamblin' man, but—ah, well. The major's office is yonder."

"I thank you, Miss."

"It's Mrs. I'm Mrs. Ser-rgeant Malloy."

"It's my tragedy I must always be too late, dear lady," said Bishop, walking his horse through.

"Ah, go along," she said. "I know ye're no good. Go 'long!"

He went along to the adjutant's office. It was a bare plank building like all the rest, raised off the ground so that it had an equally bare and dismal porch. Bishop mounted to the porch and shoved open a door, and instantly he was in a quiet office. Men wearing stripes wrote on long sheets of paper, glanced up at him incuriously, and went on writing.

He spoke to a man who wore two stripes and a bunch of foreign decorations, some having crosswise bars. "Major Jennisk, please. My name's Bishop."

The German from the Imperial Guards stood up and marched to a closed door. He received a reply, spoke, received another reply, and beckoned quickly to Bishop. The Army of the West was full of old soldiers from the old countries, on the jump; and tough young Irish punks; and battered adventurers from everywhere, particularly from the South since the defeat of the Confederacy.

Bishop ducked through that door and stood in the Presence. He heeled shut the door behind him, and said to Jennisk, "I've got over five hundred good horses to sell. You still buying?"

Major Jennisk's sharp round eyes widened. "*Five* hundred?" he exclaimed in his piping voice. A pleased look replaced his previous harried expression. As before, he made no move to shake hands. Nor did he offer friendly greetings and a chair. "That fellow Smith said three hundred."

"We picked up a second bunch," Bishop murmured. "Want 'em?"

Jennisk nodded quickly. "Yes. They'll fill my order. I've been worrying—" He stopped that, and grew cagey. "I'll take any that pass requirements."

Bishop helped himself to a cigar from a heavy brass humidor on the desk. "They'll pass. And I've got clean papers for 'em, from the original owners."

"You do a thorough job!" Jennisk's pursy little mouth quirked a knowing skepticism. "I won't look too hard at the papers. Where are the horses?"

"Comin', couple miles down the trail." Bishop fired a match for the cigar. "Might be better to send some soldiers to bring 'em in, h'm?"

"That's right." Jennisk heaved his paunchy shape up out of the chair, with a flabby man's grunt. "Wouldn't look well for Hump's ruffians to be seen coming here—especially with those rifles!"

"No, it wouldn't."

Bishop listened to Jennisk clipping orders in the outer office, and an orderly's snappy "Yessir," and the bang of a door. He gazed musingly at the brass humidor. Its lid was heavily embossed with the Stars and Stripes, the Eagle, and the crossed-sabers cavalry insignia. A patriotic cigar box. He strolled out of the major's office, deep in thought.

• • •

Troop C brought the horses up to the fort and held them for count into the corrals. A lieutenant, acting as inspecting line officer, called, "Five hundred and thirty-four, I make it," and looked questioningly to Bishop, who nodded.

Jennisk asked the veterinary what he thought of them. "Good!" was the answer. "Of course, we'll have to test them for wind and so forth, but—"

"If they weren't sound," said Bishop, "they wouldn't be here. They've come a long way." He lowered his voice to Jennisk. "I don't have time. Call it five hundred straight, an' take the odd thirty-four to allow for possible rejections."

Jennisk made some kind of sign to the vet, who grinned and nodded. He jerked his head then to Bishop and left the shade of the stable wall, and Bishop walked with him. They entered the adjutant's office, where Jennisk parted from Bishop and spoke quietly to a thin-faced sergeant at a desk. He rejoined Bishop and they went into his office.

Seating himself behind his desk, Jennisk attempted a measure of affability. He pushed forward the brass humidor. "Have another cigar, Bishop. I'm having bank drafts made out, government-stamped. Cashable at any bank, you know, without question. That's for my protection as well as yours. All right?"

Bishop nodded. "Good as gold."

The thin-faced sergeant knocked and came in. He laid two papers on the desk and withdrew, closing the door. Jennisk scanned them with care, before dipping a pen in an inkwell and signing both. He slid them over to Bishop and held out the pen.

"This one is yours. The other you endorse—that's mine."

Bishop scanned the figures. "Five hundred horses at thirty-five dollars a head, which was the price you agreed on, adds up to more'n ten thousand, Major!"

Jennisk's eyes were suddenly ugly. "Take it or leave it! The horses are here in the corrals. They're stolen horses, and we both know it and to hell with your papers!"

"This—" Bishop tapped the other bank draft— "gives you a cut of, let's see—" He peered at it. "Fifty-two thousand, five hundred dollars! I sign that over to you?"

"Yes!" Jennisk whispered. "Or would you rather be thrown into the guardhouse and wait there for trial and the warrants that are out for you?"

"You're out to get dirty rich, seems to me!"

"It's better than retiring on half pay! I'm not in this damned army for glory! Endorse that draft! Sign it!"

Bishop signed. He flirted the draft across the desk and picked up the other one, shrugging. The paper skimmed past Jennisk to the floor. Jennisk swung in his chair and reached down for it. Bishop picked up the patriotic humidor. He turned it in his fist, and glanced at it, and with one long strike he imprinted the brass Star Spangled Banner on Jennisk's thinning scalp. Jennisk bowed down to the floor and stayed there.

Bishop took a few cigars from the humidor and retrieved both bank drafts. For a moment he looked down dispassionately at the ungraceful figure on the floor. Maybe he had killed Jennisk; in that case there would be the notice: *Died in the line of duty.* And the grim chase after the killer.

He said, closing the door, leaving, "Major, it's been a pleasure. No, don't bother; I know the way. 'By!" He nodded pleasantly to the thin-faced sergeant at his desk, to the German corporal, the orderly, all the rest. He gave the corporal a cigar.

He held his horse to a walk through the parade ground and back along Laundress Row. On the porch of one of the line of little houses Mrs. Malloy inclined her head to him, discreetly. A burly sergeant sat beside her on the porch, smoking a pipe, his boots off, his red-brown face settled in the phlegmatic reverie of an old soldier taking his ease.

Bishop reined in before the porch. "Sergeant Malloy?" he inquired, and got an affirmative nod. From his pocket he drew two gold double-eagles and clinked them together. "I'd appreciate a small favor. There's a scorched little man waiting somewhere down the hill not far from the main gates. Could you send a trooper out to him with a message?" He spun the twenties over the porch rail.

The sergeant caught them nimbly. Just as nimbly, his wife plucked one from his hand. "What's the message, sir?"

"Just—'Bishop has started north.' That's all. I thank you."

He touched his hat and passed on through the small door. Once outside, he heeled his horse to a dead run along a wider and more roundabout course, using all the cover he could find.

At the camp on the Clear Fork he pulled to a sliding halt and stared somberly at the border men. They were all there, standing alertly by their horses, reading his haste as a sign of trouble.

"Where's Smith?" some of them sang out. "What's wrong?"

"Wrong?" Bishop rasped at them. "Why, you are, if you're waitin' for him to come back an' pay off! I guarantee he won't! The little cuss is headed north, fast as he can ride!"

"What? A double cross! Is this true?"

"Double cross is right!" answered Bishop. "You can wait here if you want to. He won't show up! If he was going to, he'd be here by now, wouldn't he? As for me—Manuel, give me my guns, *por favor.* I'll need 'em if I catch up with him!"

They hit into their saddles so fast their horses danced. The resentment of Smith's hot-tempered insults had not died out; it served as a ready fire-starter and flared up into raging oaths of vengeance.

Manuel, tossing Bishop his guns, snarled, "You? *We* will catch up with him! Left us guarding those two, like fools, while he—"

They whirled off, none of them giving any further thought to Sera and Red. Those two meant nothing now. Their minds were on money, on catching Smith and turning him inside out. It wasn't only Bishop's word that convinced them. It was also the fact that he had returned to the camp and Smith had not. They could see most of the road to the fort and Smith wasn't anywhere on it.

Red exclaimed to Sera, "Let's get out of here before they come back!"

"They won't," Bishop murmured. "They'll spot him soon after they pass the fort. He'll be dusting north, all right—lookin' for me! And if he gets out o' that mess, he'll be lookin' for me all the harder! We better mosey, though. There's trouble in that fort, an' they just might connect me with it."

He looked at Sera a moment, then briefly at Red. "Here's something for you. It's endorsed. Good as gold, they tell me. I won't be going your way."

• • •

They caught each other in Santa Fe, over in New Mexico, in the old Bank Bar near the plaza. It was an even catch, a stand-off. From a poker table Bishop saw Smith enter, and Smith spotted him in the same instant and stood stock-still. Because of heavy law around Santa Fe, each studied the other for his intentions.

Bishop cashed his chips and got up from the game. They came slowly face to face.

"Drink, Smeet?"

Smith nodded stiffly. He looked poor and tired. They stood up to the bar and drank in silence, till Smith said, "A hell of a trick!"

"Trick? Which one?" Bishop poured again. "Oh—that! I put a dent in that major's skull, an' had to duck out fast. Didn't you get my message?"

"Yes—and I raced north after you! Where did you go?"

"I cut back to camp, on—hum—an afterthought. To see Red and Sera about something."

Smith sighed faintly. "And to send my crew after me, eh? I've been on the run from them ever since! Who got the money for the horses?"

"Red an' Sera," Bishop admitted. "I held out ten thousand for myself, as commission—a horse dealer's cut. Those two went off together. To raise more horses. Or maybe to rob a grave, for all I know."

"I thought you were after that girl. No?"

"No," Bishop lied. "She could do too many things too damned well. Shoot, swim, climb, handle horses, an' what-all. About the only thing I could do better was shoot—an' somehow I just couldn't see that as a basis for matrimony."

Smith shook his head. "My crew think I've got that money. They hunt me out everywhere I go. And I'm dead broke. Hah! I still say—a hell of a trick!"

"Tough," agreed Bishop. He drank again, thought it over, and at last growled, "All right, damn it, I'll stake you to a thousand, Smitty."

L(eonard) L(ondon) Foreman was born in London, England in 1901. He served in the British army during the Great War, prior to his emigration to the United States. He became an itinerant, holding a series of odd jobs in the western States as he traveled. He began his writing career by introducing his most widely known and best-loved character, Preacher Devlin, in "Noose Fodder" in *Western Aces* (12/34), a pulp magazine. Throughout the mid thirties, this character, a combination gunfighter, gambler, and philosopher, appeared regularly in *Western Aces*. Near the end of the decade, Foreman's Western stories began appearing in Street & Smith's *Western Story Magazine*, where the pay was better. Foreman's first Western novels began appearing in the 1940s, largely historical Westerns such as *Don Desperado* (1941) and *The Renegade* (1942). The *New York Herald Tribune* reviewer commented on *Don Desperado* that "admirers of the late beloved Dane Coolidge better take a look at this. It has that same all-wool-and-a-yard-wide quality." Foreman continued to write prolifically for the magazine market as long as it lasted, before specializing exclusively for the book trade with one of his finest novels, *Arrow in the Dust* (1954) which was filmed under this title the same year. Two years earlier *The Renegade* was filmed as *The Savage* (Paramount, 1952), the two are among several films based on his work. Foreman's last years were spent living in the state of Oregon. Perhaps his most popular character after Preacher Devlin was Rogue Bishop, appearing in a series of novels published by Doubleday in the 1960s. George Walsh, writing in *Twentieth Century Western Writers*, said of Foreman: "His novels have a sense of authority because he does not deal in simple characters or simple answers." In fact, most of his fiction is not centered on a confrontation between good and evil, but rather on his characters and the changes they undergo. His female characters, above all, are memorably drawn and central to his stories.